Rice Wine

Rice Wine

A NOVEL

BARRY CAME

WEIDENFELD & NICOLSON
NEW YORK

Published by Weidenfeld & Nicolson, New York
A Division of Wheatland Corporation
10 East 53rd Street
New York, NY 10022

Published in Canada by General Publishing Company, Ltd.

The author gratefully acknowledges permission to reprint from "The Hollow
Men," in *Collected Poems 1909–1962* by T.S. Eliot, copyright 1936 by Harcourt
Brace Jovanovich, Inc.; copyright © 1963, 1964 by T.S. Eliot.

Published in Great Britain by Faber and Faber Limited. Published in the United
States by Harcourt Brace Jovanovich, Inc. Reprinted by permission of the pub-
lishers.

Library of Congress Cataloging-in-Publication Data

Came, Barry,
  Rice wine.

  I. Title.
PR6053.A44R5   1987   823'.914   87-21057
ISBN 1-55584-036-1

Manufactured in the United States of America
Designed by Irving Perkins Associates, Inc.
First Edition
10 9 8 7 6 5 4 3 2 1

for Mara Caruccio

On April 24, 1980, Macli-ing Dulag, a tribal chieftain of the
Kalinga people, was involved in an incident in his ancestral village, which overlooks the Chico River in the highlands of northern
Luzon, the Philippines. That incident provided the germ of the
idea from which this novel sprang. But while the Macli-ing episode was a real event involving real people, my story is pure
invention. So is the cast of characters peopling it. I have even taken
liberties with the map—both geographic and ethnographic—of
the Luzon Cordillera. This is a work of fiction. The events that I
have portrayed may never have occurred. If they did, they may not
have unfolded in the manner I have depicted. But all the same, it
might have happened this way. . . .

Between the idea
And the reality
Between the motion
And the act
Falls the Shadow

—T. S. Eliot,
"The Hollow Men"

P R O L O G U E

THE BRIDGE, or what was left of it, sobered them all for a moment, even the colonel. They stood motionless in a line along the edge of the cliff, hunched deep within rubber ponchos that glistened blackly in the driving rain, and stared silently down at the twisted ribbons of steel stretched across the gorge at their feet. All that remained of what had once been a suspended footpath was a tangled skein of metal shackled at each end to identical towers sunk into opposite banks of the river. The whole jumbled mass was rocking furiously in the gale that was hurtling down the valley's throat, groaning and screeching like something alive. Both of the heavy cables anchoring the superstructure to the gorge's granite walls had sheared loose on the far shore. They were rearing up and lashing down at the surface of the boiling river below, snapping viciously as they struck at the racing water.

The lieutenant, sensing an exit, was first to react. "How the hell are we going to get across that?" he shouted, leaning in close to the colonel's face and cupping his hands to his mouth to make himself heard above the combined din of wind, rain, river, and screaming metal. He could not see the colonel's expression in the gloom, but it was evident from the immobility of the short chunky figure standing beside him that the man had not heard. Either that, thought the lieutenant glumly, or the drink was taking its toll again.

He reached out, grabbed the colonel's shoulder, and shook it gingerly. "Colonel!" he shouted in the guttural lowland accent they shared. "The typhoon's damn near ripped out the bridge. Maybe we'd better call this whole thing off."

Abruptly, the colonel's large head, almost too large for the trunk supporting it, swiveled in the lieutenant's direction. Peering out from beneath a combat helmet tilted low over his eyes, he stared at the hand grasping his shoulder, then swung a sharp glance upward at the lieutenant's gaunt face.

Looking back into the defiant eyes under the helmet's rim, the lieutenant groaned silently. He knew there was no chance. He felt the despondency surge up from his innards. It was a sensation that had grown familiar since the battalion had been rotated into the highlands.

"You got a problem, Ramirez?" the colonel shouted accusingly. He threw an arm at the swaying steel skeleton of the bridge. "The tension cables are gone, sure enough, and the footpath and handrails are twisted all to hell. But they're still connected, at least." He looked closely at the lieutenant. "If you don't feel up to it, I'll get your squad across in one piece."

The lieutenant shrugged, but he was unwilling to let go of the faint glimmer of hope that had risen when he first saw the half-wrecked bridge. "Pinero will never make it," he shouted, playing for time. "Too drunk. And that new kid, Reyes, can barely carry his own weapon. We're gonna lose him for sure." He hesitated, wondering how far he dared go without provoking his volatile commander. When the colonel merely continued to glare wordlessly, he leaned closer. He dropped his voice, as much as the storm would allow, and said carefully, "What worries me, Colonel, is once we get over there, how are we going to get back? The river's rising fast; so's the wind. What do we do if that bridge goes once we're in there?"

"I'm not sure I'm reading you, Ramirez," the colonel answered. There was a hint of threat in his voice.

The lieutenant took a deep breath. "What I mean, Colonel, is suppose we get in there and they don't cooperate." The lieutenant spoke rapidly; the words came spilling out in a flood. "What if we have to mix it up a little to make the point? If that bridge goes, the only other way out is up over the Cordillera. Never mind we're going to have to do it in the middle of a typhoon. And what if while we're scrambling over those godforsaken hills in this mother of all storms, we also have a crowd of highly irritated people on our tail who not only know the terrain the way Sergeant Cruz there knows the backside of every whore in Ermita, but who also grew up with fathers who ran around in G-strings, lopping off heads like yours and mine just for kicks?"

As soon as he had finished speaking, the lieutenant knew he had overreached.

The colonel stiffened. "That's enough!" he barked. "We'll be going over that bridge now. Pinero and the new kid, whatever his name is, will stay this side. Post them up on the road to cover our backs. Sergeant Cruz will take the point. You take the rear. Now let's move out!"

Observing the lingering protest in the lieutenant's eyes, the colonel raised a warning hand. "I don't want to hear any more," he hissed. "We have to teach some people a few lessons tonight they should have been taught a long time ago." He reached deliberately into his poncho and pulled out a pearl-handled Colt automatic. He slipped the magazine out of the grip with a deft flourish, verified it was fully loaded, slammed it back with the heel of his hand, rammed a charge into the firing chamber, and thrust the weapon back inside his poncho. He stepped in the lieutenant's direction until their eyes were inches apart. With quiet menace, enunciating each word slowly, he said, "You got that clear now?"

The threat hovered for a long moment. Yielding at last, the lieutenant turned and beckoned to the tall figure of the sergeant standing warily a few feet away on the cliff's edge. "You've got the point, Cruz," he ordered briskly, avoiding the big sergeant's eyes.

"Send Pinero and Reyes back up to the road. Tell them to keep their eyes peeled." As the sergeant turned, the lieutenant shouted, "And for Christ's sake, Sergeant, make sure Pinero doesn't have a bottle stashed someplace. We may need even those two clowns before this night is over."

Moments later, the party clambered over the cliffside and down a long flight of stone steps hacked crudely out of the gorge wall. It was not a quiet descent. The squad cursed loudly as they slipped and slithered down the primitive staircase, the steps slick in rain that cascaded down in near solid sheets.

Bringing up the rear, the lieutenant listened uneasily to the sound of the descending troops. He was grimly aware that, like the colonel, they had been drinking heavily and, like the colonel, they were balanced on a knife edge, capable of slipping out of control at any moment. Chilled by a sudden foreboding, he hurried downward.

The scene that greeted him at the bottom of the gorge did nothing to dispel the disquiet he felt. The troops were gathered in the lee of the concrete base of the steel tower anchoring the bridge to the riverbank. They were muttering mutinously among themselves as they sought shelter from the elements raging around them. The rain was sweeping horizontally across the surface of the crashing river, driven by a keening wind that accelerated as it funneled between the walls of the gorge. The bridge, under constant assault by the wind, shrieked as it rocked on its moorings.

Observing the smoldering resentment, the lieutenant understood that he had to act quickly. He caught the sergeant's eye, urgently motioned him across the bridge. The sergeant stared back for a moment, his face creased in a thin smile. Then he nodded, almost imperceptibly, before slinging his carbine crosswise over his shoulders. He adjusted the strap on his chest with exaggerated care, flexed his arms to check the fit, and climbed up onto the high concrete base of the tower. He paused briefly, scanning the swaying tangle of metal stretched in front. Then he planted his feet firmly on a strand of metal, grasped another above his head with both hands, and slowly, methodically, began to work his way over the river.

The murmuring among the troops huddled against the tower base ceased abruptly. They moved out into the storm in a single mass and followed, transfixed, the sergeant's passage across the lurching threads of metal. He made it look almost easy, sliding along the steel ribbons, swaying with the bridge as it rocked in the wind. When he was roughly halfway, he stopped. He turned, looking back at the watching squad. He stretched his arms and legs wide until he was spread-eagled on the pitching bridge, a man on a demented trapeze. And he smiled, a huge, beaming grin that split his broad face from ear to ear.

The troops almost cheered, probably would have had not the colonel signaled for silence. He was quick to exploit the mood. Leaping onto the concrete base, he beckoned the troops to follow and set off immediately in the sergeant's wake. The rest of the squad stood for a time, staring sheepishly at each other. One by one, they slung their weapons across their backs, scrambled onto the base, and moved slowly across the bridge as the sergeant had done.

The lieutenant watched them go, wondering how many could offer an adequate explanation for what they were doing. As the last of the squad disappeared into the murk on the far side of the river he slung his own rifle and followed. He did not even bother to ask himself the same question: he knew he didn't have an answer.

Approaching the opposite shore, now far behind the rest of the squad, the lieutenant began to pick up fugitive scraps of noise. They tore past on the wind, whirling by before he could be certain he had heard anything. There was what sounded like the cackle of alarmed geese, barking dogs, squealing pigs. He stopped, straining to listen. He peered into the gloom ahead but could discern little. There was a suggestion of deeper shadow perhaps, black on black, that might have been the elaborately terraced cliffside he knew rose from the far bank of the river, spiraling up in constantly diminishing steps to the hamlet on the heights. He moved ahead, stepping up his pace as much as he dared. More fragments reached him, disembodied sounds that were instantly shredded by the storm. There was a heavy thud, a high sharp wail. Struggling to negotiate the tossing bridge, he felt the sweat bead on his forehead, trickle down from his armpits, pool in his groin. A tiny crystal of anxiety formed deep inside him as he strove to make some contact that would confirm or deny what was just barely eluding his senses. And then he heard it. It was clear and unmistakable, carried down by some trick of the wind, rising above the clamor of the bridge and the river and the rain: a long, chattering burst of automatic rifle fire.

The lieutenant raced off the end of the bridge. He was moving so fast that he tumbled off the edge of the concrete tower base on the far shore. Limbs flailing for purchase, he fell headlong into a strong, sturdy pair of outstretched arms.

"Christ, Lieutenant!" said the sergeant. "Will you take it easy?" The sergeant hoisted the lieutenant to his feet.

"What the hell is going on up there, Cruz?" gasped the lieutenant, struggling to regain his wind. He looked at the sergeant. "And what the hell are you doing down here?"

"Judging from the racket, I'd say somebody is kicking somebody's ass up there, Lieutenant," replied the sergeant. "And I'm down here because the colonel doesn't want me up there."

The lieutenant and the sergeant exchanged a long look. It was interrupted after a time by the sound of further commotion drifting down from the hilltop. There was crashing and banging, voices raised in anger and in fear. A dog's barking was cut short by the crack of a rifle, which was instantly followed by a single agonized yelp. Both the lieutenant and the sergeant turned to peer in the direction of the fracas, up over the shadows of the terrace walls that climbed the steep slope like stairways.

"It's the witnesses again," the lieutenant whispered, gazing upward. He added, more loudly, "That's it, isn't it, Cruz? That's why you and me are down here."

The lieutenant turned, found the sergeant looking intently back, saw the confirmation written in the man's still regard.

"Sonofabitch," the lieutenant muttered. He readjusted his poncho carefully, unslung the M16 on his back, and said briskly, "Let's go, Cruz; maybe it's not too late."

The lieutenant started off in the direction of the terraces, but he had gone only a few steps when he realized the sergeant was not with him. Looking back, he saw him standing in the rain where he had left him.

"What's the holdup?" the lieutenant shouted.

"I've been ordered to stay put."

"Well, I'm countermanding that order. I'll be responsible. Let's go."

The sergeant, a survivor, refused to budge. He stood rooted, implacable, the rain cascading off his helmet onto the shoulders of his poncho.

The lieutenant returned. He searched the sergeant's features. "What's your problem, Cruz? You know as well as I do what may be happening up there."

"The colonel ordered me to stay here," replied the sergeant stubbornly. He avoided the lieutenant's eyes.

The lieutenant shot him a look of disgust. "Have it your way." He snorted, he wheeled, and headed back toward the cliffside.

The sergeant watched him go. When the lieutenant had vaulted the first of the low stone walls at the base of the hill and disappeared into the darkness, the sergeant muttered, "You lose either way, chump."

The lieutenant might have agreed. He too had experienced the colonel's methods before. But he had made a promise and he intended to do his best to keep it. He waded across the flooded paddy beyond the wall, leading into the wind and rain, thigh-deep in water, viscous mud sucking at his boots.

The clamor from the heights increased as the lieutenant slogged relentlessly across the ascending terraces. It swelled as he clambered over the stone walls and plunged through the waterlogged paddies. It was a sound he had heard before, and he didn't like to think about what caused it.

The lieutenant's chest was hammering from the exertion of the climb when, vaulting another wall, he was nearly bowled over by an onrushing herd of pigs. The small black creatures squealed in alarm as they crashed into his legs before wheeling en masse, and barreling off into the night. He looked up and found himself at last on the edge of the village.

It was a mean affair, an untidy sprawl of rectangular wooden huts with thatched roofs scattered haphazardly up the side of a rising slope. Each dwelling was raised high off the ground on stilts and ringed with a broad balcony. A knot of villagers was gathered on the balcony of the nearest hut. Their faces were turned fearfully in the lieutenant's direction as they attempted to identify what it was that had startled the swine. Their reaction to his appearance was identical to that of the pigs. They cried out in alarm, turned in a single body, and rushed into the interior of the hut.

The lieutenant moved on, in growing despair at what he found. The village was a shambles. Doors hung ajar, ripped from their hinges. Smashed windows rattled in the wind. Jute bags, slashed open, spilled tongues of grain. Huge earthen pots lay broken and overturned, leaking rusty-colored rice wine. Like the dwellers on the balcony, the other villagers he encountered shrank at his approach. They were, for the most part, the very old and the very young. He wondered at the absence of the others.

On rounding a corner, he found out where they had gone. They were assembled on a knoll, backs turned against him. A pale corona of light flickered against the storm beyond, drawing their attention. What it illuminated the lieutenant could not see. But he could hear, rising above the sound of the storm, a loud insistent rapping and the unmistakable tones of the colonel's voice. He was raving.

The lieutenant rushed forward, frantically elbowing a path through the crowd. The tension rattled on his nerves as he pushed and shoved against the unyielding bodies. Angry, sullen faces turned in his direction. Hands reached for cleaverlike bolos strapped to waists. He struggled on, clubbing a passage with the butt of his M16. He stumbled, pitched forward, and careened into a lean figure standing at the front of the crowd. Both the lieutenant and the other man crashed to their hands and knees.

The lieutenant barely noticed the man he had bowled over. His gaze was riveted to the scene spread out at the foot of the knoll in front of him.

It was lit by a pair of kerosene lamps hanging from the eaves above the wooden door of a village hut. The lamps swung in the wind, casting two dancing circles of white light. Rain slanted crosswise through the light, racing streaks of incandescence. Scattered in a rough semicircle, on the outer edge of the revolving arcs of light, stood the lieutenant's squad. Most faced outward, nervously eyeing the crowd, which far outnumbered them on the knoll. A few looked inward, peering up at the colonel. He stood beneath the lamps on the balcony in front of the door of the hut.

The colonel was volcanic, caught in the vise of an uncontrollable rage. He had lost his helmet, and the rain plastered his hair, the color of dead ashes, to his skull. There was an M16 in his hands that he had picked up somewhere. He was using it, stock end first, to batter at the hut's door. Even from the knoll, the lieutenant, who was still on his knees, could see the flush suffusing the colonel's cheeks, the muscles bulging in strain on his neck. The colonel was roaring. The lieutenant, perhaps because of the storm, could not identify distinct words. It sounded like some other means of communication thundering from the colonel's throat—something more elemental.

There was a pause. The lieutenant heard another voice, coming from behind the door. It was also angry but more controlled. The colonel listened, head cocked, chest heaving. Then he stepped back and howled, as if he were in pain. He reversed the carbine in his hands, pointed it at the door, and fired.

The gun chattered and shook, jerking his arms, jolting his body. The rounds, ripping through the door, hurtled chips of wood and silvers of molten metal in a lethal shower through the dancing, spectral light. Long after the weapon was empty, the colonel stood with his finger clenched tightly around the trigger. Knuckles white. Teeth bared.

PART ONE

The Valley

I

AS USUAL, it was the geese that woke Frank Enright. He lay with his eyes closed, listening to the ill-tempered honking. He smiled, reassured as always by a private morning ritual that had lasted for close to twenty years.

Don't know why I keep the noisy beggars, Frank thought. But he continued to smile contentedly. His irritation was feigned. He knew full well why he kept the geese: it was because of old Tom Conlin. Frank treasured the birds for the link they provided, one of the few he had left. He could not listen to them without thinking of the Irish priest. The image conjured up was always clear and sharp, as if two decades had not passed since he had climbed down from the back of the jeepney—garish in chrome and mirrors—to meet Father Conlin.

This morning was no exception. He saw the old man painted on the back of his eyelids as he lay in the big bamboo bed listening to the impatient geese and the rhythmic creak of the ceiling fan slowly whirring above his head. The priest was standing again in the roadway as he had done that sweltering afternoon long ago. The hem of his ankle-length white cassock was dusted with the ocher soil of the valley. One arm was extended in greeting, the other raised to shield his eyes against the bright tropical sun. The man was short and round, a succession of happy circles capped by an unruly halo of fine white hair. He was surrounded by a gaggle of great gray geese. They hissed angrily at the tall, athletic-looking young man in clerical black, clerical collar around his neck.

"They're evil creatures, I know," had been Father Conlin's first apologetic words. "But I never could abide dogs, and a person needs something around these parts to keep off the snakes and the thieves. I suppose you'll be wanting dogs, Father Enright, coming from New York . . . It is New York, isn't it? . . . Oh, Rochester . . . ahh, New York State, is it? . . . Well, if you take my advice you'll stay away from the dogs . . . around here they eat 'em . . . pitiful brutes . . . stick to geese, m'lad . . . never regret it . . . I never have . . . geese!"

Frank's smile broadened at the memory of his predecessor at the mission. He had stuck to geese. As for regrets, well . . . he did not like picturing the old man's reaction to what he had done with what had been handed to him. He opened his eyes. There were bars of sunshine slanting through the louvered shutters on the bedroom window. He stretched and yawned, wondering idly what was holding up the rains this year. And then he remembered the day.

Frank glanced at the watch on his wrist, sprang from the bed. He snatched up a sarong, bright crimson on deep black, and draped it expertly around his waist. He needed to prepare the spare room, organize the others. Liz would be no problem. He frowned. Harry might, depending on how many others were sharing his bed at the moment.

Frank growled and strode across the room to where a pair of glazed doors opened onto a balcony. He threw the doors open and walked out into the daylight.

There was a clean, scoured feel to the morning. Even the air seemed to shine with a freshly burnished luster. Frank glanced down at the brown trickle of a river, imagining it as it soon would be—running full and vigorous, choked with silt and the shorn limbs of living trees. He looked up at the rice terraces, and, as always, was moved. Even after twenty years of living daily with the

spectacle, the sight of the antique hanging gardens caused something to lurch gently within him.

From Frank's vantage point overlooking the river, the terraces
rose majestically on all sides, carved from the surrounding mountains. There was not a single slope that had escaped the handiwork
of the ancient, unknown architects who had painstakingly chiseled
the hillsides into a vast network of shelves for the cultivation of rice.
They climbed the steep flanks in ascending steps, gigantic stair-
cases glittering green and gold in the sun.

In the distance, high on the shoulder of one of the hills, Frank
watched a party of cultivators move slowly along the shelves,
preparing the stone walls for the coming rains. They patched the
breeches with rocks hauled up from the riverbank and replanted the
tiny red-leafed shrub with the astonishing binding power, a power
strong enough to withstand even a typhoon. Not for the first time,
it dawned on Frank that what he was observing was as old as the
religion he had been preaching in the valley for the last twenty
years. He stared down at his sarong, struck by the irony. Though
garbed in the vestments of a native seer, in the eyes of those he was
trying to reach he was nothing but an alien priest. And an alien
priest he would remain.

Frank's gaze wandered disconsolately over the terraced hills.
He could feel his morning exaltation slipping away. He tried
to remember what it was like to feel confident. He sighed
heavily.

Frank's eyes followed the brown river toward Alfredo's village. It
was invisible from the bedroom's balcony, hidden beyond a wide
bend where the stream disappeared into a green cleft between
rising terraces. That was where the key to the future lay.

Frank stood in his sarong, watching the morning sunlight splin-
ter on the river's surface. His world was crumbling, and there
seemed little he could do to prevent it. All his efforts achieved
nothing. He smiled sadly, suspecting that the virile activism that
had once been the wellspring of his being might even have made

things worse. He wished that he could pray. But he could not do that—not any longer. Even that was past.

Frank took a deep breath, glanced at his watch. Perhaps the youngster who was arriving would effect a change. He would be approaching now, traveling up to the valley in the back of a jeepney. A suggestion of melancholy crept into his eyes. It would no doubt be as implausibly gaudy a vehicle as the one that had brought him as a confident young man to the same place so long ago.

2

PAUL STENMARK was not happy. His blue eyes glittered with a wrath as cold as winter ice on the lakes in Minnesota, where he had been born some thirty years earlier. It was not that he regarded himself as a particularly fastidious young man. He simply knew that he did not want to be where he was at the moment, shoehorned inside a vehicle he could think of no adequate words to describe. It was half truck, half jeep, painted the colors of the rainbow, plated in stainless steel, fringed with tassles, and groaning under the weight of a bizarre assortment of chromed screaming eagles, charging stallions, and beatific saints of obscure origin.

The trip had gone badly from the start. Although Paul was prepared to admit that his career had not yet taken off, he nevertheless nurtured a well-developed sense of his place. There were certain things he expected, certain prerogatives he viewed as his right. Which made it all the worse when the bank's in-country representative, a local and therefore doubly suspect, pulled rank on him, skewering him with the weapon he valued most.

It had happened almost as soon as Paul had stepped, wilting in the sudden onrush of tropical heat, from the long flight across the Pacific. Despite his relative inexperience, Paul felt skilled enough in the ways of Washington's bureaucracies to recognize the thousand subtle little gestures and barbed remarks for what they were.

He understood that no opportunity was being lost to remind him of his own position in the bank's jealous hierarchy, which was several rungs below that of the country rep. There was the question of transport. Shifting his legs with effort on his suitcase, which was jammed beneath his knees, he was certain that his current plight was no accident. His icy eyes gleamed as he plotted revenge.

Paul prided himself on his ability to rough it, even if his very few, very brief forays into the field had hardly tested that ability. His specialty, after all, was the economics of the underdeveloped world. And the underdeveloped world, by definition, was uncomfortable. About that he had no illusions. Adversity was to be expected, even welcomed. But there were limits. Discomfort did not mean humiliation. Certainly there had been no hint of that in the director general's briefing.

"I'VE GOT one that's right up your alley, Stenmark," the DG had said, utilizing his dynamic voice, the one that made all the veterans in the organization instantly wary.

Not being a veteran, but eager to achieve that status as quickly as possible, Paul was intrigued.

"Have you ever been to the Philippines?" the DG asked. Without waiting for an answer, he continued, "Well, you're gonna want to go when you've had a look at this baby. It's a classic. What we have is a major untapped river basin just begging to be harnessed. This in a country with precious few indigenous power resources, virtually no oil, starving for energy." He pushed a thick stack of papers across an enormous walnut desk. "The studies are all here: Bureau of Reclamations, USAID, World Bank, Asian Development Bank, private-sector consultants." He flashed a brilliant smile, the smile that old bank hands claimed was primarily responsible for his success. "You have a look at them, fella. I'm sure you're gonna agree that the numbers add up to something impressive."

"If it's so good, how come they can't find private-sector fund-ing?" Paul bluntly asked, not entirely aware he was being blunt.

The DG blinked. He was unaccustomed to candor, especially from underlings. A shade of the dazzle leached from his smile and he regarded the lanky young man opposite him: long legs crossed confidently; round, earnest face framed by limp, blond, unfash-ionably long hair; blue eyes gazing calmly from behind fashion-ably rimless glasses.

"Good question, Stenmark," said the DG heartily, masking his attempt to decide whether the man on the other side of his desk was merely artless or was, in fact, challenging him. He continued, more carefully, "Until recently this *was* a commercial project. The financing was Swiss. An Australian contractor had been hired— he's still in place, as a matter of fact. Initial construction had started. Then the usual happened. There was local opposition, a few nasty incidents, and, boom, the Swiss pulled out. Now the whole thing's in limbo while the authorities over there try to come up with alternative financing."

"All the same, the opposition must have been pretty fierce if nobody else in the private sector will touch it," Paul persisted.

The DG studied Paul, drumming well-manicured fingers on the edge of the desk as he did so. He decided a switch in tactics was called for. "Let me be frank," he said, discarding his dynamic voice for something more candid. "The issue now is political. You are aware, of course, that the government we are talking about is not exactly popular with certain people in this country. The man running things over there has been around for a long time and has developed something of . . . ah . . . an image problem here. You may not be aware that there is also an insurgency problem. The usual left-wing crowd, I'm afraid. It's containable, I'd say, judging from all the reports I've read. But it's there, all the same. What's worse, this particular project seems to have become entangled in the struggle between insurgents and government. So we have a complicated situation on our hands. We have a developing country with a clear, quantifiable need for locally produced energy if it is to continue developing. We have identified a major potential indigenous source capable of providing that energy at reasonable cost if the necessary funding can be corralled. But we have the kind of political equation in play that scares the daylights out of private money. So . . ." The DG paused and arched his eyebrows at Paul, as if the answer were self-evident.

Paul stared back, said nothing.

The DG shifted with irritation in the brushed leather of his chair, wondering about the accuracy of the assessment contained in the psychological profile that was locked in his desk drawer. "So we step in and perform the very role this institution was created to perform," he said, adding, with a trace of impatience, "which is, I'm sure I don't have to remind you, to guarantee the financing of worthy development projects that private funding would not otherwise consider."

Paul nodded thoughtfully. "I haven't read the studies yet, of course," he murmured doubtfully, "but I get awfully nervous about projects that nobody else will touch."

The DG gave Paul an exasperated look.

"Where exactly is this project located?" Paul asked.

"Luzon," the DG snapped.

"There's some American military bases around there—isn't that true?"

The DG looked suddenly uncomfortable. "Yes," he replied warily.

"Any connection?"

"I wouldn't think so," the DG answered, a little evasively.

Paul pursed his lips reflectively.

The DG decided to play a hunch, based on his own long experience with the seductive power of self-interest. He dropped his voice to an intimate whisper. "I suppose I don't have to remind you that if we give this one the green light, we'll be needing someone over there for the duration of the contract to ride herd on things."

Paul stirred. "What kind of an investment are we talking about?" he asked, a trifle too quickly.

The DG smiled, relaxed into his brushed leather. "Depending on the number of dams, anywhere from half a billion up to two billion dollars," he replied calmly, his faith in the unerring accuracy of his own instincts reaffirmed.

"And my role?"

"I want an on-scene, hardheaded, unsentimental assessment of the situation. I want all the factors thoroughly explored. I want the closest possible focus on the pros and cons and a recommendation, one way or the other. If I'm going to take a two-billion-dollar proposal to the board, I'll have to make sure that every square millimeter of the ground is covered." He looked into Paul's eyes. "And I want you to do that job for me."

"When do I leave?" asked Paul, rising.

"Soon as you can."

Paul strode purposefully across the wide field of pale gold that carpeted the DG's office. On reaching the door, he turned and looked back. But the DG was busy shuffling papers on his desk. He did not return the glance.

It was only after Paul had left the office that the DG raised his head. He pressed a button on the intercom on his desk. "Put through that call now—Department of the Navy." He leaned back into his chair and stared pensively at the door as he waited for the call, gently tapping on his perfect white teeth with the elegant tip of a slim gold pen.

THE CONVERSATION with the director general had been Paul's sole consolation during the long journey up into the highlands from the provincial capital. He was on the brink of a major career advance, and the realization of how tantalizingly close it was tied his stomach in knots. After all the years in graduate school, the patient slogging in deskbound anonymity through the bank's Washington bureaucracy, he was finally poised on the dizzy edge of everything he had been waiting for. He had read the studies given him by the DG and the scheme was good, on paper at least. There was local opposition, to be sure, but what was new about local residents fighting a dam, or an airport, or a nuclear power plant? He set his jaw firmly. He would deal with that problem when he arrived. He had to. He was in a hurry.

Which did nothing to alleviate the discomfort of seven hours on a hard bench in the open rear of the jeepney, winding up into a range of mountains his briefing maps told him was called the Grand Cordillera. He rumbled along a rough track—to label the passageway a road was to give it unique dignity—beneath serrated peaks rising several thousand feet into the clouds. Ascending, he traversed dark pine forests, stands of gnarled oak dripping delicate orchids, high alpine meadows. He dipped into upland valleys, watered by clear, tumbling streams, rose up again past terraced hillsides and plunging waterfalls.

Paul saw little of this passing spectacle, however, for he was kept constantly alert contending with his fellow passengers. There were a dozen people on two narrow benches that ran along the sides of the rear deck of the jeepney. They were crammed into an area where half their number would have been uncomfortably squeezed. Paul's Nordic dimensions were a distinct disadvantage. He sat jackknifed with his feet on his suitcase and his knees jammed against his chin. His immediate neighbors on either side were the real problem, however. Both, in their separate fashions, seemed intent on making the trip a purgatory.

On Paul's left sat an ancient fossil of undetermined sex. He, or she, was chewing betel leaves and expectorating the juice over his, or her, shoulder. The breeze caught the discharge, whipped it around in a shallow arc, and sprinkled it over the passengers unfortunate enough to be seated downwind. Paul was seated downwind.

As bad was the immediate neighbor on the other side, or rather, the baggage the man carried in his lap. It was a scrawny fighting cock, the color of rusty nails with a disposition to match. The bird apparently detested Paul, a loathing it had expressed by repeatedly attempting, successfully on at least two occasions, to defecate down his trouser leg. Paul had spent much of the trip staring uncomfortably into the creature's baleful red glare.

His relief was considerable, then, when the jeepney careened around a bend in a shower of ocher dust and began to tear downhill into the little upland station that was his destination. The place was not much more than a wide spot in the road, where the track bisected a rolling meadow that shelved gently down from the foot of sharply rising hills to the rock-strewn bank of a fast, shallow river. There were a dozen buildings scattered along the roadway, mostly traditional native dwellings on stilts but also a medical clinic marked by a large red cross, a school fronted by a play-ground, and a grain depot bearing a billboard in Chinese script. Two structures dominated the scene, confronting each other across the track. On the riverside stood a framed church, clapboards painted a sparkling white, that was topped by a tall steeple. On the steeple there was a huge metal cross. It glinted in the sunlight. Facing the church on the other side of the road sprawled a low, L-shaped building made of raw concrete blocks. At the interior elbow of the building there was a courtyard. A flagpole rose from the center of the courtyard, flying the country's banner. In the heavy midafternoon heat, the flag hung limp.

Paul's jeepney skidded into the courtyard, sending a spray of dust over an assortment of military vehicles parked under the flagpole. When the debris settled, he saw the welcoming party he had been briefed to expect. There was a tall, burly, middle-aged priest in a soiled white cassock. He was accompanied by a man who might easily have been his elder brother. He was equally massive, but in place of a cassock he wore tan slacks and one of those loose embroidered shirts that Paul had discovered to be virtually a uniform in the country. It was the third member of the group, however, who caught his attention. Between the two strapping men stood a slight, dark woman in a white smock, of the kind favored by doctors and dentists. Neither the smock nor the raven hair tied back severely could conceal the fact that the woman was disturbingly attractive.

Paul sprang for the rear exit, at precisely the same moment the rest of the passengers did precisely the same thing. The result might not have proved quite so calamitous had it not been for Paul's bulky suitcase. He tripped over the bag, which sent him crashing into the other passengers, which sent the lot of them tumbling out the end of the jeepney. They fell to the courtyard, where they lay in a squirming, muttering heap. Paul lay among them, splattered with red dust, brown spit, and multicolored chicken shit.

3

"JESUS, MARY, and Joseph!" said Frank Enright, watching the crowd tumble from the rear end of the jeepney.

"Oh my God!" said the dark woman at his side.

"Bloody hell!" said the big man in the embroidered barong.

The three gaped at the crumbled heap of figures in the dust for a moment, unsure how to react. When Paul rose from amid the bodies and peered around in confusion, the big man began to chortle.

"Will you cut that out, Harry!" Frank ordered. "He could have hurt himself."

"D'ya reckon 'hat's our boy, Frank?" replied the man called Harry, attempting, without much success, to suppress his mirth.

"If it is, he certainly knows how to make an entrance," said the dark woman, unable to contain a chuckle.

"You too, Liz!" Frank commanded. He turned a disapproving look on his two companions and, seeing the merriment written on their faces, only avoided catching the infection himself by looking rapidly back in Paul's direction. "C'mon now, let's try and behave for once," he said gruffly. "That poor fella looks in need of a helping hand."

Frank hiked the skirt of his long white cassock in a brawny fist and strode across the courtyard. His companions followed, having some difficulty mastering their expressions.

"I hope you haven't hurt yourself," Frank said solicitously on reaching Paul.

"Uh . . . no . . . I don't think so," Paul mumbled stiffly. He was acutely embarrassed. He had, in fact, suffered injury, but to his dignity, upon which he placed great value. He glanced myopically down at the ground at his feet. "But I do seem to have lost my glasses."

"Are you looking for these?" asked the woman Frank had called Liz, offering Paul his rimless spectacles and a disarming smile.

"Yes. Thank you," said Paul, a little awkwardly. He replaced his glasses and noticed Liz's smile. He added, more affably, "I'm afraid I can't see much without them."

"You must be Paul Stenmark," said Frank, noting with satisfaction the effect of Liz's smile.

"That's right," Paul replied. It was only with reluctance that he took his eyes off the dark woman and looked at the husky priest. When he did, he found himself being regarded by a pair of friendly gray eyes set in a deeply tanned, heavily lined face. The overall effect was faintly nautical. There was a sailor's squint in the eyes and a weatherbeaten look about the man.

"My name is Francis Enright," the priest said. "I run the mission across the way. The young lady is Elizabeth Buenaventura." He paused, amended, "Sorry, that's *Dr.* Elizabeth Buenaventura. She runs the clinic you might have noticed on your way in. As the locals say, Liz mends broken bodies. I try to do the same for broken souls." He looked fondly at the woman. "I confess she does a better job."

"Yes," Paul said, vaguely puzzled by the look the priest and the woman exchanged. There was something intimate about it, not the kind of regard he would have expected. "I'd been told you would be meeting me."

"I trust you've also been warned about the unlovely creature approaching like a breath of foul air," Frank continued, gesturing at Harry's looming hulk. "His name is Henry Quayle and he's responsible for most of our woes. If you have trouble understanding him, don't worry. Everybody does. It's because he can't speak English, only Australian." He grinned at Harry. "Harry and me are the twin pillars of the foreign community around here. I try to uplift things. Harry does his best to make my task impossible."

"Pay no attention to the papist," said Harry, stretching out a beefy welcoming paw. "He blames everything that goes wrong around here on me and me poor little dam." He winked at Paul. "Besides, he's always a touch ornery between shipments of altar wine."

There was no rancor in the exchange between the priest and the Australian, who clearly shared more than the same robust dimensions. The insults were delivered genially, received in the same spirit. But the atmosphere puzzled Paul. He had expected anything but jocularity between two individuals who, he had been forewarned, stood in opposing camps regarding the issue he had been sent to study. The priest was fighting the hydroelectric project. The Australian was building it. In view of what was at stake, Paul found the behavior of Frank and Harry frivolous. He was nonplussed and did not know how to respond.

Noticing Paul's discomfort, Frank intervened. "You probably want some time to clean up and rest," he said. "You'll be staying with me at that big house behind the church across the road. I'm afraid you don't have a lot of choice. I've got the only place around here with the space to put people up in reasonable comfort." He paused. "Except for Harry's bungalow, of course." He shot a withering glance at the Australian. "But that always seems to be occupied, despite my best efforts."

Harry smiled cheerfully into Frank's wintry glare.

"I'm sure I'll be comfortable with you, Father Enright," Paul interjected, perplexed once again at the byplay between the priest and the Australian.

"Please call me Frank," said the priest. He motioned toward the church. "Shall we go?"

"I'll be right with you as soon as I retrieve my bag," Paul replied, adding with deliberate emphasis, "*Father* Enright." He had no wish to be impolite, but he harbored a certain respect for titles. When it came to questions of rank of any kind, he was something of a stickler.

"Okay," said Frank with a mildly amused grin. "Let's try and get you settled in before folks around here start breaking down the door to see you." He raised an eyebrow at Paul. "I've got to warn you there's an awful lot of people who have been waiting for your arrival."

ONE OF them was, at that moment, studying Paul and the others with more than simple curiosity. He stood at a window in the L-shaped building that overlooked the courtyard. There was a Venetian blind on the window, which was partially closed. It screened the man's presence from outside scrutiny and threw alternating bands of light and shadow across his broad, almost square face. Beads of perspiration speckled his brow and temples.

The man was short and stocky, dressed in olive-green military fatigues that were darkly stained on the chest and back and underneath the armpits. On his outsize head he wore an outsize hat. It was black, styled like an American baseball cap. Inscribed across the hat's brim were brilliant yellow letters and symbols. For those who could decipher such runes, they indicated the man's name was Rosales and he was a lieutenant colonel of infantry attached to the 58th Battalion of the Philippine army.

Colonel Rosales remained absolutely still as he observed the conversation going on outside his window between Paul, Frank, Harry, and Liz. There was no expression on his face when the conversation ended and the four began to walk out of the courtyard in the direction of the church on the other side of the road. But the colonel followed their progress attentively, with eyes as cold as those of a night creature tracking its prey.

THE MAN sat by an open fire in a little jungle clearing, cleaning a military carbine made of black synthetic material with a metal folding stock. He was young and slim, dressed in torn lightweight trousers and a ragged sleeveless tunic crudely fashioned out of the same fabric. His legs were crossed in front of him. The carbine rested on his feet, which were bare. The soles were encrusted with a thick callus. As the man bent over the weapon, a lank of oily black hair fell across his lean face. His hair gleamed in the firelight.

The man did not look up when the young woman entered the clearing. She nodded at the circle of young men squatting around the fire. They were all as youthful and threadbare as the one cleaning the gun. The woman walked to him, sat down at his side.

"He's here," she announced.

The man finally glanced up, regarding the woman with large eyes as black as the night beyond the fire's reach. His features were even, attractive. He asked, "When?"

"He came on the afternoon jeepney."

"What's he like?"

"Younger than I expected." She shrugged. "Otherwise very American. You know the type: tall, blond, blue eyes." She smiled. "I think he's a little clumsy."

"Why do you say that?"

The woman chuckled. "He knocked everyone out of the jeepney."

The man grunted. "Don't let that fool you."

"What do you mean?"

"They're all like that at first," the man replied. "It's why we underestimate them so often." He turned, gazed into the fire. "Sometimes I wonder if they do it deliberately, just to throw us off guard."

The woman sat considering this. After a time she asked, "What are you going to do?"

The man smiled, revealing a large space between his even front teeth. "We've prepared a welcome for him."

"May I know what?"

The man looked from the fire to the woman. He continued to smile. "You'll know when it's time for you to know." His smile disappeared. He rose to his feet, lifting his weapon. "There's something I have to do first."

The woman looked up, watching the man carefully. "What?"

"See Alfredo," the man replied tersely.

"Tonight?"

"Yes."

"Why?" the woman asked with a trace of irritation.

The man raised his gun, inspected it in the firelight. "Because we still need him."

The woman studied the man's hands as they fondled the weapon. Her eyes, as always, were drawn to the extraordinarily long nail on one of his thumbs. "For how long," she asked, staring at the thumb, "are we going to have to cater to the whims of that man?"

The young man unclipped a magazine from a web belt at his waist. He checked that it was fully loaded, slammed it into the weapon. His eyes moved back to the woman, and his smile returned. He said softly:

"Until we don't need him anymore."

4

FRANK ENRIGHT sat in old Tom Conlin's rocking chair, cradling in his hand a glass of his precious Laphroaig. Both were bad signs, he knew, but he could not help it. He was not enjoying himself. He was bored and more than a little disappointed after spending an entire evening in the company of his newly arrived guest.

Frank took a deep swallow of the Scotch he normally handled with parsimony and stared bleakly at Paul. He could not escape a sinking feeling that the hopes he had pinned on the young man facing him had been misplaced. Frank was uncertain about Paul's precise brief, but his organization was well-known, widely respected even. It was no secret that he had come to judge whether or not Harry's cursed dams deserved the money to proceed. He had supposed that Paul would want to explore the affair thoroughly. To Frank, that meant mainly listening. Paul, instead, appeared to be intent on talking.

Which is what he was doing at the moment, sitting in Frank's spartan living room, nursing a San Miguel beer, the same beer he had been nursing for hours. It was what he had been doing since dinner, virtually nonstop.

Even Rosales had not managed to halt him. The colonel had shown up, unannounced as usual. He had been accompanied, as

usual, by the stunning Concepcion, who, as usual, had remained
totally silent. But the colonel's sinister presence, which could
subdue even Harry at his most garrulous, had only briefly derailed
the man's headlong monologue. Rosales had soon retreated, dragging his beautiful, mute mistress with him. Harry and Liz had
followed not long after. Each made a flimsy excuse and departed,
Liz with a sympathetic grimace, Harry with a wry smirk.

It was the nature of the conversation, as much as the sheer flow,
that mystified Frank. Paul was rattling on about something he
repeatedly referred to as "the global dietary energy supply." He
pronounced the phrase ponderously, as if it were in quotation
marks, the title of a learned discourse. As far as Frank could make
out, it was mostly a fog of dense jargon. Paul talked of catchment
areas and population pressures, rice yields and balance-of-
payments constraints, import requirements and export availability.
He discussed the production of millions of kilowatt-hours of electricity and the per-barrel price of Saudi Arabian crude. He never
mentioned, however, what to Frank was the fundamental issue.

Frank sat, savoring the smoky whisky he regarded as his only
concession to luxury, and studied Paul. He watched him solemnly
declaiming. The kid had all the answers. Frank had spent his life
looking for answers. He had even gone to the point of submerging
his own personality in a great professional brotherhood in an effort
to find them. All he had discovered was questions. The young man
in front of him did not have *any* questions. This irritated Frank. He
suddenly grew impatient.

"And what are you planning to do with the poor wretches who
have the misfortune of living in your bloody catchment area?"
Frank cut in, more acerbly than he intended.

"Huh?" replied Paul, startled by both the question and the tone
in which it was posed.

"There are eighty thousand people living along this river," Frank
continued, more mildly. "Correct me if I'm wrong, but I believe
the plan is to build four dams at separate locations across the river.

Now, I'm no expert, but it doesn't take a whole lot of foresight to realize that if this project goes through, a fair-sized chunk of this valley is going to be under water. Is that right?"

Paul paused and blinked.

"Well, it's true the prefeasibility studies identified four potential development sites in the river basin," Paul replied uneasily. "But there's still some question, due to what I understand are adversities obtaining at some of the sites, whether to proceed with all four. In fact, the order of merit in terms of production cost is—"

"Spare me the details," Frank interrupted with a wave of his hand. "Is it or is it not true that the valley is going to be flooded?"

"Certainly you can't have a hydroelectric project without reservoir storage," Paul answered. "Offhand, I don't know the precise figures. Judging from the design capacity, however, I'd say we're talking somewhere in the neighborhood of eight hundred million cubic meters per dam. That's total, not usable, storage, of course—"

"So the valley's going to be under water," Frank broke in again.

"No," Paul replied, a hint of impatience in his voice. "Not all of it."

"Some of it, then?"

"Well . . . yes, of course."

"And what happens to the eighty thousand people whose lands, whose homes, are going to be inundated?"

"That's an exaggeration. Nowhere near eighty thousand people are going to be directly affected, even if all four dams are built."

"How many then?"

"That's difficult to say exactly without knowing how many hydro sites will be developed to tie in with the provincial grid."

"I'll settle for ballpark estimates. Thirty, fifty, eighty percent?"

"I'm afraid I don't really know what you're driving at," said Paul, irritated. "I didn't come all this way to face an interrogation."

"Good Lord, man!" Frank cried, exasperated. "Maybe if you try to answer my questions you'll find out."

Paul's eyes grew round. "If all four sites are developed, about half the population of the river basin is going to be affected in one way or another," he answered quickly. He was a little taken aback.

"You mean forty thousand people are going to lose their lands?" Frank demanded. His voice was rising.

"No, no, no," said Paul hastily. "Nowhere near that number. Ten, maybe fifteen thousand at most."

"But you said half the people in the valley."

"I said half would be affected. Ten thousand or so will have their properties flooded when the lakes rise behind the dams. The rest will be touched only indirectly."

"Indirectly?"

"There will be land-use restrictions on the forests above the reservoirs," Paul replied. Noticing the look in Frank's eye, he added nervously, "To protect the watershed."

Frank grew suddenly aware of the menace in his voice and the effect it was having on Paul. He relaxed. "Sorry," he said with a sheepish grin. "As you can see, all of this is very close to me." He rose and walked across the room to where a rattan table stood, bearing a single bottle. He took the bottle, poured three fingers into the empty glass in his hand. He looked at Paul. "Want another San Mig?"

"Pardon?" Paul asked, a shade breathlessly.

Frank gestured at the glass of beer, clearly stale, in Paul's hand. "A San Miguel. It's the name of the beer you're drinking, or not drinking, by the look of it. You care for another one?"

Paul glanced quizzically down at his glass, as if surprised at finding it there. "Oh yeah . . . sure . . . that'd be fine." He did not really want another beer, but he was now wary of his host.

"Wait right there. I've got some on ice in the kitchen."

Paul watched Frank pad, bearlike, into the kitchen. The priest was dressed in faded blue jeans, worn sneakers, and an old Notre Dame football jersey. Paul thought the man didn't look much like a priest. In the sweater, he looked more like a college fullback. He was unaware of how close to the mark was this observation.

"Sorry if things got a little heated there," said Frank on his return. He handed Paul a fresh glass of beer. "Mind if we start over?"

"Not at all," Paul answered, even though he no longer relished pursuing the subject. "But I'm not certain what the point is you're trying to make."

"My question is, what is going to happen to the people in this valley who are going to be pushed off their lands to make way for this project?" Frank asked patiently.

"They'll be relocated. I can assure you now that you have nothing to worry about on that score. There is already a resettlement scheme in place. Nobody's going to suffer. The reverse, in fact."

"How's that?"

Paul leaned forward eagerly, once more warming to the subject. "I don't know whether or not you're aware of it, but this is not just another hydroelectric project. It's also a massive irrigation scheme. Once the dams are in place and the artificial lakes are full, we'll have the capacity to irrigate thousands upon thousands of hectares of flatlands now lying idle. I don't have the figures at my fingertips, but I'd be surprised if each and every cultivator displaced will not eventually be farming seven or eight times the number of hectares he is at the moment."

Frank watched Paul. He asked quietly, "And the terraces?"

"The terraces?" Paul replied, puzzled.

Frank felt the gloom descending. "Those shelved rice paddies climbing up the mountainsides you may have noticed on your way here."

"Oh, those terraces." Paul shrugged. "They disappear, of course. No great loss. They're pretty, but they must be a backbreaking way to cultivate wetland rice. Awfully inefficient, too."

Frank slowly closed his eyes.

Paul, noticing this, continued, "Once we get these people down on good, rich, level ground, you'll see the progress. Give them plenty of water for irrigation, good seedstock, the latest in machinery, fertilizer, pesticides and so on, why, I guarantee that yields will skyrocket. Not only that, but the real beauty of this scheme is that while we're making a new life for those poor farmers we are also transforming the energy of that river outside, now completely wasted, into electricity to fuel the development of the entire country. Everybody benefits."

Frank gazed mournfully down at his glass, which was once again empty. "I think we'd better arrange for you to see Alfredo."

"Alfredo?"

"Alfredo Dantog," Frank replied, rising. He shambled across the room for refill.

"Who's he?"

"A local tribal chief down the river a ways," Frank answered over his shoulder as he poured Scotch into his glass.

"Is he important?"

"Yes," said Frank, turning to face Paul. "He's important."

5

THE YOUNG man raised a hand and brushed the lank black hair from his black eyes. There was a hint of frustration in the gesture. "*Apo Pangat,*" he said patiently, "I don't think you understand."

"The problem is, I understand too well," replied the man sitting opposite on the floor of the hut. He was much older but he had the same black hair and eyes and the same lean, hard look.

The young man took a breath. "*Apo Pangat*—"

"I've already given you my answer," the older man interrupted calmly. His bony face was the color of hammered bronze.

"But . . ."

"No matter what you say, the answer will remain no." The older man folded his arms across his chest, revealing cords of wiry muscle beneath the rolled-up sleeves of his faded denim shirt.

The young man closed his eyes, as if struggling for control. He reopened them, regarded the older man. "I have killed. I have taken heads. I have respected the *bodong*. I have married into your people. My child's veins run with your people's blood. Am I now to be denied a voice in the councils?"

There was glint of amusement in the older man's eyes. "What councils?"

"This."

"This is not a council."

"It amounts to the same thing, does it not?"

The older man fingered the triple string of multicolored coral lozenges wrapped tightly around his neck. He said evasively, "And the taking of heads is now frowned upon."

"I know," the young man said, sighing, "but it is sometimes hard to abandon the old ways." He paused, fixed the older man with an intense look. "I do not need to remind you that I was there with your son."

The older man's brow furrowed, as if in pain. He glanced away, let his gaze wander around the room where they sat. It was a simple room. Floors and walls were made of the same rough, unfinished planking, weathered a dull gray. The ceiling was constructed of thatch. There was a single window with a cracked pane of glass. There were no furnishings of any kind other than a lantern on the floor. The lantern emitted a low, steady growl and cast a stark white light. It threw harsh, achromatic shadows across the men's faces.

The older man looked back at the younger. "You may speak."

The young man took care not to betray any sign of satisfaction. "If this thing is to be stopped," he said, "you must allow us to act now."

"Why?"

"The American brings the money that will permit them to build their dams."

"That is not my understanding of his role."

"Do not believe them when they tell you he is here merely to investigate."

"I have no reason to disbelieve *them*, as you say."

"They have told you nothing but lies before."

"Frank has never lied to me, nor has Liz. Not even Harry has tried to deceive me."

The young man shifted uncomfortably. "The priest deals in half-truths," he muttered. "You are still led astray."

"Even if that were true, which I do not believe, the American is here, is he not?"

R I C E W I N E

"Yes."

"I am willing to accept that as evidence that the issue remains undecided. He did not need to come all this way if they already know what they are going to do."

"It is camouflage."

"Perhaps."

"So you will talk to him."

"Yes. I will try to convince him of the justice of our cause."

"And when he does not listen?"

"How am I to know that until I have tried?"

"But what if I am right?"

The older man shrugged. "Then we will stop them by other means."

"How?" asked the young man with a dry laugh. "With the priest's prayers?"

The older man smiled. "Frank has given us more than prayers."

"Yes," replied the young man scornfully, "evenings of political reflection, protest meetings, letters to the press."

"It has been successful so far."

"Has it?" the young man demanded. "Do you really think that's what has stopped them in the past?"

"I will not deny the effectiveness of your methods," the older man answered placidly. "You have been of great help."

"Then why do you prevent me from acting now, before it is too late?"

"Because I do not believe it is too late." The older man placed a finger on his chest. "*I* will talk to this American"—he swung the finger until it was pointed at the young man—"and *you* will do him no harm."

The young man looked away.

The older man contemplated the younger for a moment. "There's another reason I do not want you to act," he said quietly.

The young man glanced at him quizzically.

"We are not fighting the same battle."

"What?"

"I'm trying to stop these dams," replied the older man. "You're trying to do something else."

"I don't understand," said the young man warily.

"At the moment, we share certain interests that lead us in the same direction. That's fine with me as long as it lasts. But I am under no illusion. There will come a time when our paths will diverge."

The young man opened his mouth to protest.

The older man silenced him with an upraised palm. "While we are traveling together, you can continue to count on my support. You are a useful companion. That's why I have taken pains to give you shelter, not because of your apparent attempts to become one of us." He paused, cocked an eye at the young man. "How are your wife and child, by the way?"

The young man shrugged uneasily.

"How long has it been since you have seen either of them?"

"I've been busy," the young man muttered, averting his eyes.

The older man studied the younger silently for a time. "You warned me earlier of people who would deceive me," he said at last. "Remember that I am not easily fooled."

The young man's eyes swung back to the older man's.

"And remember this, too," continued the older man. "When we go our separate ways, as we inevitably will, you will go alone. In the meantime," he added coldly, "if you abuse my hospitality, you risk losing it."

The black eyes locked. In the older pair, there was a calm self-assurance. In the younger, a gleam of something less pleasant.

6

PAUL STENMARK was uncomfortable. The cause was sitting next to him on the front seat of a battered Land Rover, handling the steering wheel and complicated gearshifts with a rough skill surprising for so delicate a woman. Initially, Paul had been delighted to learn that the exotic Dr. Elizabeth Buenaventura, or Liz, as everyone seemed to call her, had been appointed his guide for the trip to see the man Father Enright had called Alfredo. Now he was not so sure. For the doctor was angry, waspishly so. Her lips were set in a thin line, her almond eyes narrowed, and she was flinging the Land Rover around a rutted dirt track with a reckless abandon. Paul was not sure exactly what he had done to irritate the lady. But he was aware that he was the agent of her distress.

Things had gone awry from the start, as soon as Liz had arrived at Father Enright's house shortly after dawn and had seen the priest's condition. Frank looked like hell. The gray eyes were streaked with blood and rimmed by dark circles. His hair was a wild tangle of curls the color of iron filings. There was a pallor beneath the mahogany tan, and all the lines on his face sagged downward, giving him a forlorn appearance. A simple hangover, Paul had assumed, not without a certain righteous superiority. But Liz had been instantly concerned. She hovered around the priest, clucking and cooing. She straightened his collar, brushed a thicket of curls from his forehead with her hand, and spying the empty bottle of Laphroaig, nagged him gently.

Attempting to strike what he regarded as a chummy note as the pair set off on their journey, Paul had made a crack about "whisky priests." Liz's reaction had been instantaneous. The Land Rover skidded to a halt in a cloud of red dust. She turned and raked Paul with her eyes.

"Just what the hell do you mean by that?"

"Why, nothing," Paul stammered. "Only that Father Enright had a lot to drink last night. . . ." He smiled lamely. "Sort of like the proverbial Irish priest." Finding only a stony glare for response, he added, "Sorry if I've offended you. I guess it was a stupid remark."

"Yes, it was," Liz replied contemptuously. She continued to glower at Paul, elegant nostrils flaring, black eyes aglint.

Paul wilted under the look, which did not, however, prevent him from noting once again the woman's appeal. She was older than he had originally thought, a maturity betrayed by a tracery of fine lines running from the corners of her eyes and mouth. But she was still lovely. She had an oval, olive colored face, with feline eyes arching upward and outward beneath a prominent brow, high cheekbones bracketing a narrow, sculpted nose, and a wide, full mouth. Even in repose, it was a haughty face, suggesting arrogance, like that of an insolent cat. When animated by the look that was being leveled at Paul, it spoke eloquently of disdain.

Which accurately mirrored what she was feeling. She had spent a good part of her life among people like the American sitting beside her. They were blunderers who trampled upon the sensitivities of others, usually leaving a trail of devastation in their wake. Her father had been one of them. The husband she had abandoned in Manila had been another.

The memory of her husband inflamed Liz's ire. She accelerated the Land Rover far too fast into a tight curve in the track, venting her anger. He had not been an unkind man, simply vacant. Like the life they had shared. There had been no passion; not in bed, nor in relation to the malaise she saw creeping over her native land. It was this, she had come to realize, that had finally driven her away. She had fled an existence she believed to be as false as the sense of security provided by the high walls, topped with barbed wire and pieces of jagged glass, that surrounded her villa in the Manila suburbs, identical to the fortresslike homes of her entire circle of friends in the capital. At the time, she was not sure what she was running away from. But she sensed, obscurely, a gathering storm and suspected that it was likely to be of such magnitude that a few strands of twisted wire and bits of broken glass would offer no protection.

Two years later, she was firmly convinced that a convulsion was approaching. She had never regarded herself as particularly political, certainly not as a revolutionary. She had, in fact, always kept a discreet distance from the young radicals at the medical school preaching blood and fire, most of whom were now languishing in the huge military prison on the outskirts of the capital. But two years in the valley, working with Frank among the locals, had changed Liz. It had sharpened the edge of the social conscience that first led her to question her previous life. Much to her own amazement, it had also given birth to a keen political awareness. She now believed, with the near-fanatic conviction of the late convert, that peaceful change in her country was impossible, and therefore violent change was inevitable. She could not envision the form that it was likely to take. The source, however, she felt she could identify. Surveying the surrounding hills through the cracked and dusty windshield of the Land Rover, she suspected that it was up in those mountains somewhere, in the hands of a ragged, barefoot band of her compatriots.

Liz cast a furtive look at Paul, wondering how much he knew of the local situation. She decided to find out. "I suppose you're aware," she said, "that we're right in the heart of bandit country now."

"Bandits?" asked Paul, uncertain whether to be pleased at the passing of Liz's sulk or nervous about her reference to the terrain.

"This is NPA territory—the people the government calls CTs, communist terrorists. These hills are supposed to be infested with them."

"NPA?" queried Paul. "Terrorists?" He was still struggling to cope with the woman's mercurial change of mood.

"The New People's Army—the armed wing of the Communist Party of the Philippines." She paused, asked incredulously, "You don't mean to tell me you've never heard of them?"

"Of course I've heard of them," Paul snapped. He was irritated by her tone. "They're a bunch of left-wingers who have been mounting some kind of low-intensity insurgency all over this area." He snorted. "I believe they're more of a nuisance than a threat."

Liz glanced quizzically at Paul. "Where did you hear that, the part about being a nuisance?"

"I was briefed back in Washington." He added, "You surely don't think people like me are sent out to places like this without a thorough grounding in local conditions?"

"Of course not," Liz answered quietly as a tiny smile crept across her face. "How silly of me."

Paul did not catch the smile. But he felt mollified by her reply, enough to persuade him that another attempt at establishing some kind of rapport with the enticing, if prickly, woman might not be fruitless. He said tentatively, "There *are* some serious gaps in my knowledge you might help to fill."

"For example?" asked Liz, not unpleasantly.

Paul was encouraged. "This fellow we're on our way to see, for example. Alfredo something or other. I'm afraid I know nothing about him except what Father Enright told me last night."

"And what did Frank tell you?"

"Only that he's some kind of local honcho who carries a lot of weight and is against the hydro project."

"That about sums it up. What else do you want to know?"

"Who is he? Why is he so important? What's he got against this project?"

Liz blew out her cheeks, whistling softly. "Now *that* will take some time. You're asking for a history lesson."

"I'm here to learn," Paul said, displaying a disarming smile, "if you're willing to teach."

Liz regarded Paul thoughtfully. She glanced up the road, then down at the steel watch on her wrist. She said at last, "All right. But there's something you must see first."

Liz drove on for several minutes, scanning the hillsides until she spotted whatever it was she was looking for. She pulled the Land Rover into a small widening in the track. "Here we are," she announced. "I hope you don't mind a short hike."

PAUL LAY on his stomach atop a bed of flat pink granite, gazing at Liz with unconcealed admiration. He knew that if he continued to do so the quickening in his loins could develop into something embarrassing. But he found it difficult to take his eyes off the doctor.

Liz was standing waist-deep in a pool of clear water beneath a miniature cataract, which was cascading upon her head and crashing down over her shoulders. Her head was thrown back. Her shoulder-length black hair was plastered shinily to her skull and neck. Her eyes were closed and her wide mouth relaxed in a dreamy, almost erotic smile. Through the fabric of the white T-shirt she wore, Paul could see the outline of her small breasts.

It was not what he had expected to find at the end of Liz's "short hike." The length of the journey had not bothered him as much as the direction. He had followed Liz straight up the near-vertical flank of a heavily jungled mountain. By the time they reached their destination, he had been drenched in sweat and panting with fatigue.

Which had prevented him from appreciating the site. They were perched on a wide granite shelf partway up the side of the mountain. A spring burst from the face of the cliff above the shelf, forming an iridescent waterfall as it tumbled into a shallow pool scoured out of the living rock. From the pool, the spring rushed across the shelf in a bubbling stream to the far edge, where it plunged a thousand feet to the floor of the valley below.

The peaks of the Cordillera marched off to the horizon, dark green in the foreground, dissolving gradually into a blue haze in the distance. The river, far below, meandered in a narrow brown ribbon between hillsides blanketed with rice terraces. Directly below the shelf, it ran in a wide loop that almost completely encircled, like a natural moat, a terraced hill with a sloping crest. Upon the crest sprawled a village. Thin plumes of blue smoke drifted lazily skyward from a dozen hearths beneath a collection of thatched roofs.

Paul saw little of this, however. On arriving, he had begged a moment to recover his breath, then collapsed thankfully onto his back. He had closed his eyes and, lulled by the smooth, sun-warmed granite, had dozed briefly. On awakening, he had found Liz beneath the waterfall, where his attention remained.

Paul decided regretfully that the activity in his loins called for preventive action before it was too late. He rolled, sat upright.

Liz saw the motion. She dove headfirst into the pool, offering a fleeting glimpse of a round bottom beneath a bikini and a flash of long coppery thighs. A moment later, her head, sleek as an otter's, bobbed to the surface. She breast-stroked leisurely to the water's edge.

"I guess I fell asleep," Paul called.

"I know," Liz replied as she stepped from the pool like a dark forest sprite. Her sleek head dripped water onto shoulders draped in a mantle of glistening hair.

"Sorry," said Paul, running his eyes over the curve of her belly between the bottom of the T-shirt and the top of the bikini.

"Don't be," said Liz. "It gave me a chance for a swim. I couldn't resist. I never can when I come to this place."

"It does look marvelous," said Paul, his glance drawn to the small breasts beneath the wet T-shirt.

Liz caught the look. She crossed her hands over her chest. "You want to turn around for a minute?" she said, a little curtly.

"Sure," Paul replied with an amused grin.

After a moment, Liz spoke to Paul's back. "You ready for that history lesson now, or would you prefer a swim first?"

"I guess I'd better have the lesson."

"Be right with you."

Liz walked by Paul, knotting a man's blue shirt around her waist above the khaki shorts. "Come look at this," she said over her shoulder as she moved toward the edge of the precipice. On reaching it, she sat, pointed down.

Paul followed. "You mean that village on the top of the hill?"

"Yes," Liz answered. "That's where we're going. That's Alfredo's *barrio*. You asked me earlier who he is. That's why I brought you here." She paused, swept an arm around the surrounding vista. "That's who he is: that village; that river; those terraces. You can't ever hope to come close to understanding Alfredo unless you can understand the context in which he lives. He's not like you or me. The missionaries were the first ones to make that mistake."

"Missionaries?"

"Yes. He's very bright, you see. The missionaries spotted it right away, when he was only a child. They thought they had a candidate for their own work. They lavished an expensive education on him, sent him off to the university. They even wanted to send him abroad for higher studies. But they did not understand him. He refused to go anywhere, came back to these hills. He has no independent existence apart from what we are looking at right now."

"I'm afraid I'm not following you."

Liz sighed. "Maybe I'm getting ahead of myself." She pushed

herself to her feet, walked toward Paul. "Let's start with the bare facts. Alfredo Dantog. He's a *Pangat*—a tribal leader, a chieftain if you like. He's somewhere between fifty and sixty years old. He's not sure exactly. None of the people of his generation know their precise birthdates. It gives you an idea of how recently this place has been *civilized*." She stressed the last word ironically, arching her eyebrows. "When Alfredo was a baby, the main pastime around here was headhunting."

"Did you say headhunting?"

"Yes. All the tribes in the highlands practiced it. Some of them still do. They lopped off heads for dozens of reasons: revenge, pride, prestige, proof of manhood, anguish over the loss of a loved one. It must have been pretty frightful. A young man's voice couldn't be heard in the village councils until he had taken a head. A relative accidentally killed could not rest easy unless a stranger's head was offered to the spirits. For those who—"

"But these hills must have been drenched in blood."

Liz shrugged. "I suppose they were. But the system was not without its benefits. The tribes' reputation was so fearsome that it saved them from the depredations of all our conquerors. The Spanish were in this country for four hundred years and they never really penetrated these hills. Neither did the Japanese during the war. You Americans made some inroads. But it was really the missionaries—Belgians at first, then Americans, some Irish—who were responsible for introducing the twentieth century and all its *glories*." Again there was the ironic stress.

"You sound as if you're not convinced that it was beneficial."

"You're right. I'm not convinced."

"Why?"

"I think the answer is self-evident."

"You've lost me again."

Liz regarded Paul thoughtfully. "Your very presence here is proof of the evil that awaits these people."

"*My* presence?" Paul exclaimed. "Evil? But I'm here to offer them a better way of life. I want to give them an opportunity to break out of their misery."

Liz walked to the edge of the cliff and looked down at the river and the terraces. "Does this look like misery?" she asked quietly over her shoulder.

Paul began to grow impatient. "Oh, it's pretty enough, I'll grant you that," he said sharply. "But behind that pristine loveliness is dire poverty, serious inequality of income, a culture that is steadily declining due to a host of interconnected factors: population growth, diminishing soil fertility, receding forests. All I want to do is to arrest the decline and give these people a chance to raise their living standards."

"At what price?" Liz asked.

"At hardly any price at all. A year or two of discomfort adjusting to a new environment, which doesn't seem to be an awful lot to pay to save a people from an endless cycle of want."

Liz threw an arm behind her back, pointed down at the terraces. "But if you destroy those, you destroy these people," she cried.

"Are you trying to tell me that if I trade one miserable rice paddy halfway up the side of an inaccessible hill for seven paddies on good, flat, easily worked ground, I'm going to extinguish a people?" Paul asked.

"Yes!"

They stared mutely at each other across the flat expanse of granite. There was a tense silence, broken only by the gurgle of the tumbling waterfall.

Paul turned finally, walked to the edge of the pool, sank onto a large boulder. He muttered, "Well, that just doesn't make any sense to me."

"It might not make any sense to you, but it certainly does to people like Alfredo," Liz replied, more calmly.

"What's so bloody special about those terraces?" Paul asked grumpily.

Liz sighed. "Do you have any idea how old they are?"

Paul shook his head.

"It's still a matter of debate, but some experts argue they were begun around the time of Christ, maybe even earlier."

"So?"

"So would you flood the Great Wall? The Pyramids? The Roman Forum?"

"If it meant a better life for deprived people, I probably would."

Liz threw up her arms in exasperation. She declared, "Well, I don't agree with you, and neither does Alfredo."

"You keep carrying on about this guy. Why is he so important to you?"

"It doesn't matter whether or not he's important to me. He is important, however, as far as the opposition to your little project is concerned."

"It's not *my* little project," Paul answered. "Seriously, I would like to know why Alfredo is important."

A look of malice slid into Liz's eyes. "It's because of the *bodong*."

"The what?"

"The *bodong*," replied Liz, satisfied.

Paul dropped his head into this hands. "More mumbo jumbo."

"It's not mumbo jumbo, and it's not that complicated if you keep in mind the history of these hills. It's a system the tribes evolved to break the vicious cycle of blood feuds that arose during the head-hunting days when any death, even an accidental one, required another head to avenge it. As you can imagine, the vendettas that resulted were horrific. Tribes were locked in conflict for generations. Well, somewhere along the line some bright, pacific soul came up with the idea of a *pagta ti bodong*."

"A what?"

"It means, literally, a peace pact. Warring clans agreed to cease killing each other off. To enforce the peace, a pact holder was appointed. His job was to kill any member of his own clan who broke the peace. Revenge was thus kept within the clan, and the endless rhythm of vendetta was ruptured. It worked remarkably well. Still does, as a matter of fact." Liz gestured down at the village. "That little place alone has more than a dozen peace pacts in operation at the moment with other clans scattered all over the hills. In most cases, Alfredo holds the *bodong*, which gives you an idea of how widely trusted he is among the tribes."

Paul shrugged. "What on earth does all of this have to do with a perfectly straightforward hydroelectric project?"

"Everything," Liz replied. "Not long ago virtually all the tribes in the valley agreed to take part in a massive peace pact directed against your project. It's probably the first time in their long and bloody history the tribes have united in a single *pagta ti bodong*. They have, in effect, agreed to defend each other against your scheme."

"That doesn't explain Alfredo's importance."

"Alfredo holds the *bodong*."

"I'm not sure I understand what that means."

"That's the point," said Liz. "Nobody does."

"Huh?"

"It's never happened before, so nobody knows for certain how it will work, or even *if* it will work."

Paul shook his head in confusion. "You've lost me again."

"In theory," said Liz, "any tribesman who violates the *bodong* by acting against the interests of his people, which in this case means acting in favor of your project, Alfredo has the authority to kill."

"Christ!" Paul exclaimed.

"Now do you see why he is important?"

"But this can't be happening—not in this day and age."

"That's the general opinion of most people outside of these hills. I don't happen to share it."

"Why?"

"Because of Alfredo."

Paul gave Liz a puzzled look.

"Let me tell you a story." Liz paused, swept her eyes around the hills. "Two or three years ago a member of Alfredo's clan killed a member of another clan. It was no accident: it was an outright murder. There was a peace pact in operation between the two clans, and Alfredo held the *bodong*. As a result, he was faced with a choice. He either killed the offending member of his own clan or he was responsible for the outbreak of tribal war. Alfredo did not flinch. He killed the culprit with his own hands. He beheaded him." Liz stopped.

"So?" Paul asked after a time.

"Alfredo loved that man very much." Liz looked back at Paul. "It was his eldest son."

7

HENRY QUAYLE lay on his back, head propped upright with hands folded behind his neck. He watched the pair of them at work with a certain critical detachment, as if admiring their technical virtuosity while reserving a final judgment on the overall impact of the performance. Gloria, or it may have been Lourdes, had his penis in her mouth. Lourdes, or it may have been Gloria, was doing the same with his testicles. Each young woman, neither of whom was older than twenty, also cradled an ice cube on her tongue. It was what the sailors of the Seventh Fleet gleefully referred to as a "bee jay on the rocks," a specialty of the little club where Quayle had found the two of them, on the raucous strip just beyond the electrified fence protecting the manicured lawns and white-painted curbs of the big United States naval base at Subic Bay.

Dropping his head back onto the pillow, Quayle closed his eyes in an attempt to luxuriate in the melange of heat and cold that was being applied to his genitals. As he feared, it didn't work. His eyes opened grudgingly after a moment and he was forced to admit that the novelty of the sensation had long ago worn thin. He sighed wearily, reaching for a bottle of San Miguel on the nightstand beside the bed. The trouble is, mate, he told himself, you're getting too old for this bloody nonsense.

Raising himself on an elbow, he pulled at the beer and looked down at the girls fighting what was clearly developing into a losing engagement. They're all so alike, he thought, as if assembled on some gigantic production line churning out dark-haired, dark-eyed nymphets. And there had been so very many of them, scattered across three continents, in all the Third World backwaters where his slide rule and his voracious appetites had led him for more than thirty years.

"Oh, Harree!" cried Gloria/Lourdes, stringing out the last syllable of his name. "I think maybe you not too interested today." There was a tone of mock complaint in her voice.

"I think maybe you be drinking too much, Harree!" cried Lourdes/Gloria, pronouncing his name with the same singsong intonation, in the same birdlike voice.

"I think maybe you're both bloody near right," Harry replied gruffly in a heavy Australian twang. "Why don't you ladies stop playing with me privates long enough to make us all some breakfast."

The girls rose, giggling and chattering brightly. Harry watched the bare brown bottoms disappear through the bedroom door. He looked at his watch, counting the seconds. On cue, the radio in the kitchen burst into deafening life, blaring synthetic international pop. Harry smiled resignedly, vaguely disappointed by the predictability of his companions. He resolved, once again, to put them both on the afternoon jeepney back to the provincial capital, where they could catch the bus to Olongapo. At least they wouldn't have to work as hard with all those eager young Yank sailors, he thought glumly.

He took a sip of beer, found it warm, put the bottle aside. He shook a cigarette from a crumpled pack of filterless Camels, lit it, looked at it with distaste after a single puff, and angrily stubbed it out. Agitated by a nameless disquiet, he rose from the bed and strode into the adjoining bathroom, where he peered carefully into the mirror above the washstand.

He was not particularly pleased with what stared back. It was still a strong, intelligent face, but the line of the jaw was fading, the square chin with the cleft at the point had acquired a companion or two, the broad cheekbones and bent nose wore tiny red starbursts, and the once-crisp black hair was shot through with gray. It was the brown eyes beneath the bristling brows that he found most disturbing. They were set in dark, puffy pouches and glazed with something indefinable, conveying ennui.

"You're tired, my old son," he said aloud to his image. He spoke fondly, as if talking to an old and doddering uncle. "There's nowhere else to go, nothing else to see."

Taking a last, long look at himself, he thought suddenly of home, which surprised him. It seemed like centuries since he had left Hobart. At the time, there had been no regrets. He had been only too eager to stretch his wings in the world outside provincial Australia. But he had subsequently flown so far and so high that he found there was no longer anyplace to alight. There was nothing he could call home: there was nothing he wanted to. He had spent his life moving, always moving. It had been a reckless, carefree odyssey, short on self-examination perhaps, but long on the sheer joy of existence. He exulted in the day-by-day, minute-by-minute accumulation of experience. He delighted in whatever was bizzare, which had led him down strange, ill-traveled byways and, in the end, exacted a price. There were three wives he had picked up along the way who could testify to that. As each of them had done, he thought wryly, in divorce courts from Singapore to Santiago.

Remembering his wives did little to improve his mood. He ambled back into the bedroom, ruefully recalling that each of the three had profited from the experience of living with him. None more so than that mercenary Vietnamese bitch now comfortably ensconced in the beachfront house among the Monterey pines, for which he was still paying. He glanced disconsolately around the sparsely furnished bedroom, built to standard company specifications. It was like all the impersonal rooms he had camped out in for the last three decades. There were dams, roads, and bridges bearing his personal imprint all over Asia, Africa, and South America. Yet all he had to show for it was a room like this, a distressingly meager bank account, and a long string of memories. It wasn't much, he thought bleakly. Maybe when this job was over he would take up that offer from his current employers. Melbourne was not such a bad town. Sydney was better. But they were not far apart.

Harry's forlorn calculations were suddenly interrupted by two naked brown streaks crashing through the bedroom door, uttering shrill twitters. Long black hair flying, the girls collided repeatedly as they tore frantically around the room in what was apparently a desperate search for panties, bras, and blouses.

"What's got into the pair of you?" Harry shouted, narrowly sidestepping a flying nymph.

In answer to his question there was a loud bang as the front door of the bungalow swung shut and a deep, gravelly voice, clearly that of Frank Enright, called, "Anybody home?"

Harry grinned at the girls, who looked back pleadingly, trapped sinners on the brink of retribution. He chuckled. "Maybe it's true what they say. You people will never recover from four hundred years in a Spanish convent followed by fifty in Hollywood."

Still chortling, he pulled on shirt and trousers and went out to receive the priest, framing a good-natured insult with which to greet him. But after one look at the expression on Frank's face, he changed his mind. "Jeez, mate," he said with concern. "You're looking a bit bloody crook."

Enright, attuned to Harry's Australianisms, smiled wanly. "I've had better days, I've got to admit."

"What's the problem?"

"Just about everything. Got time for a chat?"

"Pull up a chair, your eminence. We're here to serve." Harry eyed Frank. "But aren't we reversing the roles?"

Frank gave Harry his wan smile again. "I suppose we are, but there's nobody else around this place I can talk to."

"Where's Liz?" asked Harry, instantly regretting the query.

Frank looked quickly aside, momentarily flustered. After a pause, awkward for both, he replied, "She's off with our new arrival. I asked her to take him downriver, to talk to Alfredo."

Harry nodded slowly, asked gently, "You want to talk about Liz?"

Frank studied his hands, folded in his lap. "No," he murmured at last. "That's one I have to figure out for myself." He sighed and glanced admiringly at the Australian. "Not much gets by you, does it, Harry?"

"Not much," Harry agreed cheerfully. "It's been a matter of survival. I learned through bitter experience that I wasn't likely to last very long in the kind of business I do, dealing with the unsavory crowd I deal with, unless I kept my eyes wide open." He searched the priest's craggy features for a moment. "But surely you didn't come here to compliment me on my personal radar?"

"As a matter of fact, that's precisely why I wanted to talk to you. I'm having some doubts about the efficiency of my own radar, as you call it, and I'd like to get a second opinion."

"I'm all ears."

"It's about this Stenmark fellow."

"Mmmm. I take it our young friend from Washington has not lived up to your expectations."

"You're right. He's not at all what I expected."

"What did you expect?"

"I'm not exactly sure. I suppose someone a little older, a little more . . ." He hesitated, searching for the right word. "Polished."

"Is that your complaint?"

"No. It isn't his youth or his clumsiness that bothers me. He seems bright enough. And he certainly appears to know his stuff. He nearly drove me bananas last night after you and Liz abandoned me. I got an incredibly long and detailed lecture on the fundamentals of underdevelopment, from A to Z, the works."

"Then what is the problem?"

Frank paused. "I know this may sound ridiculous, but I think that his very expertise is the problem. He's got all the facts and figures at his fingertips. Believe me, he can bury us both in the jargon and statistics of underdevelopment. He not only thinks he has a cure for mankind's ills, he *knows* he has one, at least for the ills afflicting that part of mankind that happens to be colored black or brown or yellow."

"So?"

"So he's so bloody cocksure of himself that he seems to be totally incapable of listening. And *that's* what worries me."

"Why?"

"Unless my radar is malfunctioning, I'd say the fellow has already made up his mind about our little problem here. I thought he'd come to listen to us. Now I'm afraid he's here to convert us."

Harry grinned, amused by the incongruity of Frank's complaint, a missionary objecting to proselytism.

Abashed, Frank raised a hand in defeat. "All right, all right," he said. "I concede the point. Call it a bad choice of words." He looked at Harry. "But seriously, does any of this make sense to you, or is my imagination overwrought again?"

"It makes perfectly good sense. What surprises me is that you're surprised."

"What do you mean?"

"Judging from the symptoms you describe, our friend appears to be suffering from a common enough malady. It's one, I might add, to which your own countrymen seem to have become peculiarly susceptible in modern times."

"I'm not following you."

Harry gazed thoughtfully at the priest. He said suddenly, "How about a cold tube?"

"What?"

"A beer. You want a nice cold San Mig?"

"No, I don't, Harry," Frank said impatiently. "What I want is an answer to the question I just asked."

"You're not going to like it."

"Try me."

"I'd rather not. Let's have a beer instead."

"Harry!"

Harry sighed in resignation. "All right. But don't say I didn't warn you. It sounds to me like our friend Stenmark is a victim of something you, of all people, should be able to understand."

"Me?"

"Yes, you. Forgive me, Frank, but Stenmark's affliction if that's the right word, is an updated version of your own. He's suffering from the missionary syndrome, pure and simple. The only difference is that his is more difficult to diagnose than yours because it's cloaked in all of the flummery of the technological age."

"You make it sound like a disease."

"I'm sorry for that. Believe me, I'm not trying to pass judgment."

"Even so, I fail to see any similarity."

"Do you really?" Harry snorted. "I doubt that. Why did you complain a moment ago about his attempts at conversion? That was your choice of words. Personally, I thought it was an extremely shrewd observation."

Frank spread his hands wide. "But I've spent a lifetime trying to help these people."

"Do you think Stenmark doesn't want to do the same?" Harry replied with a trace of irritation. "Oh, I'm sure he's assailed by the same doubts as the rest of us, but at bottom, I suspect he's probably as much motivated by a desire to do good as you are." His voice grew louder. "If you want my personal opinion, that's your problem. Yours and Stenmark's." He paused. "And I might as well include the other zealot up in the hills. You all feel in possession of revealed truth, and you'll move heaven and hell to convince the rest of us that your way is not merely the right way, it's the *only* way."

Frank contemplated Harry, intrigued by the heat that had crept into his voice.

"You're all priests," Harry continued, with feeling, "practicing your black arts upon a people who didn't invite you in the first place and who would be much happier if you'd all pack up your strange vestments and alien creeds and take them off to meddle in somebody else's life."

Frank smiled sardonically. He said, "I'm glad you don't want to sit in judgment."

Harry glanced back, a little disconcerted.

Frank asked, "Don't you believe in anything?"

"Only in what I can touch," Harry declared. "I believe in what I build, and I build bloody good roads and bridges and dams. They're real, they're tangible. Whether or not they're of benefit to anybody, I don't know. To tell the truth, I don't really care anymore. Those are the kind of questions I leave to philosophers like you."

The two men stared silently at each other for a time. Then each grinned, at precisely the same instant.

"Maybe I'll have that beer now, Harry," said Frank.

"Could have been me speaking, Frank," said Harry.

8

PAUL STENMARK glanced into the bowl and nearly retched. It was full to the brim with tiny creatures. They appeared to be some kind of fish fry but without mouths, only slimy suckers. They also appeared to be alive, judging from the fact that all were feebly squirming. Paul regarded Liz by his side with alarm, fearing the worst. When she dipped her long, elegant fingers into the bowl, extracted a pair of fry, and breezily popped them into her mouth, his heart sank. For he knew he was confronting two choices, equally unpalatable. He could either follow the doctor's lead or risk seriously offending his hosts.

Most of whom were jammed into the room, a large, wooden-floored affair under a thatched roof, closely watching his behavior. Young men, women, and children lined the walls, craning for a view of the tall blond stranger. Squatting in a semicircle on the floor directly in front of him were several older men. Most were clad in dungarees and blue workshirts, but one or two of the eldest wore nothing but brightly colored loincloths. Everybody in the room was silent. All but one stared at Paul with curious, expectant eyes. The exception was a wiry, middle-aged man with black hair brushed straight back and a bony face the color of bronze. He sat cross-legged on his haunches, regarding Paul with a look that was more than curious: it was mercilessly appraising.

Aside from the intent gaze, there was little about the man's appearance that set him apart. He was dressed in faded denims, his feet were bare, and around his neck he wore strings of colored coral. But he radiated an air of easy authority, and he was treated with clear deference by his fellow villagers. Paul assumed he was the man he had come to see: the *pangat*, Alfredo Dantog. There had been no introductions as yet, however. Only a hastily muttered warning from Liz as they mounted the steps leading into the wooden hut. She had told him to do exactly as she did to avoid inflaming the notoriously prickly sensitivities of the people he was about to meet.

Despite the admonition, Paul was on the point of refusing the proffered fingerlings. But something in the lean man's unflinching scrutiny and the hushed silence of everyone else in the room made him hesitate at the last moment. Surprising even himself, he suppressed his squeamishness and reached into the bowl. He pulled out a wriggling fry, gingerly, by the tail. He looked at it for an instant, unable to conceal his horror. Then he closed his eyes and swallowed the thing, barely managing to avoid gagging as it slipped coldly down his throat.

The tension in the room broke immediately. Even before Paul reopened his eyes, he heard a sudden buzz of conversation. When he finally looked up he saw a smile of relief on Liz's face and a quiet grin creasing the features of the man he supposed was Alfredo.

"You have done well, Mr. Stenmark," the man said in a low melodious voice. His tone was surprisingly cultivated but curiously outdated, as if he had acquired his language in a different era. "The dish is a delicacy for my people. The creatures, you see, are very small and agile and thus difficult to gather. They must be picked off the rocks in the river one by one. And it can only be done at this time of the year, just before the rains. My people are greatly pleased that you come to us at a time when they can provide such a rare luxury. They would have been greatly disappointed if you had not enjoyed the experience." A gleam of amusement twinkled in the coal-black eyes. "You did enjoy it, did you not?"

Paul smiled weakly, appalled at the prospect of having to gulp down more of the fry if he agreed. He found himself saying, nevertheless, "Why yes, of course." He felt the sweat beading on his upper lip as he did so.

"That pleases me. So many of your people seem unable to share in what delights us." He shot an arch look at Liz. "I'm glad you are not one of them, Mr. Stenmark."

"Please call me Paul."

"As you wish."

"And am I correct in assuming that you, sir, are Alfredo Dantog?"

The man in the coral necklace silently nodded his agreement.

Paul sat expectantly, anticipating a continuation of the conversation, but the *pangat*'s attention was diverted at that moment by the appearance of a woman, who knelt by his side, placed a hand familiarly on his shoulder, and whispered into his ear. The woman was old, with a deeply lined face. The hand on the *pangat*'s shoulder was rough and calloused and discolored with dark circular patches of skin. She was however, still handsome, and she carried her age with a certain dignity. She was wrapped from breast to thigh in a sarong with red and black horizontal stripes. Her hair was long and black, bunched at the nape of her neck in a scarf of the same color and material as her sarong. In the parting that ran exactly down the middle of her head, there were heavy streaks of gray.

Alfredo gave the woman an indulgent smile, then turned back to Paul. "My wife," he said, with a trace of pride.

Paul nodded at the woman.

The woman swung a pair of black eyes in Paul's direction. There was neither warmth nor welcome in the look. She regarded Paul with a mix of resignation and melancholy, as if his presence cast a shadow of approaching woe.

"Excuse me for a moment," Alfredo said to Paul with an apologetic shrug. "Domestic concerns." He turned back to his wife.

Unsettled by the woman's look, Paul let his gaze wander around the room. Most of the earlier throng were departing, leaving a crescent of squatting elders in the middle of the room and a scattering of loiterers around the walls. Off in a far corner a few bare-chested women, girls probably, judging by the impertinent upthrust of their breasts, tended a gigantic pot suspended over an open fire. Two emaciated gray dogs skulked near the pot, nervously testing the air with raised snouts.

As the crowd dispersed, Paul began to take in his surroundings. He found himself inside a large thatched hut, raised several feet off the ground on stilts. The interior was divided in two, joined by a doorway hung with strings of colored beads that served as a curtain. The sleeping quarters were beyond, Paul assumed. If they were similar to that part of the hut where he was sitting, he did not envy the occupants. Everything was built of the same rough, unfinished planking, weathered a uniform dull gray. There was little else to relieve the monotony: a single, glazed window; a lone chair; a few large earthenware pots. A weeping Madonna hung from one wall. A crucified Christ was suspended opposite. Mother and Son gazed mournfully across the room at each other, sharing a special grief that was theirs alone.

Paul shivered with distaste as he absorbed the scene. The village had looked attractive enough from a distance, perched in Arcadian splendor atop a living green staircase of rice terraces. For a moment, he was even moved. A tiny flicker of doubt flared in the back of his mind as he flirted with the possibility that there might well be merit in the arguments of those who would preserve these strange, sculpted hills. But the flame wavered and finally died once he had crossed the suspension bridge linking the road with the village on the other side of the river.

As he mounted the terraces, working his way upward by means of protruding flat stones built into walls for the purpose, he found his old attitudes returning. He crossed whispering shelves of bright green rice, watered by an intricate network of tumbling brooklets and minute waterfalls, and he saw not a primitive engineering miracle but merely inefficiency. He watched the villagers, bent double in the knee-deep muck, and he was not moved by the timelessness of human endeavor as some might have been. He was outraged at the monstrous waste of human resources.

By the time he approached the village, he no longer had any doubts. He could smell the place before he saw it. A barnyard stench, a reek of feces, drifted down over the terraces that screened his view as he climbed. Mounting the last of them, he understood why. The village was as much a site of animal as of human habitation. Man and beast shared a kind of hierarchical coexistence, the human inhabitants occupying the huts raised on stilts, the animals roaming freely the ground beneath. Geese, chickens, ducks scratched the mud, competing for space with lolling black pigs covered with spiky bristles, packs of mangy gray dogs, and here and there a huge, somnolent water buffalo.

Carefully picking his way through this malodorous menagerie, Paul saw no rural charm in the meager dwellings that lined the noisome alleyways he trod, only squalor. It was ignorance that was written in the faces of the inhabitants, not rustic innocence. Now that he had a chance to examine at close range the living conditions of these people, Paul was more convinced than ever that something had to be done to improve the situation.

The limitless vista of opportunity that was unrolling in his mind's eye made Paul smile, until his glance fell upon Alfredo. The *pangat* was studying him closely again. Paul attempted to hold the man's gaze, but he could not. He felt uncomfortable, unable to rid himself of the notion that Alfredo had been reading his thoughts.

As in confirmation, Alfredo abruptly asked, "Are you a very ambitious man?"

The question rattled Paul. He looked in surprise at Alfredo, then quickly dismissed the thought forming in his mind. It was too ridiculous. He replied breezily, "I suppose I am."

"And what are your ambitions?"

Paul answered quickly, flippantly. "To be rich and famous."

Alfredo persisted. "And how will you achieve your riches and your fame?"

Paul began to suspect that there might be more to the conversation than he first imagined. He replied, with more care, "In the normal way, with a little luck and a lot of hard work."

"Can you be more precise?"

"Precise?" Paul asked uneasily. He noticed out of the corner of his eye that Liz had turned with interest in his direction.

"Yes, I would like to know how one becomes rich and famous in your society." Alfredo leaned forward. "I confess it is a topic that has been mystifying me of late. I am having difficulty identifying the underlying reasons why it seems to be such a compelling force among your people." He leaned back, and a self-deprecating smile crossed his features. "But forgive me if I am pressing you. I merely seek enlightenment."

Paul stared at Alfredo. He was impressed by an eloquence he had not expected. He was also stuck for an answer. The timely arrival of the bare-chested girls who had been tending the caldron in the corner of the room saved him. There were three of them. Two carried large earthenware bowls, one piled high with a steaming mound of white rice, the other stacked with fist-sized chunks of something gray and unappetizing. The third woman wrestled with a large clay jug.

"Aha!" exclaimed Alfredo, rubbing his hands together with gusto. "Our meal." He looked at Paul. "A most interesting discussion, which we will pursue if you are agreeable. But first, something to eat. It is simple fare by your standards, but nourishing all the same." He reached a calloused hand into one of the bowls and pulled out a wedge of gray material, the outer skin of which was covered with black bristles an inch long. "This is boiled pig,

slaughtered in honor of your visit." He pointed at the other bowl.
"That, of course, is rice. It is from our own *payaos*, what you call
the rice terraces." He motioned to the woman with the jug, who
poured a clear russet liquid into a small bowl. Alfredo dropped the
chunk of pig, took the bowl, and drained it in a single swallow.
"And this," he said, smacking his lips with satisfaction, "is *tapoy*."
He held out the bowl until it was refilled, then passed it to Paul.

Paul accepted the bowl. Emulating Alfredo, he downed the
bowl's contents. Instantly, he regretted this uncharacteristic act of
recklessness. It felt as if liquid fire had been poured down his
throat. He gasped, coughed, opened his mouth, desperate for
something to quench the flames consuming him—but found he
had no voice. Eyes aflood with tears, he raised a hand in blind
supplication. He felt himself being pounded on the back and heard
Liz urging him to drink from a bowl of water that was being pressed
to his lips. He gulped greedily, spluttering as the water gradually
soothed him. Wiping away the tears, he looked up into the concerned face of Alfredo.

"I'm terribly sorry," Alfredo said. "Are you all right?"

Paul nodded weakly. He attempted to speak, but his raw throat
emitted merely a feeble croak.

"You need some air," said Alfredo solicitously. He reached
down, grasped Paul by the arm, and gently raised him to his feet.
"Come with me. We will walk." The others seated on the floor
began to rise as well, but Alfredo halted them with an upraised
palm. "No, no, no. Please don't interrupt your meal. I will tend to
the young man."

Alfredo led Paul out onto the balcony ringing the hut and down
a flight of rickety stairs to the ground. The pair moved off among
the thatched dwellings in the direction of the summit of the slope
upon which the village sat. Linked arm in arm, they made an
incongruous sight. Paul, pale and gangling, towered over the dark
figure he leaned upon.

On approaching the crest of the hill moments later, Paul found his voice. "I really must apologize," he said awkwardly. It was the question of his dignity again.

"Nonsense," Alfredo answered. "I'm completely to blame. I should have warned you about our *tapoy*. It is a potent wine, made from our rice, which can be unkind to those who take its powers lightly."

They reached the top of the hill. Behind them the village fell away, sprawling untidily down the slope. In front, the rice shelves plunged on three sides down to the brown loop of the river. The terraces shimmered, green on green, in the afternoon sun.

Alfredo dropped Paul's arm and gestured downward. "Sometimes I forget, you see, that our wine is like our *payaos*. They are both gifts of Kabunian, and, like all of his bounties, they are double-edged. Handled with care, they provide solace. Abused, they bring grief."

Paul looked at Alfredo. "Gifts of whom?"

"Kabunian."

"Kabunian?" Paul asked, having some difficulty with the pronunciation.

"Yes."

"Who is . . . Kabunian?"

"The greatest of our guardians." Alfredo swept an arm around the hills. "We believe that all you see here was gifted to our ancestors by him."

Paul followed Alfredo's gesture with his eyes, looked back at the *pangat* suspiciously. He was reluctant to believe what he was hearing. He asked hesitantly, "This . . . Kabunian . . . is a . . . a god?"

Alfredo shrugged. "Call him that if you like. The name really doesn't matter. He is like all the spirits that inhabit everything you are now looking upon—those trees, the rocks, the river. But he is also unlike all the others in that he is greater than they are."

Paul looked away.

Alfredo chuckled softly. "It bothers you to talk of these things, I see."

Paul frowned.

"Why is that?"

Paul shifted uneasily on his feet.

"You do not approve?"

Paul glanced at Alfredo, looked quickly away again.

"You find what I am saying farfetched perhaps?"

Paul cleared his throat.

Alfredo sighed. "It has always been the same with your people. I suppose it always will be."

"What's that supposed to mean?" Paul asked, a little sharply. He was beginning to resent Alfredo's tone, which he found patronizing.

"Ever since I was a child I have been listening to your people. You come to us with your beliefs, which you treat as everlasting truths, and you expect us to embrace them wholeheartedly. When we do not, you are insulted. When we tell you of things we hold sacred, you are embarrassed."

Paul eyed Alfredo. "I suppose this god of yours kicked me in the head when I drank his rice wine."

Alfredo chuckled again. "Do not be so quick to condemn what you do not understand."

Paul muttered something unintelligible.

"I was merely trying to tell you that your ignorance of the power of the wine led you to treat it with less than the respect it deserves."

"I see," Paul replied. He was rankled by the reference to ignorance, which he found presumptuous in view of what he was listening to. "Do you mind telling me what the wine has to do with those paddies?"

"Simply that both are gifts of Kabunian, demanding the same respect."

Paul drew an irritated breath. "Which is why you are opposed to the dams on the river, I suppose."

"In a sense, yes," Alfredo answered evenly. "Let me try to explain. Kabunian gifted us the land. Our ancestors built the terraces in celebration of the gift. In our tongue, they are known simply as 'the fields of our forefathers.' So, you see, the terraces are a constant reminder of what we are, where we have come from, even where we are going. They are our eternal link with our past and our promise of a secure future. To lose them is to lose ourselves."

"Even your ancestors had to start somewhere."

"Of course."

"Then why can't you begin anew?"

"That is impossible," Alfredo responded. For the first time, a hard edge entered his voice. "Our role during our brief sojourn in this world is to preserve and maintain the link with our past. This we must do at all costs, so that we can pass it on intact to those who come after us. It has been thus for countless generations, beyond memory."

"Maybe it's time for a change."

"The trust is sacred!" Alfredo snapped. "If we succeed, we have done our part and can rest. If we fail, we are doomed. Failure would mean extinction."

Paul looked at Alfredo, startled by the depth of the conviction he had glimpsed in the man's tone. He asked hesitantly, "Is there nothing that would change your mind?"

"Nothing," Alfredo declared.

9

THE BOY, who had not quite reached the age when he might safely be called a man, was naked. He was fastened to the iron frame of a small stripped-down bed by means of steel cuffs attached to his wrists and ankles. The cuffs were arranged so that the boy was spread-eagled upon the bed's bare metal springs, like a gutted chicken on a grill.

Colonel Rosales approached, causing the boy's eyes to widen with an emotion that was beyond fear. The colonel leaned over him, placed his hands on the bed's frame on either side of his head. Their faces were close, so close that a drop of sweat rolled down the colonel's chin and dripped onto the boy's cheek. "All right, my friend," said Rosales quietly. "It's time."

The boy stared up into the broad, square face beneath the wide brim of a black cap. His eyes rolled, exposing the white, the way most animals' eyes respond to unmastering terror.

"Who took them?" Colonel Rosales asked in the same quiet voice. "Where are they now?"

The boy's mouth twitched uncontrollably, but he said nothing.

"It's no use now. You must be aware of that," Colonel Rosales continued. "You will tell me everything." He paused. "Sooner or later."

The boy swallowed, the muscles rippling along his throat from the effort. He did not respond.

"Have it your way, then," said Colonel Rosales flatly. He removed his hands from the bed and rose. He stared down at the boy. "Okay, Sergeant," he called over his shoulder. "Douse him."

"Colonel . . ." began a voice from the corner of the room, which was small, windowless, and constructed entirely of concrete.

"What is it, Lieutenant?" Colonel Rosales asked without moving his eyes from the boy's face.

"He's very young."

"Old enough to steal an M203."

"But we're not even sure it was him."

Colonel Rosales's eyes swung from the boy on the bed to the lieutenant, who was a slim figure standing in the shadows beyond the naked bulb that hung from the room's ceiling. He was dressed in similar olive-green fatigues but wore no hat. The colonel peered at him. "He had the weapon, didn't he?"

"We found it in his house."

"And that isn't proof enough for you?"

"Anybody could have put it there."

"Then why the hell won't he tell us who that might have been?"

"He's scared."

Colonel Rosales looked back at the boy, smiled thinly. "He should be."

The boy shuddered as a whimper escaped his lips.

"Sergeant?" Colonel Rosales called.

A figure emerged out of the shadow, moved toward the colonel. He was dressed like the others, in fatigues, but he was tall and hefty. In one hand he carried a large plastic bucket full of water.

"Colonel," said the lieutenant.

"What is it now?" Colonel Rosales asked, with a trace of impatience.

"Is this really necessary?"

Colonel Rosales looked back at the lieutenant, who had moved closer to the light but whose chest and face remained obscured by shadow. "You're beginning to worry me, Ramirez.."

"It's just—"

"How many weapons were taken when that truck was ambushed?" Colonel Rosales interrupted.

The hands in the light spread.

"How many?" Colonel Rosales demanded.

"Six M16s, four M203s, a case of grenades, and a few hundred rounds of ammunition."

"You have any doubts about who did it?"

"No."

"I guess I don't have to remind you what damage they can do with that kind of gear."

"No."

"Then don't you think we'd better find out pretty quick the whereabouts of those weapons?"

"Yes . . ."

Colonel Rosales turned his back to the boy. "Go ahead, Sergeant."

The sergeant lifted the bucket in his hand. He tossed the water in it over the boy.

The boy gasped, spluttered.

"You feel like talking now," Colonel Rosales asked the boy, "before we begin?"

The boy stared.

"Bring the phone, Sergeant," said Colonel Rosales.

The sergeant moved into the shadows, reemerged a moment later. He carried with him a portable telephone with an attached battery, of the kind used by soldiers in the field.

"Hook him up," said Colonel Rosales.

The sergeant moved to the boy, casting a furtive glance at the lieutenant. He knelt, unrolled two wires that ran from the telephone's battery. He attached one wire to the boy's nipple with a metal alligator clip. He clipped the other wire to the boy's testicles.

The boy moaned.

"Give it a crank," said Colonel Rosales.

The sergeant returned to the telephone. He grasped a handle attached to it. He hesitated, looking quickly from the colonel to the lieutenant.

"Colonel," said the lieutenant urgently. He stepped into the light. He was young, with a narrow, angular face. In his dark, intelligent eyes there was a look that mixed anger and despair.

"Look, Ramirez," said Colonel Rosales wearily, turning to face the lieutenant. "How long has this man been in your custody?"

"He's a boy," the lieutenant answered.

"I don't give a damn how old he is!" Colonel Rosales shouted. He threw a hand behind him at the boy. "That little sonofabitch is a CT!"

The lieutenant's lips formed a thin line.

"Now, I asked you, how long have you been interrogating him?" Colonel Rosales demanded, his voice tight.

"A day," the lieutenant replied grimly.

"Have you extracted a single piece of information out of him in that time?"

"No."

"A single word?"

The lieutenant shook his head.

"Then you'd better button up, because we don't have any more time to waste."

The lieutenant took a breath, as if to speak.

Colonel Rosales regarded him with narrow eyes. "If you don't have the balls to do this job, you'd better leave it to somebody who does."

The lieutenant's jaw clenched.

Colonel Rosales spun. He took a step toward the bed, reached down, and grasped the boy by the hair. He yanked the boy's head up, leaned close to him. "I'm through fucking around with you," he hissed. "You ready to talk?"

The boy's lips trembled, but he did not say anything.

"Right!" Colonel Rosales snapped. He threw the boy's head down. It rang against the bed's iron frame.

"Now, Sergeant," Colonel Rosales commanded.

The boy stiffened and began to buck against the bed. The screeching of the metal springs was no less human than his screams.

PART TWO

Monsoon

IO

"WE'LL THROW the dam across right there, between that rounded bluff on the far bank and the cliff face behind us," said Henry Quayle, motioning toward a sheer wall of granite that rose from just beyond the shore of the river where he and Paul Stenmark were standing. He pulled a yellow hard hat from his head and wiped the sweatband with a handkerchief. The handkerchief was gray and frayed from overuse, much like the man wielding it.

"It won't be anything fancy," Harry continued in a professional, no-nonsense kind of way. "One hundred and fifty-five meters high, eight hundred eighty along the crest. I reckon around eighteen million cubic meters of rock fill should do the job." He put the hard hat back on, reached down for a flattened pebble among the scree at his feet, and sent it skipping across the river's mud-brown surface.

"The spillway might be a little dodgy, but I'm thinking a gated chute is the best bet. Net width, eighty-five meters. Radial gates, ten and a half by fifteen. The rest is a piece of cake." He glanced up and west, running his eye over thunderclouds gathering there. "Diversion tunnels there . . . and there," he said, jabbing twice with a gnarled paw, forefinger extended. "Each one eight hundred meters long, twelve in diameter." He jabbed again. "Powerhouse over there. Open-air type. That's what you want in this kind of place. Six turbines, sixty megawatts apiece."

"What's the electricity output when it's all in place?" Paul asked. He was enjoying himself. He liked the Australian's professional manner. He found it comforting. He did not have to argue. Harry was precise, unambiguous—unlike just about everything else Paul had encountered in the valley up to the present moment.

"Eight hundred and forty-five million kilowatt-hours per year, on average," Harry answered promptly.

"For how long?"

"Thirty years—probably longer if I could count on materials."

"You can't do that?"

Harry snorted. "You must be joking."

"How bad is it?"

"Bloody awful," Harry replied with disgust. "No matter what I order, there's always some clever wanker on the supply line only too ready to adulterate the specifications."

"For example?"

"You know, sand in the cement, that kind of thing."

"Is there no way you can control that?"

"How?"

Paul shrugged. "Well, you'd think the government would have an interest in assuring the integrity of projects like this."

"Not *this* government," Harry replied with contempt.

"Surely you're exaggerating."

"I wish I was," said Harry. "The thieves in this country don't worry about the government. They *are* the government."

Paul gave Harry a skeptical look.

"Believe me, my friend," Harry continued, "you can rest assured that the jackals are already squabbling with each other to see which one is going to get the biggest bite out of whatever funds you may see fit to pass along."

Paul stared thoughtfully at Harry, considering the remark. His gaze drifted out across the river. The light was fading, he noticed, and raindrops were beginning to pebble the water's surface. He glanced upward. Dark clouds were moving in rapidly from the west, rolling down in great billows over the mountain peaks above.

"We stay here," said Paul, "I think we're going to get wet."

Harry followed Paul's look. "Yep," he agreed. "Looks like the monsoon's finally arrived. Let's get inside."

They started off in the direction of a construction shed, picking their way around workers scurrying for shelter and gigantic pieces of earth-moving equipment. Neither spoke until they entered the shack, just beating the rain that, as if furious at missing its prey, pounded angrily on the shed's corrugated metal roof.

"Can I get you something?" Harry asked. He was forced to shout to make himself heard above the noise of the rain hammering above. "A drink, maybe?" he added hopefully.

"Got any coffee?" Paul shouted back.

"Coffee, huh," Harry replied without enthusiasm. He was unable to conceal his disappointment.

As the Australian busied himself with a blackened pot, a portable stove, and a jar of instant coffee, Paul asked, "What about the reservoir?"

"The reservoir?"

"What's the capacity?"

"Seven hundred ninety million cubic meters," replied Harry, who was back in his professional mode.

"Is that total or usable storage?"

Harry glanced up. "So you're not just a pretty face after all."

Paul smiled. He was beginning to warm to the Australian. He was the only person he had yet met in the valley who did not answer direct questions with a riddle.

"The seven hundred and ninety million is total storage," Harry went on. "Usable storage is around four hundred and thirty million."

"That's going to irrigate a whole lot of land."

"Yep," Harry confirmed. "To be exact, forty-nine thousand

hectares during the rainy season, thirty-six thousand in the dry."

"How does that compare with the present situation?"

"You mean how much land is currently under irrigation?"

"Yes."

"For the whole project or just this one dam?"

"Let's start with just this one for now."

"Now you've got me. I'll have to look that up," Harry answered, handing Paul a steaming mug of coffee. He rummaged among papers scattered across a desk. "Here we are," he went on, sipping from the mug in his own hand, then looking down at it with distaste. "Six thousand, six hundred and eighty hectares during the rains, four thousand, three hundred and sixty-five in the dry season." Harry yanked a calculator from his breast pocket, sipping from the coffee as he punched figures into the device. Once again, he looked down at the mug with distaste as soon as he swallowed a mouthful of coffee. "That's around fifty-five hundred hectares on average."

As Harry continued to stare bleakly at the mug in his hand, Paul said, with warmth, "So what you're telling me is that once this dam is in place there will be the capacity to irrigate ten times as much land as at present."

"Mmm-hmm," Harry murmured absently, glancing around the shack as if in search of something. The rain continued to rattle noisily on the tin roof outside. Inside, the light was growing dim. Muttering, Harry rose and flipped a wall switch, flooding the shack with a bright fluorescent glare.

"And how much land will be lost?" asked Paul eagerly. He was growing excited.

"Lost?" Harry asked with distraction. He was preoccupied, rooting through a row of cupboards on the wall.

"Yes, lost," said Paul impatiently. "Submerged beneath the reservoir."

"That depends on whose figures you use," answered Harry, continuing to inspect the cupboards.

"What are the figures?"

"The authorities estimated three hundred hectares."

"Why, that's hardly anything!" Paul cried. "You think that's an accurate estimate?"

"Nope."

"You don't?" Paul was taken aback.

"Nope."

"Then what is an accurate estimate?" Paul was becoming frustrated, an emotion heightened by being forced to direct his question at Harry's broad back, since the Australian was now busily engaged in rifling the contents of a line of metal filing cabinets stacked at one end of the shack.

"You want the tried and tested Harry Quayle formula for ferreting out the truth in government statistics?"

"If that will give me an answer," Paul nearly shouted, this time at Harry's large rump, which was raised high as he stooped to rummage through the bottom drawers of the filing cabinet.

Without turning, Harry said, "If it makes the government look bad, double the official figure. If it makes them look good, divide it in half."

"What is that supposed to mean?" Paul shouted. He was now exasperated.

"Simply that if the government says three hundred hectares," Harry replied evenly, "in this case you can bet six hundred is closer to the mark."

Paul was absorbing this when he was suddenly startled by a loud cry from the Australian.

"Aha!" Harry boomed. "That evil, slant-eyed bastard! I knew I'd find one somewhere." He rose with a triumphant grin, mitt wrapped around the neck of a bottle of clear, tawny liquid, which he held aloft. He looked lovingly at the bottle, shaking his head in admiration. "The cunning cock filed it under M—for Mekong, of course. I should have known." Chuckling happily, he strode across the room toward Paul. "This is a particularly lethal brand of whisky from Thailand. It belongs to Ot, my foreman, who is also a nasty product of that benighted land."

Paul stared, speechless, as the Australian poured a healthy measure of the whisky into his coffee. He sampled the result and grimaced. He looked down at the mug for a moment, studying it. Then he walked to the door, opened it, and tossed the contents into the driving rain. He poured another couple of inches of whisky into the now empty cup, sampled this, and smiled. "That's better," he proclaimed with satisfaction. "A modest brew, without irritating pretensions. Care for a dollop?"

Paul shook his head negatively.

Harry shrugged, sat down opposite him. "Now where were we?"

"You were talking about the unreliability of the official estimates."

"Right," said Harry. "The government claims three hundred hectares will be lost and seven hundred and fifty families will have to relocate if this dam goes ahead. I'd say twice the number of hectares, maybe triple the number of families."

"That's still pretty negligible compared to the overall benefits."

"I suppose that depends on your point of view."

Paul raised his hands. "I hope *you're* not going to get metaphysical on me too."

Harry chortled. "You've been talking to Frank and Liz."

"*And* Alfredo Dantog."

"Ahh . . . now *there* is an interesting character."

"You may find him interesting," Paul replied. "I find him confusing. A little frightening too. He looks intelligent. He sounds intelligent. Then he opens his mouth and out comes all this . . ." He paused, searching for the right words. "This primitive obscurantism." He hesitated again. "For that matter, I have to admit that the priest and the doctor leave me a bit mystified as well."

Harry smiled. "They speak a different language, that's all."

"You can say that again."

Harry contemplated Paul for a moment. "It may sound strange to your ears, but I warn you, don't underestimate any of them, nor the sentiments involved. We are tampering with very powerful currents here, and they run deep."

"I'll try to keep that in mind," Paul replied curtly. He continued, "But what I'd like to talk about now are some unromantic things— the hard facts, the dollars and cents of this whole project."

"Easy enough." Harry pulled out his calculator. "The electrification phase is a straightforward case, remembering that this is a country without oil resources or much of anything else in the way of indigenous energy supply." He punched the machine. "To produce the eight hundred and forty-five million kilowatt-hours of electricity that my little dam here will churn out we'd need somewhere in the range of one to one and a half million barrels of oil a year." He punched the calculator again. "At current prices, the project would save close to twenty million dollars annually." Another punch. "Assuming oil prices remain constant, in the first thirty years of the life of the plant that's six hundred million dollars."

"Multiply that by four power plants and you're saving a mountain of foreign exchange," Paul interrupted vehemently. He rose to his feet, thrust a finger at Harry. "Never mind the fact that only one-third of the households in this country are served by electricity at all right now."

Harry regarded Paul silently with an amused air, not unlike avuncular tolerance.

Paul began to pace. "And what about the irrigation phase?"

"You already have those figures."

"No, no. I mean in terms of cost effect."

Harry punched his calculator. "Balancing the loss of, say, six hundred hectares against the gain of close to fifty thousand, I'd estimate the annual net value of rice production should rise by a factor of seven."

Paul slammed a fist into his palm. "There you have it. Just what my own investigations have told me. No matter how you look at this project, this country cannot afford *not* to proceed." He whirled, cast a fierce look at Harry. "Can you tell me why the hell nobody else around here but you and me seems to be able to see that?"

As Paul stood staring at Harry, waiting for an answer, he was astonished to see the Australian suddenly tilt sidelong in his vision and careen horizontally, still seated in his chair, across the shack toward the far wall. At the same instant, he realized that he himself was being hurtled with great force and speed in the same direction. Before blackness engulfed him, he heard a deafening roar and felt a rush of hot air that seemed, somehow, to glitter with thousands of spinning, knifelike shards of glass.

II

FOR A paralyzing few moments, Paul thought he was blind. He could hear a disembodied voice calling his name, faintly, as if from a great distance. He could feel pressure on his arm, a firm grip. But he could see nothing, absolutely nothing. On the edge of panic, he raised a hand to his eyes and found them sealed shut with something wet and viscous. His hand recoiled in horror, and he sobbed, loudly.

"Easy, lad . . . easy," he heard in a soothing whisper.

"Harry?" he cried, his voice catching. "Is that you, Harry?"

"Yes, it's me. But for Chrissakes keep quiet."

"But I can't see!" he moaned loudly.

He felt a broad hand close gently over his mouth. "If you don't stop hollering it's going to be permanent," Harry whispered urgently. "Now try and control yourself for a minute and listen. Will you listen?"

Paul nodded.

Harry withdrew his hand. "You can't see because there's blood all over your face. There's not much light in here, but I don't think it's serious. Looks like you caught some flying glass in your forehead, that's all. Now I'm going to get something to clean you up a bit. In the meantime, stay where you are. Don't move. Don't say a word. I'll be right back. Then I'll explain."

87

Despite the admonition, Paul began to cry, "But what—"

"Shut up, damn it!" Harry cut in fiercely. "Or we're both dead."

Stifling an urge to whimper, Paul relented. He felt overwhelmed by his confusion, unmanned by his fear. There were icy talons grasping his heart. But as he lay struggling with his dread, he heard the rain clattering on the tin roof above. It triggered his memory. He recalled the roaring rush of hot air that had flung him across the room and realized there had been an explosion of some kind. The realization helped to calm him. He squirmed upright, carefully flexing his arms and legs, testing for injuries. He gently probed his face, wincing as he jarred slivers of glass embedded above his eyes. He rubbed gingerly at his eyes, wiping away the congealing blood that had sealed the lids shut. He almost shouted for joy when he could finally pry them open and understood that he was not blind.

"How are you feeling now?" Harry asked in a whisper, looming out of the obscurity.

"Better," Paul replied in a normal voice, then dropped it to a whisper when Harry urgently shushed him. "I think my glasses must have saved my eyes. I've got some nasty cuts in my forehead, just as you said. Elsewhere, I think it's nothing worse than bumps and bruises." He paused. "But why are we whispering?"

"Can't you hear it?"

"Hear what?" Paul asked, understanding in the same instant that he had, in fact, been picking up sounds other than the rain without realizing it. There were sharp cracks, deep-throated rolls, reverberating booms, all muffled by the steady monsoon downpour but clearly distinct when he paid attention. He felt the talons tighten their grip. "What is it?"

"New People's Army, I reckon. Sounds like they're in a firefight with the PC detachment up on the road." Harry poured liquid from a bottle onto his graying handkerchief. "Lay back a minute while I clean you up."

"New People's Army?" asked Paul shakily. "You mean those guerrillas?"

"None other," replied Harry, daubing at Paul's eyes and brow. "The blast knocked me out for a while too, but near as I can make out they hit us first with something heavier than usual . . . RPG, mortar maybe. Now they're having a go at the PC post."

"You mean we were attacked?" asked Paul, unbelieving.

"Well, you don't feel like you've just been asked to dance, do you?"

"But they haven't done this kind of thing before."

"Bound to happen sooner or later. But we don't have time to go into all that now. At the moment, our first priority is to get the hell out of here. Unless I miss my bet, once they finish with our gallant guardians in the Philippine Constabulary, they're going to come on down here and polish off the survivors." Harry took a final daub at Paul's forehead. "Which is you and me."

Paul was about to respond when Harry, with a sudden fierce grip on his arm, silenced him. He looked at the Australian, saw him staring fixedly at the shattered door of the shack. Then he heard it too. It was a quiet creak, as if someone was carefully mounting the steps leading to the shed. With Harry's warning fresh in his mind, he gaped in terror at the door, which hung bent and twisted on its hinges. When he saw it move, responding to pressure from out-side, he sucked in his breath. He stared, horrified, as it swung slowly inward, groaning on its hinges, scraping the floor. He saw a widening wedge of falling rain outside, then a hand, finally a head, indistinct in the gloom. Beside him, he felt Harry tense, as if ready to spring. Then he heard a voice.

"Boss?" it said in a low querying whisper. "You in there, boss? You all right?"

Paul heard Harry's breath expelled in relief. "Ot, you sonofa-bitch!" The Australian leaped to his feet, bounded across the room, and wrapped the figure in the doorway in a bear hug. "I never thought I'd see the day when your ugly puss looked good to me."

"Jeez, boss, am I glad to see you," the figure answered. There was a suggestion in the voice of American wheatfields, but it was slightly askew, as if the accent had been picked up far from those wheatfields. "I thought for sure you'd bought the farm this time."

"Bloody close run by the look of things." Harry jerked a thumb over his shoulder at Paul, lying panting against the wall. "Knocked me and me mate here ass over teakettle."

The man Harry had called Ot peered into the obscurity in Paul's direction. Paul, drained, rose shakily and staggered toward the two. He grimaced with a pain that screamed through his muscles.

"This is Ot, my foreman," said Harry, pointing to a man that Paul, on approaching, saw was a tall, hulking Oriental with a hideously pockmarked face. "Paul Stenmark," added Harry, gesturing at Paul.

Ot flashed a mirthless smile, displaying a row of broken, blackened teeth. He studied Paul's face and turned back to Harry. "He don't look too good," he said, as if Paul were not standing right there.

"Yeah, well, none of us do right now," answered Harry. "And I reckon if we keep standing around here nattering like schoolgirls we're going to look a lot bloody worse." He glanced at Ot. "NPA hit us, am I right?"

Ot nodded. "Looks like they may be finally coming out of the woodwork. They've laid their hands on a few M203s and found someone to teach 'em how to use 'em. They just missed this shack. Plunked it down nicely right on your doorstep, which is probably why you're still able to stand here talking to me." He paused, looked Harry in the eye. "But they scored a couple of direct hits on the dorm."

"Oh Christ, no!" exclaimed Harry. "Was anybody in there?"

"Wiped out the whole crew. I've just been down there. Awful mess. Teeth, hair, and eyes all over the place. Would've got me too, but I was under the Land Rover working on that cracked pan."

"Ahh, no," Harry groaned, slumping back against an overturned desk. "Fifteen men." He stood staring at the floor for a long

moment. Then he raised his head, looked suspiciously at Ot. "You
sure there are no survivors?"

"Well, you can go look for yourself, boss," Ot replied evenly.
"But I'm thinking we don't have a whole bunch of time to hang
around here if we don't want to end up in the same fix."

Harry nodded, pulling himself erect. "You have any idea of the
size of the opposition?"

"A lot, for these guys. I counted a dozen moving up the trail to
the PC post. I figger there's probably at least that many more in the
bush judging from the rumpus."

Harry whistled softly. "And carting M203s as well. They're not
fooling around this time." He paused, calculating. "Transport?"

"Your Toyota's a wreck. The Land Rover's probably all right. Got
no roof nor much of anything else but it should be running."

"Okay," Harry replied decisively. "Then I reckon we have two
options. Number one, we swim the river and hump it over the
terraces to that little village on the rise around the bend. It's rough
going, three or four klicks across the paddies. But the rain will
cover our movements, and I think we can get through without
being seen."

"What's the second option?" Ot asked.

"A shade more dicey. We wait until the firefight dies down. Then
we take the Land Rover up the road at something near the speed of
fucking light and bust through at the PC post. If the boys went up
the trail to hit that post, I'm guessing they'll come back down it. It's
shorter and there's more cover than on the road. We'll have two
elements in our favor—surprise and mobility. If we can make it
past the post we're home free all the way to the mission."

"I vote for Plan B," said Ot promptly.

Harry glanced up. "Why?"

Ot looked uncomfortable. "You know I can't swim, boss."

"Oh, shit!" Harry answered in disgust. "Right, then. I guess it's
up the road." He looked at Paul, as if suddenly aware of his
presence. "If that's all right with you."

Paul, who had been listening to the exchange in a growing alarm that now bordered on panic, nodded tightly. The talons were clawing at his chest, there was a fluttering emptiness in the pit of his stomach, and his mouth was as hot and dry as scorched sand. He personally favored swimming the river, anything that would take him as far and as fast as possible in the opposite direction from the noise he now understood was the sound of men dying violently. But he feared that speaking aloud might tilt his control, which was balanced on a razor edge, out of his grasp.

"All right," continued Harry. "No sense waiting around here. Let's get down to the Land Rover."

They set off into the night. Outside, the rain pelted down. Paul clung to Harry's side, hampered by the loss of his glasses and terrified that he would lose contact with the one sheet anchor in the nightmare in which he now found himself.

Harry seemed to sense Paul's need. He continued to whisper encouragement as they moved through the night, even pausing at one point to fling an arm around the younger man's shoulder and murmur, "Don't worry, lad. I've been in worse fixes than this before."

"Not *much* worse, boss," muttered Ot.

As if in confirmation, he and the Australian froze, so suddenly that Paul collided with the pair of them. In the gloom he sensed rather than saw their concern and glanced wildly around looking for the cause. Unable to discern more than dim shapes outlined hazily in the falling rain, he silently cursed the loss of his glasses.

"You hear anything, Ot?" asked Harry.

"No," the Thai answered, tense.

Paul strained to listen. He realized he could hear nothing now but the damp hiss and splatter of the rain. The faint, muffled sounds of the firefight had ceased.

"I think we'd better get a move on," said Harry urgently. He grabbed Paul's arm and began to trot. Within moments, the three of them had reached a battered, stripped-down Land Rover, missing roof and doors. The Australian guided Paul onto the rear bench, said to Ot, "I'll drive."

For an agonizing instant, Paul feared the vehicle would not start. Harry flipped the ignition, but the engine failed to come to life. The starter whined with ever diminishing strength. Paul stared at Harry's hand as he worked the controls, willing the motor to respond. But when it finally did, he was immediately alarmed, for it roared with a noise he was certain could be heard for miles.

Harry looked bleakly at Ot. "No bloody muffler."

Ot looked back, shrugged.

Harry threw the vehicle into gear. "Hang on!" he yelled as they flew forward.

Unprepared, Paul was flung sharply against the uncushioned bench where he had been crouching. He managed with difficulty to secure foot and hand holds as he bounced heavily around in the rear of the Land Rover. Once upright, he peered into the darkness ahead, over the shoulders of Harry and Ot sitting in front of him. He saw that Harry was driving without lights but could make out little else. He felt the vehicle's progress slow as they began a steep incline. Harry geared down noisily and they leaped forward again.

As they continued to churn uphill, Paul was staring ahead, straining to see, when the Land Rover's windshield abruptly disintegrated with a loud crash. He heard Harry curse at the same time as Ot was lifted and hurled against the rear of his seat, with such force that his head snapped back to within inches of Paul's face. Paul watched as the back of Ot's skull exploded in front of his eyes, showering him with fragments of something hot and slimy. The Thai slumped forward and began to slide sideways out of the vehicle. Paul, reacting instinctively, reached forward and yanked him in. As he did so, Ot's head fell backward into his arms. Paul looked down at the pockmarked face staring up at him, mouth agape in surprise, a jagged hole in his forehead above his lifeless left eye.

Paul was staring down in horrified fascination at the face in his arms, feeling the gorge rise in his throat, when he realized that Harry was screaming at him. "Down! Get down!" the Australian was shouting, voice frantic. He heard gunfire, the ping and thud of projectiles striking the body of the Land Rover. Lurching forward, he became aware the vehicle was now hurtling in reverse down the slope they had just climbed, engine shrieking in protest. He looked up. Through the shattered windshield, he saw the machine's headlights suddenly pierce the darkness, then die. In that instant, captured in the twin shafts of pooled light like figures frozen in a snapshot, he glimpsed a half-dozen armed men, hands raised to shield their eyes from the bright, blinding glare.

The Land Rover hit level ground. Still racing rearward, it wheeled hard to the right. Paul heard Harry groan in agony as he changed gears. When the vehicle jumped forward, he lost his grip on Ot, watched him slide in an untidy dead heap onto the floorboards.

"We're going into the river," Harry shouted. "It's too deep to get all the way across in this. When I tell you to jump, get into the water and head for the other shore. When you get there, don't stop. Get up the side of the hill as far and as fast as you can."

Paul opened his mouth to reply. He wanted to tell Harry about Ot's head exploding in his lap. He wanted to scream in protest. He wanted out of the mayhem. But before he could say anything, the Land Rover tilted forward violently and, with a mighty splash, plunged into the river. Almost immediately, it struck something, slithered, and tumbled onto its side, tossing Paul headlong into the dark, flowing stream.

There was a moment of shock as Paul hit the river, found himself sinking through cold water. He fought his way upward, gasping for breath when he finally broke the surface. Then despair engulfed him as he glanced around in a frenzy and understood he now had no idea which shore offered haven. He could feel the river's current tugging at his legs, threatening to drag him under again. He knew he could not long delay making a choice. But the memory of the frozen figures in the Land Rover's lights, and what they had done to Ot, immobilized him.

Harry solved his dilemma. Paul felt a touch on his shoulder and saw the Australian's reassuring head bobbing on the river's surface beside him.

"This way," said Harry. "But quietly. They'll be right on our tails."

Paul followed Harry, feeling the current gain strength as they moved through the water.

"Let the current carry you," Harry urged. "It's not far."

Within minutes they stumbled onto a rock-strewn beach.

Paul sank gratefully to his knees, muscles aching. But Harry quickly dragged him upright again.

"We don't have a lot of time," he said, pulling Paul up the beach to a black mass of hill that loomed out of the darkness in front. "They'll have lights. We have to get up onto the terraces before they find the Land Rover and guess where we've gone."

They reached a stone wall, chest high. Harry placed a hand on top, as if to vault it. He quickly withdrew it, groaning with pain.

"What is it?" asked Paul, worried.

"Dunno exactly," answered Harry, cradling his forearm. "I think it's my wrist. I may have taken a shell fragment. Maybe a piece of glass. Hurts like blazes."

"Let me see," said Paul.

"Later. We've got to get up these terraces first. There's a village at the top where the locals owe me a few favors."

Paul scrambled onto the wall, reached back a hand, and helped hoist Harry up. Once on top, Harry paused, grimacing as he held his arm tightly against his chest. He nodded into the gloom. "That way."

Paul took a step off the wall and immediately sank to his knees in thick mud and water, out of which was growing something grass-like and waist high. He stood, confused, as Harry landed with a squelch beside him.

"Nothing to worry about. It's only a rice terrace. Not the easiest thing in the world to negotiate under the circumstances, but it's harmless."

Paul had no chance to respond. At that moment, he heard a voice shouting in the distance behind. He turned in dismay, saw a thin pencil of light stabbing the darkness on the far side of the river, then another.

Harry grunted. "They found the Land Rover. We'd better get moving."

Paul remained standing. He was mesmerized by the moving beams of light and the voices, now calling urgently to each other. Watching and listening, he realized it had stopped raining. He looked skyward, idly wondering why he had not noticed before. He glanced back across the river and suddenly felt defeated, completely spent. He wanted the voices with the lights to stop hounding him. He looked at Harry, who was regarding him closely, and experienced a surge of petulant animosity. He was angry with the big, grizzled Australian who, despite his size and strength, could not make them stop chasing him.

Harry reached out and grasped Paul's arm. "Come on," he said gently.

Paul did not move. He stared at Harry, mouth working.

Harry slapped him, hard, across the face. "We don't have time for that," he growled. He turned and began to slosh across the flooded ricefields, the grain rustling against his thighs as he moved.

Paul watched him go for a moment, then hurried after. Slogging through the mud, he gradually regained his control. But with it came a deepening sense of shame. He moved mechanically in Harry's footsteps, so appalled at the lapse in his behavior that he scarcely noticed as they climbed another wall, traversed another soggy terrace, repeated the process a dozen times. He was barely aware they had reached dry land, far up the side of the hill, until Harry spoke.

"There it is, finally. The village. I think we can breathe a little easier now."

Paul looked up, saw etched onto the skyline in the gloom the dim outlines of a scattering of huts raised on stilts. All were darkened except one, where lamplight visible through a window cast flickering shadows across an interior wall.

"Harry . . ." Paul began tentatively. He wanted to explain.

"Forget it," interrupted Harry gruffly. "It wasn't exactly a picnic back there."

"But . . ."

"Listen, Paul," Harry broke in again. There was kindness in his voice. "Stress works strange things with people. I'll tell you I was pretty close to losing my own grip on more than one occasion tonight. And I think I've seen a lot more nastiness in my misspent life than you have in yours. There are times, my friend, when I have to pinch myself to believe that I've survived it all, more or less intact. So there's no use fretting over things. It's over now. Nothing but a bad memory. Something to build your character."

After a moment of silence, Paul said quietly, "Thanks, Harry." He paused, added, "Sorry about Ot."

"Yeah," answered Harry tightly. He drew in a deep breath, let it out slowly. "I'm gonna miss that bastard. Best damn foreman I ever had. Bloody good mate, too."

Paul noticed that Harry continued to cradle his arm tenderly, wincing with every step he took. He asked, "You want me to look at your arm?"

"Let's get inside that hut first," replied Harry, nodding at the lamplight in the window they were approaching. "Look's like somebody's awake. Might even get a drink, even if it is that awful rice wine." They reached the foot of the staircase leading up to the entrance on the balcony ringing the hut. Harry shouted, "Anybody home?"

Paul heard a scuffling sound from inside the hut, but there was no answer.

The Australian called again. "It's me, Harry Quayle. I've got a busted wing and a terrible crying thirst. Both need tending."

Silence.

Harry looked at Paul, a puzzled expression on his face.

"Why don't we go up and knock?" said Paul.

Harry peered around carefully at the surrounding huts. "There's something not right here," he said slowly, pondering.

Paul waited.

Harry shrugged. "Probably my imagination. These people tend to be skittish at the best of times. No doubt they heard the ruckus down at the damsite." He mounted the steps, motioning Paul to follow. They reached the doorway on the balcony. Harry raised his good hand to knock, then froze. "The dogs!" he whispered, his voice tense.

At that instant, the door flew open. In the entrance stood a bushy-haired, barefoot young man. Tied around his forehead there was a red bandanna. In his hands, leveled at Harry's midriff, he held an automatic rifle.

Paul sprang back, wheeled for the stairway. Blocking his path was a similarly unshod, similarly armed young man. Paul looked back frantically at Harry. Over the Australian's shoulder he saw a third figure and the black, staring hole of a gun barrel, pointed at his head.

"Oh, shit!" he heard Harry say.

12

HARRY LAY slumped against the wall inside the hut, cursing quietly but vehemently as he stared at the three young men squatting around an oil lantern on the far side of the room. Weapons cradled across their knees, they were arguing heatedly among themselves, gesturing and glancing at Harry and Paul as they did so. Their movements, in the yellow lamplight, threw eerie shadows across the bare, unfurnished room.

Paul, sitting cold, wet, and morose on the floor beside Harry, could understand nothing of the language they were speaking. As for Harry's dark mutterings, it seemed to Paul's ear that he was complaining about dogs for some inexplicable reason. Adjusting his soggy clothing, Paul asked, "What did you say?"

"I said I must be getting old," Harry muttered angrily. "Only a senile fool would forget about the dogs."

"The dogs?" queried Paul listlessly. He was uncomfortable in his dank clothes. He was overwhelmed by his plight. And he half suspected that Harry had taken leave of his senses.

"Of course. You can't just stroll into these villages at night without the dogs creating havoc."

"But I didn't hear any dogs," said Paul.

"That's just the bloody point," Harry grumbled. "If the dogs aren't howling their fool heads off at a stranger's approach, it means they're all dead or holed up somewhere with their tails between their legs, rigid with fright."

Paul turned to Harry, understanding beginning to dawn. He remembered the Australian's whispered ejaculation, the shock of belated recognition in his voice, just before the three gunmen pounced. He was about to comment when he noticed Harry tenderly holding his arm across his chest. He said, instead, "How's the arm?"

Harry glanced down, as if suddenly recalling his injury. He began a careful examination of a large gash just above his wrist, which was leaking blood. "Looks like a ricochet," he said with an air of professional detachment. "Probably a hairline fracture. Could've been worse, I suppose."

"You'd better do something about it."

Harry nodded. He looked across the room, raised his damaged arm, and complained, in tones Paul found excessively belligerent, "Hey, you lot, I'm bleeding to death over here."

The three youths stopped talking and glanced at Harry. The one with the bushy hair and red bandanna rose, crossed the room. He dropped to his haunches to inspect Harry's arm. "I send for somebody," he said tersely after a moment. Returning to his companions, he uttered brief instructions, and one of them left the room.

Watching him go, Paul whispered anxiously, "Are they NPA?"

"Mmm-hmm," murmured Harry, following Paul's gaze. "But there's something strange about them."

"Strange?"

"Yeah. They're not locals. That dialect they were speaking. If I'm not wrong, it's something from the Visayas. Samar maybe."

"Is that bad?"

"Not necessarily, but it's unusual for these parts." Harry continued to gaze thoughtfully at the two remaining gunmen.

"That's not all, is it?" asked Paul nervously. Something in Harry's manner was beginning to make him feel uneasy.

"No," Harry replied slowly. "It's their demeanor, the way they handle themselves. Did you notice how that character swaggered when he walked over here? Too damn cocksure. And their eyes. There's a mean, hard look in them."

"So? They're NPA, just killers."

"On the contrary, your normal 'red fighter,' as he likes to style himself, is a starry-eyed, idealistic peasant. He'd just as soon wax poetic about sunsets as blow somebody's brains out."

Paul glumly regarded his two captors. "They don't look like poets to me."

"No. This lot we've fallen in with is cut from different cloth." Harry shook his head.

"You mean they might not be NPA after all?" asked Paul hopefully.

"Oh no. You can rest assured they're NPA." Harry looked at Paul. "Just a lot worse as far as you and I are concerned."

Paul was staring at Harry, fighting despair, when the door to the hut creaked open behind him. He saw Harry's gaze shift and watched his eyes widen in surprise. Turning, he saw the third gunman reenter the hut, followed by an emaciated Oriental, who was carrying a white enamel bowl and an armful of bandages. The gunman returned to his companions seated around the glowing lantern. The Oriental moved toward Harry and Paul, advancing with a curious kind of slithering, sideways motion. He had a bald head that glistened in the lamplight, as if oiled, and a wedge-shaped face the color of old amber.

"Hello, Harry," he said cheerfully in unaccented American English.

"Chan!" whispered the Australian through clenched teeth. Hostility dripped from his voice. "What rock did you crawl out from under?"

"More to the point, Harry, what brings you here?" the man answered equably. He glanced down at Harry's forearm, oozing blood, and clucked. "Tsk, tsk. I see you've been having more wonderful adventures. My oh my, you *do* lead an interesting life."

The man knelt, placed the bowl and bandages on the floor, and looked at Paul. The gaze chilled him. It was glacial, heavy-lidded, like that of a lizard contemplating its helpless prey. "Your friend is too preoccupied to remember his manners," the man said, extending a hand. "My name is Winthrop Chan. My business is rice." He flashed a wintry smile, light glinting on fragments of gold embedded in his teeth. "Your business, I am told, is *progress*." There was an ironic stress on the last word.

Transfixed by the man's reptilian stare, Paul meekly reached out a hand. He suppressed a shudder as it was brushed lightly by skin the texture of sandpaper.

"Count your fingers, Paul," muttered Harry.

Chan emitted a dry, rasping sound from his throat that resembled, distantly, a chuckle. He took Harry's forearm and began to tend the wound with bandages and a clear liquid in the enamel bowl.

Harry looked down at Chan with unconcealed distaste. "I might have known you would be mixed up in this somehow."

Chan smiled enigmatically, continued to dress Harry's injury. "Mixed up in what?"

"You know perfectly well what I'm talking about, you miserable weasel." Harry winced suddenly.

"Did I hurt you?" Chan said with apparent chagrin, pausing in his ministrations.

Harry grunted.

Chan resumed working. "You are so cruel, Harry," he said, seemingly affronted. "You know the harvest is upon us and I have to calculate the paddy, keep my suppliers content." He shrugged. "I'm a simple merchant, performing his mundane chores."

Harry snorted. "In the back of beyond? In the middle of the monsoon? In the depths of the night? On this particular night of all nights? When I've just lost my entire crew," he paused, "including Ot."

Chan's hands hesitated for a moment over Harry's wound.

"Yeah, that's right, Chan. They're all dead."

Chan began very deliberately to wrap a bandage around Harry's forearm. He murmured, "I'm sorry."

Harry leaned forward, lowered his voice. "If you're so bloody sorry, what are you doing cavorting with that shower of shit on the other side of the room?"

Chan bent to his task, concentrating, "These are difficult times, Harry," he said. "I'm a businessman. To survive I require good relations with all the . . . er . . . participants."

"Come off it," Harry whispered fiercely into Chan's ear. "Those are not your normal barefoot revolutionary boys over there."

Chan raised his head, stared at Harry with cold eyes. "What do you mean?"

Harry looked back into the hooded gaze. "You know who they are as well as I do."

Chan continued to stare frigidly, mutely.

Harry moved forward until his face almost touched Chan's. "Sparrow," he said quietly.

For an instant something flickered in the reptile eyes. Chan glanced away. He sighed. "How often I have underestimated you, Harry."

"It is a sparrow unit, isn't it?"

Chan stole a look at the three young men around the lantern, who were still arguing, but less strenuously. He nodded.

"But I thought they were urban operatives. What are they doing out here?"

"They're in transit."

"In transit from where? To where?"

"It's worth my life to tell you that."

"Not if you're talking to a dead man. What makes you think I'm going to survive this night?" He gestured at Paul, sitting quiet and tense at his side. "Or him either." Paul paled. "From all I've heard, me and my friend here are the kind of targets that make their mouths water."

"You will survive," said Chan, putting the finishing touches on Harry's bandaged arm. He sat back to admire his work for a moment, then raised his eyes and smiled maliciously. "This night, at least."

"You know something we don't?" asked Harry.

Chan glanced furtively at the three gunmen, who had ceased arguing and were gathering their meager belongings, as if preparing to depart. "They want to kill you, true enough. It's what they have been arguing about." He looked at Paul speculatively. "But it seems that your young companion here has powerful allies."

Harry looked questioningly at Paul, who stared back, mystified. His glance returned to Chan. "Who?"

Chan raised an eyebrow at Harry. "Who else?"

Chan rose to his feet. He reached down to retrieve the enamel bowl and remaining bandages, murmuring as he did so, "Be very, very careful with the *kasama* in the red bandanna. His wishes have been frustrated. He is not used to that." He stood erect, cradling the bowl in his arms. He bowed his head formally at Harry and ran his veiled gaze one more time over Paul, thoughtfully. Turning, he nodded to the three gunmen. Then he slid noiselessly out of the room.

Paul watched him go, feeling an immense relief. He whispered to Harry. "Who was that?"

"The slimiest toad in the Cordillera," said Harry, staring pensively at the doorway through which Chan had just exited. "He's an ethnic Chinese, not the most popular crowd in the country. Ostensibly, he's a rice merchant. He buys from the locals, sells on the Manila markets. Cheats at both ends."

"He's not with these people, with the NPA?"

"He's with everybody. And nobody. Whenever he can see profit for himself. He has his long, sticky fingers in more pies than you can count. He's mixed up in every piece of dirty work there is in these hills. Whenever there's something murky going on, you can bet Winthrop Chan will not be far away."

"What's he doing here?"

"I don't know exactly. I have a number of hunches, none of them very pleasant."

"But he said they weren't going to . . ." Paul paused, swallowed. "To kill us."

"He pretends to know more than he does."

"You don't believe him?"

"Up to a point. I don't believe they would have allowed him to patch my arm if they were going to sling us into a couple of shallow graves."

Paul had a brief, bleak vision of himself interred under a thin layer of paddy mud. It unsettled him. "Then what is going to happen to us?"

Harry looked at the three gunmen approaching from the other side of the room, weapons poised. "I think we are about to find out."

13

PAUL SAT cross-legged, attempting not to dwell on his plight, which he found too distressing for close examination. He was loosely chained by the wrist to an iron ring embedded in something remotely akin to the horse-drawn sleds of his youth. It was flat, square, wheel-less, made of roughly hewn timbers lashed together with loops of stout hemp. In place of a horse, however, there was a huge, plodding water buffalo. And the beast was dragging the conveyance not over crisp Minnesota snow, but through Asian mud.

At the creature's head, guiding it, was one of Paul's three captors. The other two walked a few paces behind, including the bushy-haired one in the red bandanna. Recalling Chan's warning, Paul avoided the man's gaze, which seemed to be permanently etched in a scowl. He pulled disconsolately on his chain, disturbed more by the implications of the device than by any discomfort it was giving him.

"Hey, take it easy there, mate," complained Harry. "I'm attached to the other end of this thing, you know."

"Oh, sorry," Paul apologized. He glanced at Harry squatting next to him, gently rocking with the sled's motion as it tobogganed over the mud. He wondered what was passing through the Australian's mind. Ever since they had been hustled out of the hut and plunked unceremoniously down behind the buffalo the man had been silent and pensive.

As if responding to Paul's unspoken query, Harry asked, "Do you know any important *kasamas*?"

"*Kasamas*?" asked Paul, remembering that Chan had used the same word to describe the sullen guerrilla in the red bandanna.

"It means 'comrade' in the local lingo," Harry answered. "All the NPA use it when they're talking to each other. They usually shorten it to 'Ka.' You're Ka Paul. I'm Ka Harry. Everybody's Ka something-or-other." He shrugged. "I guess it makes them feel chummy."

"How would I know any of these people?"

"I've been trying to figure out who Chan was referring to when he said you'd attracted the attention of somebody important."

"But I thought you didn't trust Chan?"

"I don't," Harry conceded. "But I'm beginning to suspect that his information may be reliable this time. Otherwise, I think we'd be swallowing this mud right now instead of slipping along comfortably on top of it."

Paul cast a nervous glance down at the black, rain-sodden slime oozing from beneath the rear of the sled at his feet.

Harry regarded the two gunmen trudging in their wake. "Have a gander at the expression on the face of our keeper, the one with the blow-dried hair."

Paul followed the look. The night was dark, heavy with moisture. Moon and stars were veiled by a low cloud cover. But there was no rain, and even without his glasses, he could discern the scowl on the gunman's face. He admitted, "He doesn't look very happy."

"Nope, he sure doesn't. That is one furious fellow we have on our hands." Harry paused, added, "But there's something else. Look at him again, carefully."

Paul looked again, squinting to focus his impaired vision. The guerrilla was leaning forward slightly as he slogged through the mud. There was a small backpack slung over one shoulder, an M16 over the other. Occasionally he muttered something indistinguishable to his companion, jerking angrily at the backpack or the weapon. Paul offered, tentatively, "He seems a little jumpy."

Harry nodded with satisfaction. "The strut is gone. I'd say the man is frightened now."

Paul turned to Harry, studying him with a mixture of interest and resentment. Watching the Australian run a beefy paw over his battered face, scratching noisily at the gray stubble on the lantern jaw, he grudgingly admitted to himself that he had come to trust the big man's surprisingly perceptive insights. It was not a comfortable admission, however, for it made Paul feel inadequate, which irritated him. He asked, a little testily, "Where the hell are we going?"

"I haven't the slightest idea," Harry replied.

The answer did nothing to improve Paul's mood. He glanced rearward. "Just who are these guys, anyway?"

"They're a sparrow unit."

"Sparrow?" queried Paul, recalling the mystifying exchange between Harry and Chan.

"It's a euphemism for a delightful weapon in the NPA arsenal. Our three friends are nothing but a hit squad, an assassination team."

"Assassination?" Paul whispered, stealing an anxious look at the two gunmen behind.

"Yeah," said Harry. "They're small teams, usually two or three members, who are supposed to operate in urban areas. Their task is the selective liquidation of isolated targets who are so-called 'enemies of the people.'"

"What kind of enemies?"

"Corrupt politicians, police torturers, exploiting landlords, soldiers who rape and plunder. That kind of enemy."

Paul cast another furtive glance at the gunmen. "If they're supposed to operate in urban areas, what are they doing here?"

"That had me stumped for a while too," Harry replied. "Until Winthrop Chan showed up."

"What's he got to do with it?"

"It's not unknown, you see, for a sparrow unit to undertake a freelance hit or two just to make ends meet. They have to live off the land, which is not always easy. So they'll occasionally accept an under-the-table payment for knocking somebody off—whether or not the target is one of the revolution's enemies. An honest mayor, for example. Or a ballsy peasant. A businessman who decides not to pay the revolutionary taxes the local commanders levy. Often the target would be on their list anyway. If not, nobody's any the wiser."

"You don't think Chan is paying these three?"

"That's *exactly* what I think. It's just a hunch, mind you, but I suspect that our three happy warriors were on their way to, or returning from, a liquidation job arranged by Chan, probably a business rival, a creditor, somebody who knew too much."

"Then they weren't part of the attack on the damsite?"

"No, I'm pretty sure now that they weren't." Harry added, with scorn, "That particular kind of performance is definitely not part of a sparrow's repertoire. They may have known about it and planned to utilize it as a diversion to cover their own activities. On the other hand, they may have been just as astonished as the rest of us."

Paul pulled absently at the chain on his wrist, troubled by a dim presentiment. "You're not suggesting that we accidentally surprised these people in the midst of something they wouldn't want even their own crowd to know about?"

"Yep," Harry confirmed. "I think we stumbled into a nest of vipers."

Paul looked in the direction of the two guerrillas. He said apprehensively, "If what you say is true, they'd want to get rid of any . . . uh . . . witnesses."

"That was my original thought."

"Then why haven't they . . ." Paul could not complete the question.

Harry looked meaningful at Paul. "That's where you come in."

"You mean all that stuff about somebody important who's interested in my welfare?"

Harry nodded.

Paul shifted his weight on his legs crossed beneath him, pondering. "But that just doesn't make any sense," he said at last. "If I'm supposed to be protected, why did they do their best to kill me not so long ago?"

"Maybe they didn't try to kill you."

Paul gaped at Harry. "But—"

"Look," Harry interrupted. "Maybe there was no intention to kill you back at the construction site. Maybe the whole point was *not* to kill you."

"What?" Paul exclaimed.

"Let me ask you a question," said Harry. "Why are you here?"

"Because a bunch of murderous assholes chased me here, that's why!"

"No, no," said Harry, calming Paul with a restraining arm on his shoulder. He continued patiently, "I mean, why did you come to the valley in the first place? What's your mission?"

"You know that as well as I do," Paul replied impatiently.

"Refresh my memory," Harry persevered.

"I came here to determine the viability of your project," Paul responded rapidly, as if the answer was tedious and unnecessary. Annoyed, he added, "To be perfectly frank, I was trying to find a way to recommend in favor until tonight, when . . ." His voice trailed off.

"Yes?" Harry asked quietly.

Paul glanced away, shook his head dazedly. "But your man, Ot. And the others. How many . . ."

"Fifteen."

"They killed sixteen people tonight."

"And they missed us. Maybe that was intentional. Their aim wasn't so bad with the rest of my crew."

"But Ot . . . the way he died."

"The heat of the moment. We must have surprised the shit out of them, roaring up that road the way we did. Remember another thing. They didn't follow us across the river. They could have, if they had wanted us badly enough."

Paul's gaze drifted off into the distance. "They'd go to those lengths," he murmured in awe.

"It worked, didn't it?"

Paul jerked his eyes back to Harry, struck by a sudden insight. "But it would have worked just as well, better even, if they *had* killed me."

"I agree."

"Then why didn't they?"

"You are being protected."

"By whom?"

"I can think of only two individuals in this valley who are powerful enough to tell the NPA what to do."

"Enlighten me, for God's sake."

"Well, you don't know any of the *kasamas*, and you haven't been around long enough for the *kasamas* to get to know you, so I imagine that rules out one of the persons I'm thinking of."

"And the other?"

"Alfredo."

"Alfredo!" Paul exclaimed, incredulously.

"Yes."

"Don't tell me Alfredo runs the NPA too?"

"No, he doesn't run them," Harry replied, "but he is in a position to control their activities to a certain extent."

"How?"

"Simply because they could not exist without him. The NPA

live in this valley because Alfredo has enough influence with his people to convince them to permit it. If the NPA did anything to incur Alfredo's wrath, they would soon be run out."

"Then he's one of them."

"No," said Harry. "There's a kind of symbiosis in the relationship. Alfredo tolerates the NPA because they are useful to him at the moment."

"Useful?"

"They are another weapon he can employ in the fight to prevent the construction of those dams." Harry gave Paul a rueful look. "We can both now testify to the effectiveness of that weapon."

Paul nodded slowly. "Yes," he mused. "I think I'm beginning to understand."

"You'd understand a lot better if you could have seen the pitiful state of the NPA when I first visited this valley, before the dams became an issue." Harry shook his head. "There were barely a handful of cadre here then. They lived no better than beggars, cadging scraps of food off the villagers and peddling ornamental nose flutes to the tourists."

"You're not suggesting the insurgency would just fade away if there were no plans to harness that river?"

"No, I'm not," Harry admitted. "But I *am* saying that our project has allowed a pathetic little crowd of wandering mendicants, preaching a bizarre Occidental faith, to become Robin Hood and his band of merry men in the space of a few short years."

Paul's gaze wandered off into the night, which was beginning to lighten imperceptibly. "Can anything be done to reverse the process, or at least slow it down a little?"

"Alfredo's the key to that in my view," Harry replied. "Convince *him* and you have a good chance of convincing the rest of his people. Convince *them* and the NPA would no longer be as welcome in their midst."

"It's not too late?"

"Maybe it is." Harry sighed regretfully. He swept his eyes around the surrounding mountains, which were outlined in black against a pale, oyster-colored flush that was beginning to suffuse the darkness. "He's one tough sonofabitch."

The sled struck a rock, jouncing Harry and Paul. Paul steadied himself with a grasp on the iron ring to which he was chained. It reminded him of more immediate concerns. He looked back, saw the two guerrillas maintaining their pace. They moved through a foot-thick layer of ground mist, leaving gauzy eddies and whirlpools behind them.

Paul glanced at Harry and was about to speak when the sled jerked to a sudden halt. He looked quickly back at the two guerrillas, who had unslung their weapons and were peering uncertainly into the crepuscular gloom. He watched a figure materialize, trailing threads of mist as it moved toward the gunmen. Then another appeared, and another, until there were a dozen surrounding the two originals. Paul's bushy-haired captor, the one with the red bandanna, attempted to speak but was silenced when each of the spectral figures raised a weapon and leveled it at him.

Beside him, Paul heard a sharp intake of breath. He turned and saw a shadelike figure hovering over Harry. It was a lean, spare man. He had a long mop of black hair that hung lankly over even, almost pleasant, features. The man ran his gaze wordlessly over Harry's face, shifted to Paul's, then settled it upon the chain linking the pair of them through the iron ring. Something flared briefly in his eyes, and the muscles along his jawline tensed. He wheeled, strode rapidly toward the gunman in the red bandanna, and slapped him across the face with an open hand. In the eerie, mist-shrouded stillness, the slap rang out like a rifle shot.

14

"WHO'S HE?" Paul managed to whisper when he had recovered his breath.

"Robin Hood," drawled Harry, his voice drenched in sarcasm.

"What?" asked Paul, glancing at the Australian seated beside him on the sled, to which they were both still manacled.

"You remember I told you there were only two people in this valley who could tell the NPA what to do?"

"Yes."

"Well, he's the other one," said Harry, his attention fixed on the subject of Paul's inquiry, who, after slapping the gunman in the red bandanna, was now energetically engaged in haranguing him.

Paul followed Harry's look. The target of the Australian's unwavering gaze was loudly dressing down the guerrilla who had held them captive for most of the night. Paul could not understand the tirade, which was being delivered in dialect, but it was clear that whatever was being said was having a devastating effect. The bushy-haired gunman was disintegrating under the verbal onslaught. Paul murmured, "What's his name?"

"Lorenzo Ortigez," Harry answered. "But when he gets through demolishing our friend with the pretty red ribbon in his hair he will no doubt introduce himself as Ka Larry, which is how he prefers to be addressed."

"He seems to swing a lot of weight."

"He should," Harry replied dryly. "You're looking at the overall commander of the New People's Army in the valley. Not only that, but an exalted regional secretary of the Communist Party of the Philippines."

"You mean he's in charge . . . of everything?"

"Of everything in these parts."

"You know him?"

"Yeah, I know him," Harry answered wearily.

Paul surveyed the slim figure standing in the pearly predawn light. The morning mist curled lazily around his feet, which, Paul was surprised to note, were bare. The man had apparently finished dissecting the errant guerrilla, for he now imperiously stretched out an upturned palm, into which his victim deposited an object before turning and shuffling morosely off into the fog with an armed escort on either side. The NPA leader watched him go for a moment, lightly juggling whatever it was that had been placed in his hand. Then he wheeled, issued brisk orders to the rest of his team, and strode toward the sled. As he neared, Paul saw that what he juggled was a key. In the other hand he carried a paratroop model M16, with the metal stock folded.

On reaching the sled, the man Harry identified as Ortigez nodded curtly at the Australian and tossed him the key. Turning to Paul, he said brusquely, as if reluctant to pronounce the words, "My apologies."

"What are you apologizing for?" Harry cut in, with a vehemence that startled Paul. There was something approaching a sneer in the Australian's voice. He jangled the chain in his hands. "This little fucking thing?"

The man ignored Harry, continued to address Paul. "I believe your name is Stenmark. I am known as Ka Larry—"

"What'd I tell ya," Harry interrupted with a joyless chuckle.

Ka Larry took a breath, as if making an effort at control. He swept his eyes rapidly over the sled, returned his gaze to Paul, and said carefully, "None of this was intended. Those responsible will be severely punished."

"Oh no!" cried Harry in mock horror. "Not another reeducation session!"

Ka Larry sighed. Turning to Harry, he said patiently, as if addressing a willful child, "The sooner you unlock that chain, Mr. Quayle, the sooner we can get out of here." He looked back at Paul, smiled apologetically. "I'm sorry—"

"Don't be sorry," Harry broke in, inserting the key into a rusting padlock on the chain. "It was a brilliant victory," he said derisively.

Ka Larry attempted to begin again. "Mr. Stenmark—"

"You must be very proud."

Ka Larry moistened his lips.

"You managed to murder sixteen unarmed men last night."

Ka Larry's eyes swiveled, shot a cold look at the top of Harry's head, which was bent over the padlock and chain.

"It's true," Harry continued, "they were not *quite* sleeping peacefully in their beds . . ."

"Those men, like you," Ka Larry snapped, "were agents of bureaucratic capitalism."

"He always talks like that when he's nervous," said Harry to Paul, as if Ka Larry were not standing there. He returned his attention to the padlock.

Ka Larry's jaw clenched.

"Of course, there were no women and children this time," Harry went on, seemingly unconcerned, fiddling with the lock. "But all the same—"

"All right, Mr. Quayle," said Ka Larry tightly.

"But all the same it must have given you a warm—"

"That's enough!"

"—a warm glow of satisfaction—"

"I said that's enough!"

"—of real achievement—"

"Quayle!"

"—something the central committee—"

"Count yourself lucky *you* survived," Ka Larry spat. He raised his gun, pointed it at Harry's head, which was still lowered over the lock.

Harry raised his eyes slowly and looked into Ka Larry's. He gave his head a small sideways jerk in Paul's direction. "But I was with *him*."

The anger in Ka Larry's eyes sparked.

Harry reached up, pushed aside the gun barrel pointed into his face. He asked softly, "And you couldn't do anything to him, could you?"

Ka Larry's nostrils began to flare.

"Not unless you wanted Alfredo to slap your wrist again."

Ka Larry glared at Harry, lips whitening.

A smile crept quietly across Harry's features.

"Get out of that chain," Ka Larry hissed between his teeth, "and follow me." He spun, strode off into the mist.

Harry released the chain, reached down, and hauled Paul to his feet. "C'mon," he said with a grim satisfaction. "We got some more walking to do."

Paul regarded Harry with something approaching wonder as he was hustled upright. He admired the Australian's courage, but found his deliberate attempt to bait the guerrilla chieftain fool-hardy under the circumstances. He wished he had time to make that point absolutely clear. Instead, he was being frog-marched toward another rendezvous that would no doubt prove as hair-raising as everything else he had recently experienced. Wading through the ground fog, staring bleakly into an uncertain future, he felt his heart sink. He asked plaintively, "Where are we going now?"

Harry gestured east, to where clouds mantling a serrated line of peaks were beginning to blush with the palest shade of pink. "The sun's coming up," he said. "They'll want to lie low today. After what happened last night, Rocky will be screaming for blood. If I know that crazy little bastard, he'll already have his lads out scouring these hills."

"Rocky?" Paul asked, nearing despair. The last thing he wanted was the introduction of another perilous character. "Who the hell is Rocky?"

Harry quickly shushed Paul, glancing furtively ahead as he did so. "You've already met him," he murmured. He stole another look at the guerrillas scattered around. "Best not to mention his name too loudly. He's not exactly the most popular fellow with this lot."

"I've met him?"

"Lieutenant Colonel Ricardo Rosales, the military commandant. Remember the sinister runt who showed up at Frank's the day you arrived? The one with the pearl-handled Colt and the built-in bird who doesn't talk?"

"Oh yeah, him," said Paul, more calmly. He found a kind of vague solace in the notion of a uniformed presence. It reminded him that his links with established authority were not completely severed. He scanned the landscape, not really expecting to spot the colonel's troops charging to his rescue, but comforted all the same by the thought they were out there, somewhere, searching for him.

Even with his myopic vision, Paul could see they were now very high. Ka Larry was leading them up the steep shoulder of one of the hills flanking the western side of the valley, far above even the uppermost level of terraces. The night sky was brightening rapidly, shading from blue-black above his head to a deep indigo in the east. There was a freshening breeze, warm and heavy with the scent of rain. It was dissipating the ground fog. In the half-light, Paul saw they were moving through what looked like burned-out jungle.

"It's *kaingin*," said Harry, noticing the direction of Paul's inquiring look. "The slash-and-burn system of agriculture the locals use to supplement their diet."

Paul was panting from the exertion of the climb up the sharply ascending slope. He was also beginning to sweat. "They hike all the way up here?"

"No," Harry responded. "This was not a local *kaingin*. It was an NPA enterprise."

Paul shot Harry a puzzled look. "These guys are farmers too?"

"In a sense," Harry answered. "They plant cash crops, use the money to buy supplies, arms even."

"Arms?"

"Since they don't have any foreign sugar daddies shipping them guns and money, what they fight with they either steal from the army or buy on the black market." Harry bent, yanked a withered plant from the soil. "Looks like they were growing garlic here," he said, examining the plant. He waved it at Paul. "Two thousand of these buys an M16."

"Without which there would be no armed struggle," interjected an emphatic voice. Harry and Paul looked up. Ka Larry was standing in their path, contemplating them coolly. "And that is the primary form of struggle we must wage if we are ever to rid ourselves of the curse of imperialism, feudalism, and fascism."

Harry groaned. "Do you always have to talk like a bloody directive from the Politburo?"

Ka Larry responded with a wintry smile. "Only when it's necessary." Turning to Paul, a trace more warmth crept into his expression. "You will come with me."

Paul glanced anxiously at Harry.

"He'll follow with my men," said Ka Larry, observing Paul's worried look. "We don't have much time, and there are some matters I would like to discuss with you." He eyed Harry coldly. "Alone."

"But where are you taking me?" asked Paul, a tremor in his voice.

Ka Larry motioned silently with his weapon up the slope to where a large stand of pine forest stood, dark and brooding.

Paul peered nervously at the wood, cast another look at Harry.

"Go along, lad," Harry urged with a soothing pat. He nodded

disparagingly at Ka Larry. "Don't let his melodramatics spook you. He can do you no harm. Remember, you're protected."

"Come with me, Mr. Stenmark," Ka Larry snapped, glaring at Harry.

Paul cast a stealthy look at Ka Larry as they ascended the slope together, moving at close to a trot. The taut line of muscles along the man's jaw and the pinched look around his eyes and mouth persuaded him that conversation was not required. He climbed in silence. By the time he reached the edge of the pine forest, he was sweating profusely and breathing with effort. Just inside the line of trees, Ka Larry motioned him to stop. The guerrilla turned and began to carefully scan the valley below.

Paul attempted to do the same. But without his glasses, he could make out few details. He saw the blurred shapes of two dozen or more guerrillas scattered across the sloping stretch of burned-out jungle, all moving slowly uphill. Beyond, the valley was merely a pool of shadow in his vision, backed by a sawtoothed ridge of hills on the far horizon. He could, however, see gray puffs of monsoon scud sailing overhead through a cobalt sky and, in the distance, banks of cloud piling on the peaks that marked the valley's eastern rim. As he watched, the clouds glimmered from within, shot through with streamers of brass and rose.

"Impressive, isn't it?" asked a quiet voice at Paul's side. He turned and saw Ka Larry gazing serenely across the valley. Paul was taken aback, as much by the guerrilla's gentle remark as by the expression on his face. He seemed transfigured. The hard lines around his mouth had softened, and there was a wistful, liquid look in his black eyes.

"Dawn can be magnificent in these hills," Ka Larry went on in the same quiet voice. "It is my favorite time." He nodded down at the valley. "The people will be lighting their fires now. They will eat a simple bowl of rice, perhaps have a little wine to ward off the morning chill. Soon they will be out on their terraces."

Paul, startled by the transformation, did not respond.

Ka Larry turned and gave Paul a speculative look. "Are you a religious man?"

Paul shrugged noncommittally.

"I was once almost a priest, you know," Ka Larry said. He hefted the weapon in his hand. "Before I took this up I was studying in a seminary."

Paul regarded Ka Larry with some confusion. He was having difficulty coming to grips with the new aspect that was being presented.

"Does that surprise you?"

Paul *was* surprised, but he tried not to show it.

Ka Larry smiled, revealing a large space between his front teeth. "I can see that it does." His eyes traveled back to the valley, and his voice grew reflective. "Sometimes it surprises me too. I was raised to fear Communism. The very word used to make my hair stand on end." He looked at Paul, lifted his eyebrows. "And now I am a Communist."

Paul stared, trying to understand where the conversation was leading.

"You want to know why?"

Paul nodded. He did not know what else to do.

Ka Larry gestured with his weapon toward the valley. "Because of people like those down there."

Paul followed the gesture, looked back at Ka Larry.

"I saw them cheated out of their lands, their property, their lives," Ka Larry said, maintaining his hold on Paul's eyes. "I wanted to help them fight back, so I entered the seminary. I would become a priest. I would be in a position to serve." He paused. "And you know what I discovered?"

Paul shook his head, a little awkwardly.

"I discovered I had joined the wrong side."

Paul looked into the black eyes, where something hard was beginning to glitter.

"I discovered the priesthood I wanted to become part of was not interested in changing things. I discovered it was not interested because it was part of the structure that oppressed and exploited people like those down in that valley. I discovered the priests . . ." Ka Larry paused, his eyes boring into Paul. "I discovered the priests were the enemy."

Paul shifted uneasily on his feet. He had begun to understand where the conversation was leading.

"You can imagine my dismay."

"Yes."

"Then you can also imagine my reaction when I stumbled upon Marx and Lenin and Mao and found that I was not alone in the conclusions I had reached."

Paul waited for it.

"From there, it was but a short step,"—Ka Larry raised his gun—"to this."

Paul looked from Ka Larry to the gun and back again. "And that's your solution?"

"It's the *only* solution."

Paul bristled. "You think I don't want to help those people down there as much as you?"

"If that's true, then you know what you must do."

"You think that by refusing to supply money for those dams I will be helping them?"

"That's what I think," Ka Larry declared. "More to the point," he added, motioning toward the valley, "that's what *they* think."

"Are you sure about that?"

Ka Larry regarded Paul quizzically. "You've talked to Alfredo, haven't you?"

"Yes," Paul replied wearily, "I've talked to Alfredo."

"And you still have doubts?"

Paul's gaze drifted back to the valley. The rest of the guerrillas, Harry hulking hugely among them, had reached the stand of pine. "Alfredo is merely a man," said Paul, watching Harry and the others filter into the pines. "A single voice."

Ka Larry studied Paul with heightened interest. He said carefully, "He speaks for his people."

"That's what everybody, you included now, keeps telling me," Paul answered. He went on meditatively, "But I wonder . . ." His voice trailed off.

"What do you wonder?"

"I wonder what Alfredo's people would say if they were given a chance to say anything."

Ka Larry watched Paul.

"I wonder what they'd think if Alfredo were not around to tell them what to think."

If Paul had been watching, he might have caught the look of recognition that came into Ka Larry's eyes, noticed that he had struck a responsive chord, as if Ka Larry too had entertained such thoughts.

15

"IGNORE HER," said Colonel Ricardo Rosales. "She's just part of the furniture around here."

The woman was young, not much more than a girl. She was seated on a dingy sofa in the dingy office, behind the colonel's back and the battered tin desk at which he sat. She had just drawn her knees up under her chin and was in the process of painting with great care her toenails, as she had previously painted her fingernails, bright scarlet. She was wearing a tight white T-shirt and an ankle-length sarong, colored bronze, like her flawless skin.

Paul had been uncomfortably aware for some time, ever since entering the room for the interview with the military commandant, that there was obviously nothing beneath the fabric stretched tautly across the woman's breasts. But it was not until she drew up her knees to work on her toes that he realized with a start that she was naked beneath the sarong as well. He removed his eyes from the dusky thighs and looked into the colonel's gaze. "I'm sorry," Paul stammered. "Where were we?"

"You were with Ortigez and his band of terrorists," said Colonel Rosales. "They'd taken you and Harry to a pine forest somewhere on the western slopes of the valley." He peered at Paul from under the peak of a black baseball hat. His name, rank, and battalion insignia were inscribed in brilliant yellow across the cap's brim.

124

"There's not much else to tell," Paul replied. "We spent the rest of that day in the forest, where they had set up a camp with tents and things. Good thing, too, because it rained the whole day. They gave us something to eat, a bowl of cold rice, and some of that rusty-looking stuff they call wine. Then I'm afraid I fell asleep."

Colonel Rosales nodded. "You had no further conversation with Ortigez or any of the others."

"I didn't get a chance," Paul answered. "When I woke up it was dark again. Ka Larry—" he darted a quick look at the colonel—"I mean Ortigez, and the others, had gone, except for Harry, of course. There was a native sitting there waiting for us. He brought us to the village, and we hiked it back from there to the mission on our own."

"Which village?"

"It was Alfredo's village."

The colonel's black eyes glittered. Leaning forward, he asked intently, "Did you encounter Alfredo?"

Paul shook his head negatively. "He wasn't there. At least that's what they told us."

"Who told you that?"

"The villagers."

"Where did they say he had gone?"

"Up in the hills somewhere. There was some kind of emergency. Medical, I guess."

"Medical?"

"Yeah, they said Alfredo had rushed off suddenly with Dr. Buenaventura."

"When?"

"The night before."

The colonel regarded Paul closely. "The same night you were attacked, in other words."

Paul nodded slowly, experiencing a vague disquiet. "The doctor can fill you in on that better than I can," he said carefully. "Why don't you ask her?"

Colonel Rosales leaned back in his chair, placed two booted feet on his desk. "I'd love to," he replied, smiling thinly. "But I can't seem to find the lady."

"You can't find her?" Paul asked. "But where has she gone?"

"Good question."

"Have you tried Father Enright? He'd know where she is."

"Have you seen Frank lately?" Colonel Rosales asked softly, a still look on his face.

Paul shook his head, suddenly aware that he had not, in fact, seen the priest since he had arrived back at the mission. He stared, unseeing, at the colonel's polished boots. "It was well after midnight when I got back," he said. "I was exhausted and fell into bed. When I got up this morning it was late. I assumed Father Enright was already up and around."

"You didn't think it strange that he hadn't talked to you?"

"To tell the truth, I did find it a bit odd, considering everything that had happened. But then I got your summons and it slipped my mind." Paul looked into the colonel's eyes, reluctant to read what he saw there. "You can't find Father Enright either?"

" 'Fraid not," replied Colonel Rosales, not quite regretfully.

"Harry will know where they are."

"Harry left for Manila at daybreak, *before* we had a chance to talk to him. His, uh, companions said he had gone to oversee arrangements for the families of his men. Also something about a wound." He scrutinized Paul suspiciously. "Was Harry hit?"

Paul nodded gloomily. "In the arm. I guess I forgot to tell you that part." He swept his eyes around the colonel's dreary office, debating whether or not to fill in other missing details, like the encounter with Chan. His gaze came to rest on a gigantic photograph, heavily retouched, of the president and his wife. Both smiled radiantly, beaming down at the woman on the soiled sofa. Paul looked back at the colonel, decided the Chan episode would complicate what was already becoming a complicated story. He asked instead, "What do you think it all means?"

"I don't know," Colonel Rosales responded. He swung his feet to the floor with determination. But I am going to bust my ass, and a lot of other people's asses too if I have to, to get to the bottom of it."

"You surely don't believe they're involved in the . . ." Paul hesitated, groping for the right words. "The business at the dam site?"

"Why not?" Colonel Rosales shot back with a heat that startled Paul. "Alfredo's nothing but a goddam Communist! Frank's not much better. And where the priest is, that little lady won't be far behind."

"But simply because—"

"I deal in facts, Mr. Stenmark," Colonel Rosales interrupted. "And what do the facts tell me?" He began to crack his knuckles loudly. "They tell me that two nights ago I lost six of my best men, not to mention Harry's workers, in a murderous attack on your project. That attack was carried out, as you yourself have testified, by Communist terrorists. Shortly before it took place, Frank, Liz, and Alfredo disappeared, more or less at the same time. Now even if you don't share my opinion of those three individuals, you'll have to admit they have at least one trait in common with the CTs: they are known opponents of your project. None of the three has been seen since." Cracking a last knuckle with satisfaction, he looked meaningfully at Paul. "You tell me what I'm supposed to believe based on that kind of evidence."

Paul shrugged.

Colonel Rosales rose to his feet, as if intent on bringing the discussion to a close. Paul was surprised to note how short the man was, a deception engendered by the massiveness of his head and shoulders.

"I don't want you to worry about this anymore," Colonel Rosales said. "I'm afraid I've already taken up far too much of your time. You must be very busy." He leaned forward, supporting himself with two hands placed on the edge of the desk. "I owe you an apology for the ordeal you have suffered. Rest assured that it won't happen again. You have my word on that." He began to move around the desk in Paul's direction. "You just leave all of this to me and get on with that project of yours."

Paul rose, said regretfully, "I'm afraid that project is no longer mine."

The colonel stopped abruptly halfway around the desk. He asked, stunned, "What?"

"I'd be out of a job if I recommended committing funds to this project."

"What do you mean by that?" Colonel Rosales exclaimed with dismay. "I thought the project was good."

"I can't deny that," Paul replied. "I think it is, too. As a matter of fact, I've never seen a project that makes better sense."

"Then what's the problem?"

"Security, mainly."

Colonel Rosales began to pace to and fro in front of the girl on the sofa. She sat studying her toes with a critical air, brows knitted. "I realize you haven't had much fun in the last couple of days," Colonel Rosales said impatiently. "But let's not get carried away. That was an isolated incident. It hasn't happened before, and, believe me, it won't happen again."

"It's not that I doubt your intentions, nor your capabilities," Paul responded, still standing in front of the chair he had occupied. "But people have been killed."

"The bastards caught me by surprise," Colonel Rosales snarled. "If Cruz hadn't snuffed that little prick before . . ." He braked himself, glanced furtively at Paul.

"What?"

"Nothing," Colonel Rosales muttered evasively. "All you have to know is that I'm ready for them now." His teeth clenched. "By God am I ready!"

"Even so, the next time—"

"There won't be a next time!" Colonel Rosales shouted as he

wheeled, faced Paul. He shot out an accusing finger. "I've already given you my word on that!"

Paul raised his hands placatingly. "Look at it from my point of view," he said. "How can I recommend a several-hundred-million-dollar investment in a project when I'm not even sure the conditions exist to make it possible to build it?"

"*You* get the money," Colonel Rosales vowed, "and *I'll* make sure about the conditions." He accelerated his pacing, began to throw his arms around. "I'll saturate the goddam place with troops. I'll put a soldier, two if need be, on every one of the workers. Your people will be protected night and day. My boys will eat with them, sleep with them, shit and fuck with them if necessary."

Paul sighed. "To protect them from whom?"

"From the CTs, of course."

Paul studied the colonel. "And what are you going to do about Alfredo?"

Colonel Rosales stopped pacing, cocked his massive head. "I'm not reading you."

Paul took a breath. "Look, don't get me wrong," he said wearily. "I'm as much in favor of this project as you seem to be. Probably more. I've examined it from every angle, and for the life of me, I can't see many flaws in it." He gestured vaguely in the direction of the valley outside. "But you try and tell that to Alfredo. I've tried and got absolutely zero results. All he wants to talk about is his ancestors and his gods."

"Don't let Alfredo baffle you with all of his Igorot bullshit," Colonel Rosales retorted angrily. "The man's a CT, and *that's* why he's against those dams."

Paul did not agree, but he also did not feel much like arguing about it. "That may be," he said, "but he's also terribly influential around here. Opinion seems to be unanimous that what Alfredo wants, Alfredo gets." Voicing the thought induced in Paul a sudden wave of fatigue. He ran his fingers over the bandages plastered to his forehead and looked at the colonel. "And what Alfredo wants in this case is an end to that project. Now if you're finished with me, I think I'll go and get some more sleep. All of a sudden, I'm feeling bushed again."

Colonel Rosales regarded Paul silently as he walked toward the door. As he was about to exit, the colonel called out, "Let me get this straight. You're canceling the project?"

Paul turned, looked across the room at the colonel. "Looks that way."

"Because of Alfredo."

"No," Paul replied. "Because of Alfredo's opinions, because of Alfredo's influence." He turned to go.

Colonel Rosales's eyes narrowed. "What if something could be done to change that situation?"

"Then I'd have to think things over again."

Colonel Rosales stood contemplating the empty doorway long after Paul had departed. Eventually, he moved back to his desk, sat down, and picked up the red telephone at his elbow. "Sergeant Cruz," he said into the telephone. "I want to make two calls, top priority. First I want Subic. Then I want Manila . . . the back channel." He replaced the receiver in its red cradle and leaned back into his chair. He folded his arms behind his head, gazed distantly out of the window that looked onto the courtyard beneath the flagpole.

"Connie," Colonel Rosales barked after a moment. "Go get me a drink."

In a single fluid motion, the woman unfolded herself from the sofa. Sarong swaying, she walked out of the room. She neither glanced at the colonel nor uttered a word to him. But the shadow of something fluttered briefly, mothlike, across her lips. It might have been a smile. And it might have suggested contempt.

16

THE THREE figures moved slowly out of the grove of gnarled mountain oak onto the sloping meadow, which was carpeted with long, coarse grass. The grass was wet from the rain and whispered in the evening breeze that rippled across it. All three appeared a little shattered, especially the teenaged boy who walked between Frank Enright and Alfredo Dantog. He moved mechanically with a dazed look in his eye, as if he had just survived an ordeal beyond imagination.

Alfredo threw an arm around the boy's shoulders and gave him a shake. "Cheer up," he said. "It's over now."

The boy looked up blankly.

"How are you feeling?" Alfredo asked, gazing fondly at the boy.

The boy smiled weakly.

Alfredo chuckled. "If you think this is the hard part, you should see what's coming—Papa."

The boy took a deep breath, blew it out with relief.

"You go on ahead now," said Alfredo, giving the boy a gentle shove down the slope. "I'll be along as soon as I've had a few words with Father Enright."

The boy gave Alfredo another smile, a shade braver than his previous effort. He glanced gratefully at Frank and headed off down the meadow.

Frank and Alfredo stopped walking and watched the boy go silently for a time.

"I'm glad that's finished," said Frank.

Alfredo nodded. "Yes. I was worried for a while there. I didn't think the mother and child would survive."

Alfredo cast a glance back toward the stand of oak, where the shadow of a crude hut was visible just inside the line of trees. The limbs of the trees were twisted into grotesque shapes and draped with a feathery moss that was sprinkled with orchids of a delicate hue. Trees, moss, and flowers, sodden from the day's monsoon, dripped water.

"You think everything will be all right now?" he asked.

"Liz seems to have it under control—for the time being," Frank answered. "But she's concerned, I can tell that."

Alfredo's gaze returned to Frank. He asked, "You've grown to know that young woman well, haven't you?"

Frank darted a look at Alfredo, glanced quickly away. He murmured, "I suppose I have."

Alfredo studied Frank with interest. After a time, he said softly, "You care for her." It was a statement, not a question.

Frank stared down the hill.

"I hope you understand what you're doing, my friend."

They regarded each other without speaking for a moment, until Alfredo, drawing a breath, said, "Well, I'd better be on my way. Look after things here. I'll be back with help as soon as I can."

"Don't be too long."

Alfredo stepped in Frank's direction, grabbed his hand. "I won't."

Frank smiled at Alfredo. "They both would have died if it was not for you."

"If it was not for Liz," Alfredo corrected, releasing Frank's hand.

"All the same, you went to a lot of trouble." Frank nodded down the hill. "That boy will be grateful to you for the rest of his life."

"I did what I had to do," Alfredo replied. "They're my people. I care for them."

Frank watched Alfredo. "That's not the whole story."

"What do you mean?"

"There's something special about this case, isn't there?"

Alfredo surveyed Frank's features, as if he knew what was coming.

"That boy," Frank continued. "He reminds me of someone."

Alfredo smiled, sadly. "Yes," he confessed. "He looks a lot like him, doesn't he?" He turned, directed a melancholy gaze down the slope.

"Very much."

"He would be a man now."

"I know."

Alfredo was silent for a time. He said at last, desolately, "He was my heir, Frank, my firstborn."

Frank reached out, grasped Alfredo's shoulder with his hand.

"How much I miss him."

17

PAUL STENMARK squinted, raising a hand to shield his eyes from the bright morning sunlight. He was still groggy with sleep, having plunged into a near-coma in the wake of his encounter with Colonel Rosales. He was also nearly blinded by the glare as he stood on Frank Enright's doorstep trying to make out who it was who had summoned him from his bed. The immaculate white uniform seemed to coruscate in the sunshine, veiling the face of whoever was wearing it behind a glittering golden nimbus.

"Paul Stenmark?" asked a voice from within the nimbus. It was a clear, crisp voice, as crisp as the uniform.

"Yes," Paul replied uncertainly.

"My name is Prescott. Lieutenant Commander Anthony Adam Prescott. United States Navy. I'd like to have a word with you if I may."

Paul dropped his hand, but he continued to stare, squinting, at the shimmering figure in white. He did not respond. He was a little taken aback.

Prescott stepped forward, into the shadow of the doorway where Paul was standing. He removed his hat and placed it securely under one arm, revealing thick, severely cut hair the same color as the nimbus he had just abandoned. He looked at Paul through corn-

flower eyes and smiled. It was a dazzling smile. The man's teeth
were faultless.

"May I come in?" Prescott inquired pleasantly.

"Of course," Paul mumbled, struggling to recover his compo-
sure. He stepped back, held the door open. "Sorry."

The commander sailed past. He swept his eyes around the room,
then wheeled and looked at Paul. "Pleased to meet you," he said,
extending a hand. His grip was precise. It was firm without being
overpowering, the practiced handshake of someone used to cal-
ibrating impressions. Releasing Paul's hand, Commander Prescott
peered at the bandages on Paul's forehead. "You've hurt yourself."

Paul fingered the bandages, suddenly recalling the circumstances that had placed them there. "Yes," he replied nervously.

Prescott regarded Paul's crumpled pajamas. "And I see that I've
got you out of bed. Sorry about that."

Paul glanced down at his pajamas with some embarrassment.
They reminded him of how long and how deeply he must have
been sleeping. The naval officer's shining perfection did nothing to
improve Paul's discomfort. He felt shabby in the man's presence.
He ran a hand through his tousled hair and muttered, "I've had a
couple of hectic days."

"So I've heard," Prescott answered, radiating sympathy. "As a
matter of fact, that's why I'm here."

AMBASSADOR BENJAMIN Freed slowly removed his thick horn-
rimmed glasses, closed his eyes, and began carefully to massage
the bridge of his nose between a thumb and forefinger, as if he were
in some distress. Without opening his eyes, he said quietly, resignedly, "Please tell me this is all a very bad joke, Alison."

"I wish I could, Ben," the blond woman in the dark, vaguely
masculine suit responded, not without a degree of sympathy. Her
relationship with the ambassador was of long standing, dating from
the time when he first began to weave the web of political connec-

tions that eventually won him his current, entirely temporary, diplomatic status. During those years she had acquired the habit of suffering when he suffered.

"Jesus!" Freed whispered. He swiveled his chair until his back was to the woman. He opened his eyes and gazed out the window behind his desk at the huge bowl of ocean that lay trapped there, encircled by two sweeping arcs of low-lying land.

The woman stared at the back of the ambassador's head, dismayed anew by the alarming progress of the bald spot.

"Those . . ." The ambassador paused, spluttered. "Those jerks!"

The woman smiled wryly. She suspected that an epithet considerably more pungent had been on the tip of the ambassador's tongue. He was as new to the language of diplomacy as he was to the practice.

"What is this guy's name again?" Ambassador Freed asked, without turning.

The woman glanced down at the sheaf of papers lying atop the tooled-leather briefcase cradled in her lap. "Stenmark," she said. "Paul Stenmark."

"And where is this Stenmark character now?" The ambassador made no attempt to disguise his irritation.

The woman detached a small round watch that was clipped to the lapel of her pinstriped jacket. She looked at it, glanced down at the papers again. "He should be arriving at Subic around now."

THE HELICOPTER banked, skipped nimbly around a hill, and skittered out over the water. Paul looked down. From his vantage point directly behind the pilot, it appeared as if the sea had poked a thumb into the rolling hills, scouring out a fat finger of an inlet twice as long as it was broad. It was fringed with little crescents of white sand beach, behind which the lightly jungled slopes climbed. Where the tip of the watery finger probed the land, there was a naval base: a gigantic, geometrically precise grid of gray piers,

white buildings, and scrupulous green lawns. Beyond, where the
hills rose from the rear of the base, there was a town, large enough
that it might have been called a small city. The town's geography,
unlike that of the base, obeyed a logic of its own. It sprawled
chaotically all over the lower slopes of the surrounding hills.

"Subic Bay!" yelled Commander Prescott. He was forced to
shout to make himself heard above the helicopter's clatter. There
was a trace of pride in his voice. "You're now looking at the largest,
finest United States naval installation west of Hawaii." He nodded
down at the inlet. "There's sixty-two thousand acres down there,
twenty-six thousand of them under forty-five feet of water. This
place has everything that any sailor in any man's fleet could want."
He pointed to an interlocking network of docks, infested by a
colony of monstrous mechanical cranes. "That's the best ship-
repair facility west of Pearl Harbor." He gestured across the bay to
where Paul could see an aircraft touching down on a strip built into
the side of the hills. "Cubi Point," he said. "Big enough to handle
anything flying today." He threw an arm around with enthusiasm.
"This place has it all. There's fuel, ordnance, a hospital, schools,
teachers, doctors, dentists, lawyers. You name it, Subic's got it." He
chuckled. "We even have our own goddam private mountain just
to shoot at." He paused, directed a look at the town scattered
messily in the hills behind the base. His voice dropped. "And that
eyesore over there is Olongapo, where a weary sailor home from
the sea can rest his head." He nudged Paul and added, "Or, so I am
told, any other part of his anatomy that requires relief."

There was a sudden surge of power from the twin engines over
Paul's head. The helicopter rose, banked again. Paul glanced down
and saw an aircraft carrier passing beneath, slowly gathering way as
it nosed toward the mouth of the bay. Tiny white-hatted, blue-clad
figures scurried across the ship's immense flight deck. Multicolored pennants, snapping in a breeze, were strung in a pyramid
from the ship's lopsided superstructure.

"Now there's a sight," sighed Commander Prescott. He was

leaning over Paul's shoulder, gazing lovingly down at the carrier. As they watched, a frigate knifed past the big ship, sleek bows hurling spray. Alongside the carrier's enormous bulk, the smaller craft looked like a toy.

"What ship is that?" Paul asked. "The big one?"

"USS *Enterprise*," Prescott answered. There was reverence in his voice.

"Where's it going?"

"That's not an *it*, that's a *she*. And *her* destination is classified." Paul was treated to another of Prescott's dazzling smiles. "But since the admiral will probably tell you anyway, she's bound for Gonzo Station."

"Gonzo Station?"

Prescott continued to smile. "It's what the crews have taken to calling duty in the northwest quadrant of the Indian Ocean."

Paul carried out some rapid mental geographic calculations, looked at the commander. "You mean the Persian Gulf?"

Prescott nodded absently. His attention was fixed, wistfully, on the carrier.

Paul followed the commander's look. The carrier was picking up speed as it approached the mouth of the bay. Paul's gaze wandered westward, over the ship's gently heaving bows toward the open sea. There was a single shaft of sunlight beyond the entrance to the bay, a lone survivor of the morning's early radiance. The sea within the pillar of light danced, brightly blue. Outside, it was leaden; vanquished, like the bay and the surrounding hills, by the advancing legions of monsoon cloud.

FIFTY MILES to the east, on the shores of another great bay, Ambassador Freed sat slumped in his chair, glumly watching similar leaden clouds. They were rolling in from the horizon, where the two encircling arms of the bay outside his window reached for each other. In the gap where they almost touched, there was a speck of an island. "Damn weather," the ambassador muttered. "I'll never get used to it."

Alison followed his look but said nothing. She'd been through this kind of thing before.

"Do you think this guy knows what he's doing?" he asked after a time.

"Hard to say, Ben," the woman replied.

"What do we know about him?"

"Not much. We know who he's working for, why he's in the country. The economics people have met him, shortly after he arrived. And of course you've seen the reports about the trouble he had the other night at that construction site up in northern Luzon."

"Yes. That sounds like it might have been unpleasant." Ambassador Freed paused. "No doubts, I suppose, that it was NPA?"

"All the indications point in that direction."

"They catch any of the culprits?"

"Apparently not."

Freed muttered under his breath. He fell silent again, sat brooding.

The woman stared wordlessly at the bald spot, waiting.

It was some time before the ambassador finally straightened. He spun his chair until he was facing the woman once more. He replaced his glasses, announced decisively, "I want to see him."

"Is that wise?"

"Probably not," Ambassador Freed replied, "but I have to know what's going on. There's too much at stake right now. The whole thing could go up in smoke if this guy gets it into his head to start hollering about pressure."

"And what if he is so inclined?"

"Then I'll have to try to talk him out of it."

"You're running a risk, you know, just to pull their chestnuts out of the fire."

"Those jerks have forced my hand."

"That's what they wanted to do."

"I know," Ambassador Freed muttered. "What's his schedule?"

The woman consulted the papers in her lap. "He'll be having lunch with Carlyle . . ." She paused, raised an eyebrow, "*Onboard* the *Blue Ridge*. After that, the Navy's flying him over to Clark, where they hand him over to your favorite general."

Ambassador Freed grunted with distaste. "They're really stroking him, aren't they?"

"Certainly looks that way."

"All right," said the ambassador briskly, glancing at his wristwatch. "If we lay on a chopper, you've probably got time to catch him at Clark. Arrange it with the people in transport. I want you to run up there personally and intercept this . . ." He hesitated, asked impatiently, "What's his name again?"

"Stenmark."

"Right. When you've collared this Stenmark, you bring him on down here."

"What if he won't come?"

"I don't think that will be a problem."

"Oh?"

Ambassador Freed gave her a sour smile. "I suspect that our friend might be feeling just a little confused, maybe even angry. I have a hunch he'll be bursting with questions."

THERE WERE a lot of questions rattling around in Paul's mind as he stared at the images flickering on the screen at the far end of the room. But he was not confused, nor was he angry. On the contrary, he was enjoying himself immensely.

He was seated in a capacious leather cushioned chair in a large oval room, which was dimly lit, like a theater. His chair was one of several dozen identical chairs banked in tiers in the shape of a horseshoe around the walls of the room. At the shoe's mouth, there was a dais. On the dais stood a man dressed in the uniform of the

United States Air Force. He was a sergeant, judging by the stripes
on his arm, and he held a pointer, which he was using to empha-
size features he seemed to find salient in a succession of color slides
flashing across the screen at his side.

Paul had no difficulty understanding what it was the sergeant
was trying to tell him. The message was clear, as clear as the
message he had received earlier in the day aboard the admiral's
flagship. Although Paul was not exactly sure why he had been
singled out for this treatment, it did not take a lot of insight to
realize that it was somehow connected with the power project up in
the highlands. The fact that he could not identify the precise
nature of the connection did not bother him. Ever since he had
climbed aboard the Navy helicopter, he had felt himself to be back
on terrain that, if not his own, was at least similar enough to be
comprehensible. He knew that sooner or later, he would find out
what he needed to know. In the meantime, it was enough to be
aware that his role in the power project was suddenly opening the
doors to corridors he had long yearned to tread.

Paul stole a look at the man in the chair beside him. His eyes
traveled from the thatch of gray bristles covering the man's large
head down to the two tiny stars on his collar. The stars gleamed in
the half-light reflected from the screen. Paul smiled, a secret,
satisfied smile.

His gaze drifted back to the dais, where the sergeant was tapping
on the screen with his pointer. Paul's attention wandered. Soon he
was no longer concentrating on what it was the sergeant was trying
to explain, nor did he notice the blond woman in the dark suit slip
into the chair behind his own. His thoughts were elsewhere, back up
in the Cordillera. He replayed in his mind the events that had
overtaken him on the terraced hills. He examined his argument, the
one that had led him to conclude there was no hope for a scheme
that, however improbably, now appeared to be leading him where
he had always wanted to go. Paul began to mull over the possibility
that he might have been too hasty in arriving at his conclusions.

18

FRANK ENRIGHT scanned the slope, looking for signs of Alfredo, or at least the boy. He glanced down at the watch on his wrist one more time and, one more time, he frowned. He ran a worried glance over the heavy clouds moving in from the south and west. They advanced relentlessly around the neighboring peaks, oozing down into the valleys in gray, sluggish streams, like lava.

Frank searched the slope again. It fell away gradually for a few hundred yards before it dipped abruptly and dropped out of sight. From where he was standing, just beyond the edge of the grove of gnarled oak, he could not see the terraces. But he knew they began where the slopes ended, cascading down the flank of the valley to the unseen river far below.

Hearing someone approaching, Frank turned and saw Liz emerging from among the twisted trees. She came toward him, carrying a blanket-encased bundle in her arms.

"Have a look," said Liz as she reached Frank. She tilted the bundle slightly so that he could see.

Frank stared down at a pair of enormous black eyes that peered sightlessly up at him out of a mottled, wrinkled face. The face was framed by a forest of coarse black hair that stood crazily erect, like the bristles on a badly finished brush.

"Isn't he beautiful?" Liz crooned proudly.

Frank glanced suspiciously at Liz.

Liz ignored the look. She gurgled and cooed at the bundle.

Frank asked uncertainly, "There's nothing wrong with it?"

"Him," Liz corrected.

"Him," Frank agreed, accepting the reprimand meekly.

"Of course not," Liz continued. "He's perfect."

Frank regarded the wizened little face doubtfully. "It . . ." He paused, amended quickly, "*He* does look a little better than the first time I saw him."

"All babies look that way when they're born, Frank."

Frank grunted. He inspected the child again. "You're sure there's nothing wrong with" —he caught himself in time—"him."

"I'm sure."

"But what about his head?"

"What's wrong with his head?"

"It's all sort of squashed in there on one side, like somebody sat on him or something."

Liz laughed. "That's pretty much what did happen to him."

"Huh?" Frank asked.

"Oh, you're a stubborn little fellow all right," Liz cooed, nuzzling the baby. "You just refused to do what you're supposed to do, didn't you?"

"Huh?" Frank asked, yet again.

Liz gave Frank an indulgent smile. "You're beginning to repeat yourself."

Frank grinned sheepishly.

Liz turned back to the child. "He's been jammed up against his mother's ribs while he's been growing inside her," she said. "That's why his head is a little lopsided."

"But will it stay that way?" Frank inquired, with alarm.

"No," Liz answered. "That will take care of itself in no time at all. Same with his legs."

"What's wrong with his legs?"

Liz turned back the blanket that was wrapped around the infant.

Frank looked. "They're all bent!" he exclaimed, aghast.

"That's what all the trouble was about."

"You mean that's what made him come out that way . . . backwards?"

Liz nodded. "He couldn't get himself turned around to come out the right way."

Frank considered this. "And that's why it took so long?"

"Mostly."

Frank shuddered. "I don't want to have to go through anything like that again."

Liz looked at Frank. "Yeah," she said dryly, "it must have been rough for you."

Frank looked contrite. "Well, all I mean is it did take an awful long time," he mumbled.

Liz gave her head a shake. "I've never had a woman in labor for that long before." She glanced back toward the trees. "Nor in those conditions."

Frank followed Liz's look. He could see the outline of the hut just inside the line of trees. He asked, "How is she now?"

"Very weak, very tired," Liz replied. "But I think she's going to be all right. I've given her something to help her sleep."

"Poor kid," Frank murmured.

"It could have been worse," said Liz. "For a while I was afraid I might have to try a Cesarean, which would not have been pleasant under the circumstances." She glanced down and began to rock the infant, murmuring soothingly as she did so.

Frank studied Liz. She was arrayed in the manner he had come to regard as her working mode. Her long black hair was pulled tightly back, and she wore a knee-length white smock. But the smock was unbuttoned. It billowed gently in the breeze, revealing the curves of her body beneath jeans and a sweater. And her hair had come loose, undone by the rigors of the last days. Strands of it fell across her face as she bent over the child.

Watching her, Frank experienced a surge of affection for the woman—and something else as well, something more potent. It engulfed him so completely that he had no time to identify it. He did not even have the time to admit to himself that he did not care to give a label to what he was feeling at that moment. He reached out a hand and tenderly brushed the hair from Liz's face.

"Don't do that!" Liz snapped.

Frank withdrew his hand, as if stung.

Liz looked into Frank's eyes, saw the confusion. It augmented her anger.

"I'm . . . I'm sorry," Frank stammered.

Liz searched Frank's eyes, as if looking for something there that might give her the courage to say what she had been wanting to say for some time. She asked at last, with irritation, "What are you sorry for?"

"I didn't mean . . ." Frank began awkwardly.

"What didn't you mean?" Liz interrupted brutally.

"I didn't mean to upset you."

"You think it upsets me to be touched?"

Frank shrugged helplessly.

The response was not what Liz was seeking. "Do you think I don't want to be touched?"

"Liz," said Frank, as if pleading.

"Take a close look at me," Liz commanded. "What do you see?"

Frank did not respond. He did not know how to.

"Answer me, dammit!" Liz's voice was rising, which reawakened the child in her arms. The infant began to moan feebly.

Frank shook his head in confusion.

"All you see is a doctor standing here?"

"Well . . ."

"Nothing else?"

Frank spread his hands.

"I am a woman, Frank!" Liz cried. The child whimpered.

Frank saw that Liz was fighting back tears.

"Liz," Frank pleaded. "I'm a priest."

Liz's dark eyes bore into Frank's. "You don't look at me the way a priest looks at a woman, Frank."

Frank gaped at Liz.

"I'm not immune, you know."

Frank had no breath to respond. He was as staggered as surely as if he had been punched, very hard.

Peering into Frank's eyes, Liz finally saw what she had been seeking, some glimmer of understanding. She looked away, down over the slope toward the unseen terraces far below.

"Liz . . ." Frank began at last.

"It's all right," Liz broke in wearily. "I guess I'm just a little tired."

The child suddenly located its brand new voice. He began to bawl. Liz glanced down, as if startled by the baby's presence. She bounced the infant gently in her arms.

Frank made another effort. "I don't know what to say."

"Then don't say anything," Liz replied, not unkindly.

When she had quieted the child, she ran a glance over the valley at her feet. "No sign of Alfredo yet?"

It took a moment for Frank, in the grip of some turmoil, to understand the question. He gave Liz a puzzled glance, followed the direction of her look with confusion.

"Or the boy?"

Frank finally replied, a little distractedly, "No."

"Shouldn't they have returned by now?"

"Yes," said Frank. Gathering his wits, he added somberly, "They should have been back hours ago."

Liz looked sharply at Frank. "What is it?"

"I think something has gone wrong."

"What?"

"I don't know,"

"Oh, Christ!" Liz muttered, glancing back toward the hut partly hidden among the contorted trees.

Frank turned, stared at the trees. "You want to get her down to the clinic," he said after a moment.

"Yes."

"She can't walk, of course."

"Not in this kind of country."

"Can she be moved?"

"Not unless we get some help."

Frank sighed. "Then I better get to work on that roof."

Liz shot a questioning look at Frank.

Frank answered with a nod toward the southwest, where the masses of dark cloud were maintaining a steady advance. "It's going to start raining again soon."

Liz turned, surveyed the clouds. "Damn!" she swore. "Damn that stupid boy."

19

THE ENORMOUS blanket of menacing cloud that lay upon the bay abruptly burst, dumping the burden that had been carried clear across two oceans and, in the process, diverting Ambassador Benjamin Freed's attention as well as Paul's. They both glanced in surprise at the ambassador's window, startled by the sudden violence going on outside. They were silent for a time as they watched the rain crashing down with a ferocity that suggested it was being hurled earthward.

"Same time every day," Ambassador Freed muttered finally. "Like bloody clockwork." He turned back to Paul, who reclined in an armchair on the other side of the large teak desk. "I don't know about *you,* but it gets *me* down."

Paul managed to summon a sympathetic smile but he said nothing. He regarded the ambassador with interest, wondering when the man was going to get to the point. They had been trading pleasantries for a quarter of an hour. It was time.

Ambassador Freed cleared his throat. "You must be wondering why I've asked you down here."

Paul almost laughed aloud. His smile broadened and he replied, "Not really."

Ambassador Freed arched an eyebrow. It was not the answer he was expecting. "Oh?"

"I assume I'm here for an explanation," Paul went on breezily.

Ambassador Freed contemplated Paul before asking cautiously, "An explanation?"

Paul crossed his legs and sank deeper into the armchair. He had been waiting for this moment, and he intended to relish it. "That *is* why I'm here, isn't it?"

"I'm afraid I'm not following you, Mr. Stenmark."

"Please call me Paul."

Ambassador Freed inclined his head. "Paul."

"I don't think we have to waste any more time on the preliminaries, Mr. Ambassador," Paul said, thoroughly enjoying himself. "Some very important people, yourself included, have been rolling out the red carpet for me all day long. I'm not exactly sure why, but I suspect it has nothing to do with my baby-blue eyes. I have a strong hunch there must be some connection with that project I'm working on up in the hills. And I also have a hunch that I'm sitting here right now so that you can tell me all about that connection."

"I see," Ambassador Freed replied carefully. He leaned back into his chair, steepled his hands on his midriff, and studied Paul thoughtfully.

Paul returned the look. As he did, he noticed that the ambassador's hands were small and delicate, unlike the paunch they rested upon.

"All right, Paul," Ambassador Freed announced after a time. His tone of voice indicated that the scales had been consulted and a judgment reached. "Let's level with each other. I want you to know that I'm prepared to be quite candid, but in return for that, I'm going to require something from you."

"What's that?"

"I want you to bring me up to speed."

The ambassador's words induced a warm, comfortable glow in Paul. Even the jargon was Washington. It reinforced the sense of ease that had been growing throughout the day, his feeling that after a harrowing trek through alien territory, he was now safely back in an environment where he understood the rules. He said, "I'd be happy to do that if I can."

"Fine," said Ambassador Freed. He leaned forward, placing his small hands on his large desk. There was just a trace of accusation in his voice when he asked, "For a start, why don't you tell me exactly what you were doing hobnobbing with all that brass up at Subic and Clark?"

"I was invited," Paul replied, unfazed by the ambassador's manner.

"Why?"

"I was told the *brass*, as you put it, had learned of my . . . uh"— Paul fingered the bandages on his forehead—"*adventures* and wanted to talk."

"About what?"

"They weren't very precise, to tell the truth," Paul answered. "But I was under the impression they were anxious to discuss the people who did this." He pointed up to his bandages.

"And you bought that?"

"In part."

"Why?" Ambassador Freed came close to a sneer. "Are you an authority on that crowd?"

"I have some personal experience, as you know."

"And that makes you an expert?"

"No."

The eyes behind Ambassador Freed's hornrims took on an inquisitorial gleam. "Then didn't you think it strange that ranking officers of the United States Navy's Seventh Fleet as well as the senior levels of command of the 13th United States Air Force, with all the resources at their disposal, would want to talk to you on a subject about which you admit you know little?"

"Yes," Paul confessed cheerfully.

The answer, and Paul's tone, threw the ambassador. He eyed Paul. "Then why did you accept this . . . um . . . invitation?"

"I was curious," Paul responded. He paused, shrugged, "I guess I was also flattered."

"Flattered?"

"Mr. Ambassador," Paul said familiarly, "if you were in my position, wouldn't you have been flattered by an invitation like that?"

Ambassador Freed cast an appreciative glance at Paul, as if seeing something there he had not noticed before. He chuckled softly. "Yes, I suppose I would have been."

Paul sat, basking in the ambassador's look.

"So you were flattered and you were curious," Ambassador Freed continued. His voice had lost the hectoring edge. "Curious about what?"

"The personalities, of course. And the situation." Paul paused, marshaling his thoughts. "As you suggested, I didn't think I had an awful lot to offer these people concerning those insurgents. I was curious to see what they really wanted."

"And was your curiosity satisfied?"

"Partly."

"Go on."

"I found out what it was they wanted to tell me."

"Which was?"

"Well, it was all very pleasant and civilized, but what it amounted to was a lecture, a series of lectures actually, all designed to impress upon me the importance of Subic Bay and Clark Air Base in the overall scheme of things. You know . . . American strategic posture in the Far East, that sort of thing."

"That's all?" Ambassador Freed asked sharply.

"Pretty much."

The ambassador nodded toward Paul's bandaged forehead. "The characters who did that were not discussed?"

"Only in the most general way."

"And your project?"

"It wasn't even mentioned."

Ambassador Freed heaved a sigh, as if relieved. "All right," he said, relaxing back into his chair once again. "I think I've got the picture now."

"Good," Paul replied. "Maybe you'd like"—he could not resist stealing the ambassador's phrase—"to bring *me* up to speed."

"You mean you haven't already guessed?"

Paul smiled, a little smugly. He found the implications of the remark gratifying. "Well, as I said earlier, there must be some connection between those bases and my project."

"Mmm-hmm."

"And I can read the newspapers like everybody else."

"So?"

"So I assume the link has something to do with the current renegotiation of the agreement under which the American military operate out of those bases."

"Keep going."

Paul raised his hands pleadingly. "You can keep me guessing all day, but I don't really see the purpose of doing that. I thought I was here to have things explained to me."

"Okay," Ambassador Freed replied. "You've been honest with me, so now it's my turn." He paused, gathering an argument. "You're absolutely right, of course. It is because of those bases. The fact is, they're very important. Our military facilities in this country represent one of two major nodal points of United States security policy in the Western Pacific Basin. As you and everybody else who can read know by now, the bases agreement is being renegotiated. What is not generally known, at least not yet, is the fact that those negotiations are virtually wrapped up. I'm not giving away any secrets when I tell you that most of the terms of the new agreement are innocuous, not much more than window dressing for the nationalist-minded here and at home." The ambassador hesitated. "But there is one item that could become troublesome."

"Oh?"

Ambassador Freed regarded Paul closely, lowered his voice. "Now this part is confidential for the moment, so I'll have to ask you to keep it to yourself."

"Of course," said Paul, having some difficulty masking his heightened interest.

"It's the price the American taxpayer is going to be asked to pay for the privilege of continued access to those bases."

"How much?"

"Close to one billion dollars."

Paul whistled softly.

"You understand what that means?"

Paul nodded. He saw the problem instantly. "Congress."

"Exactly," said the ambassador. "Funds of that magnitude always pose difficulties, even if they are not destined for regimes with less than savory reputations."

"I'm beginning to see where I fit," said Paul slowly.

"I thought you might."

"My project is awfully close to those bases."

"It looks even closer on a map of Luzon, especially if that map is being waved around in front of a not entirely sympathetic congressional committee."

"Uh-huh," Paul mused. "If the bank was to reject a request for funds for a peaceful project right next door to Subic and Clark while Congress was chewing over a billion-dollar military package—"

"Particularly if it became public knowledge," Ambassador Freed cut in, "that the refusal was because of security problems stemming from a Communist insurgency."

Paul stiffened. "But hang on a minute," said Paul, eyes widening. "How would they know . . ." He stopped himself.

Ambassador Freed completed the question. "How would the United States military know your intentions?"

Paul stared at the ambassador.

Ambassador Freed arched his eyebrows. "Let's just say that we have impeccable sources, particularly with the boys in uniform on the other side."

Paul ran a hand over his bandaged forehead, searching his memory. His hand dropped. He whispered, "Rosales!"

"Please," Ambassador Freed said, raising a cautioning hand. "Don't say another word. I am already uncomfortable with this conversation, and I hope you appreciate that."

Paul shook his head in amazement. "So that's what it was all about." He looked at the ambassador. "They're afraid that a negative vote on that project will amount to the same thing for their bases."

"More or less," Ambassador Freed replied. "They were exercising a little damage control . . ." He paused, smiled. "Before there was any damage."

They certainly went to a lot of trouble," Paul complained, a shade testily.

"They're cautious people," said Ambassador Freed carefully. He was watching Paul.

"All the same, they've been trying to influence my decision."

"Which was none of their business, I agree."

Paul shifted in his chair, with irritation.

"It was an exceedingly stupid move," Ambassador Freed continued. "Particularly if it was to become widely known."

Paul gave the ambassador a close look.

"And that would be a shame, wouldn't it?"

Paul continued to regard the ambassador.

"Because there was no real harm done."

Paul pursed his lips dubiously.

"Don't forget you've been dealing with the military mind here," said Ambassador Freed in a tone that implied a faint hint of ridicule. "It's a strange beast. When confronted with a problem, it reacts instinctively by issuing an order, which it expects to be unquestioningly obeyed. It is unaccustomed to more subtle forms of persuasion." He smiled winningly. "Unlike you and me.

"And there's one more thing, Paul," Ambassador Freed went on heartily. "You've won the acquaintance of some powerful individuals today. That can be . . ." He paused, almost as if he was looking for the right word. "Useful."

Paul found that he was suddenly glad he had not communicated his skepticism about the viability of the project in the hills to his superiors. His gaze drifted to the window behind the ambassador's shoulder, beyond which the rain was sheeting into the bay. Perhaps he *had* been premature.

20

ELIZABETH BUENAVENTURA slumped against the doorway and listened to the rain hiss into the thatch above her head. Her gaze wandered gloomily around the windowless room, taking in the chinks of fading daylight peeking through the plank walls, pausing over the puddles of rainwater on the earthen floor, settling finally upon Frank. He was on his hands and knees before a heap of twigs, attempting to nurse a fire into life. She watched him for a few moments, then muttered, as she had been muttering with increasing frequency, "Damn that stupid boy!"

Frank glanced up from his reluctant fire. "Don't be too hard on him, Liz."

Liz jerked a thumb over her shoulder in the direction of the room on the other side of the doorway, as barren and wretched as the one in which she was standing. "I doubt if that girl is more than fourteen."

Frank returned his attention to the little pyramid in front of him. "The boy's only fifteen."

"That's old enough."

"Old enough for what?" Frank asked, studying the lone wisp of gray smoke that rose, pencil-straight, from the peak of his pile of tinder.

"Old enough to know you can't drag a pregnant girl to a place like this," Liz replied, sweeping her eyes around the room with disgust.

Frank did not answer. He was bent over his twigs, blowing carefully on them.

"Not unless you want to kill her," Liz went on, vaguely irritated by Frank's inattention.

Frank continued to blow on the twigs.

"Which is what surely would have happened if he hadn't panicked at the last minute and run off to Alfredo for help."

"You notice how they all eventually turn to Alfredo when they're in trouble," Frank mused, rising to his knees.

"But why the hell did he bring her up here in the first place?"

"I guess he thought he didn't have much choice," Frank answered. "I guess both of them thought that." He contemplated the mound at his knees, which was beginning to crackle quietly.

Liz grunted.

"They've been up here for weeks," Frank continued. "Both of them."

"Oh?" Liz asked, regarding Frank with renewed interest. "So you finally *did* manage to get him to say something."

"I didn't," Frank answered, watching the first tiny flames licking upward from the tinder. "Alfredo did."

"And what was the story he told Alfredo?" Liz inquired acidly.

"The usual," Frank responded, with resignation.

Liz frowned at Frank.

Frank looked up. "They're runaways. They come from warring clans, apparently."

"Oh God!"

"Yes." Frank sighed. "I know."

"Romeo and Juliet, for Christ's sake!"

"I guess the affliction *is* universal," Frank remarked ruefully.

Liz leaned a little more heavily into the doorway separating the hut's two rooms and gazed sourly at the multitude of puddles scattered around the earth floor beneath a multitude of leaks.

Frank inspected Liz. The effects of her efforts in recent days were beginning to show, in her pose and in the deep shadows under her eyes. "You must be tired," he said.

Liz continued to stare at the pools of water, watching the rain plunk slowly into them.

Frank gestured with his eyes toward a dry patch of the floor beside the fire, where a sleeping bag was spread atop a yellow rain slicker. "Why don't you try and get some sleep."

Liz looked at the sleeping bag, then at Frank. "I'm worried, Frank."

Frank looked toward the room beyond the doorway where Liz stood. "Something wrong?"

"No, they're all right," Liz replied. "As well as can be expected, anyway. The girl's asleep again; so's the child. They'll both probably be out for hours now." She heaved a frustrated sigh. "But we can't stay up here forever. We've got to get them down to the clinic, or at least a *barrio,* and the sooner we do that the better."

Frank glanced up at the porous thatch. "We're not going any-where right now."

Liz followed his look. "Oh, where the hell *are* they?" she com-plained.

"I don't know," Frank answered. "But I *do* know that something serious has gone wrong. There's no other explanation."

"But . . ."

"Alfredo would have been back with help long ago if there was any possible way he could. He would not abandon us like this. I know that man, Liz. He's been my best friend for twenty years. As a matter of fact, he's been practically the only real friend I've ever had . . ." He paused, lowered his voice. "Until you came along."

Liz stared at Frank, momentarily disconcerted. She averted her eyes, murmured, "Well, we're going to have to do *something.*"

"The rain will break sometime tonight," said Frank. "We'll have a few clear hours in the morning. If Alfredo or the boy hasn't returned by then, I suggest that you and I will have to manage as best we can on our own."

Liz's glance returned to Frank. "What do you mean?"

Frank nodded toward the hut's only other room. "We'll have to carry those two in there down to the nearest *barrio*."

"*Carry* them?"

"Can either of them walk?"

"No."

Frank shrugged. "Then you got any better ideas?"

"But how can we carry those two in this kind of country?"

Frank smiled mischievously. "What's the matter, you can't manage a three-day-old baby?"

"Well . . . yes."

"Oho, then you're of the opinion that *I'm* the problem."

Liz caught the twinkle in Frank's gray eyes.

"You may not believe this, lady," said Frank, flexing his shoulders theatrically, "but there was a time when I terrorized playing fields across the entire midwestern United States."

Liz ran an admiring gaze over Frank's hefty shoulders.

"So I don't want you thinking I'm too old and decrepit to cart a mere slip of a girl over a few piddling little hills."

Liz's eyes traveled from Frank's shoulders up over his rugged face to the tangle of untamed curls tumbling onto his forehead. Liz was not thinking Frank looked old and decrepit. That was not even close to what she was thinking.

THERE WAS something missing in the face nestled within the folds of the down sleeping bag on the floor of the hut. Gradually it had dawned on Frank that Liz, in repose, wore no trace of the quick-to-flare passion he had so often glimpsed in her. With her eyes closed, a curtain had been drawn over that part of her, leaving only a vulnerability he found both surprising and touching.

Frank looked back at what was left of the pitiful fire in front of him. He picked up a twig from the dwindling pile at his side and stared at it morosely. The wood was not really dry; there were leaves still attached to the slender branch. It would not burn, he knew, but he tossed it on the embers anyway. It was better than nothing. He pulled the collar of his thin windbreaker more tightly around his neck and blew into his hands. The chill was damp and bitter. It gnawed into his bones. He hunched and watched the stick smolder. The leaves curled and withered.

Frank's gaze was drawn back to Liz. She was still sleeping on her side, with her face peeping out of the heavy bag. But her lips had parted slightly. The suggestion of sensual languor aroused in Frank emotions he did not like to contemplate. They made him feel breathless.

He suddenly realized that the lips he was staring at were moving, were being moistened. He glanced up and found himself the object of an intent regard by a pair of enormous sloe eyes. The look in them was blissful, without a hint of the fervor he had been wondering about earlier.

Frank marveled at the rush of welcome warmth he was experiencing. He smiled. "Hello there."

"Hi," Liz replied dreamily.

"Sleep well?"

"Mmm-hmm."

"The rain's finally stopped."

"Good," Liz murmured, closing her eyes again. "What time is it?"

"A few hours before dawn."

The eyes snapped open. "Omigawd!" Liz exclaimed. "Have I been asleep that long?"

"Yep."

Liz struggled to sit upright in the sleeping bag.

"Relax," said Frank. "Stay where you are. It's warmer."

"But the girl," said Liz, fumbling with the bag's zipper. "The baby."

"They're fine."

"Not if they've been sleeping all this time," Liz answered, finally mastering the zipper. She began to open the bag but stopped abruptly, as if suddenly remembering something.

"They haven't," said Frank.

"Haven't what?" Liz asked distractedly. She seemed to be searching the interior of the bag with her feet.

"They haven't been sleeping all this time," Frank replied, wondering at Liz's efforts.

Liz halted whatever it was she was doing, glanced at Frank. "They're awake?"

"Not at the moment," Frank responded. "They woke up a couple of times during the night. I went to have a look, but it was obvious I wasn't needed."

"What?"

"The girl was feeding her child." Frank shrugged. "I'm no expert on these matters, but I'd say mother and son had the situation under control. They both looked pretty happy about things, anyway."

Liz breathed a sigh of relief. "That's good." She resumed her struggles within the sleeping bag.

Frank observed for a time until his curiosity prevailed. "What are you doing?"

"Nothing," Liz muttered, which was patently false, since her hands had now joined her feet inside the bag. All four limbs were engaged in what appeared to be some kind of mysterious combat.

"Is there something in there with you?"

"No."

"It sure looks like it."

"If you must know," Liz replied tersely, "I'm trying to get back into my jeans."

"You took them off?"

Liz gave Frank a wry look. "Sometimes you really do amaze me, you know that, Frank?"

Frank watched silently as Liz continued to writhe within the sleeping bag. After a time, she slumped onto her back and stared with frustration up at the underside of the thatch roof.

"I can't do it," Liz announced.

"Why?"

"Because they're too bloody tight, that's why, you idiot."

"Oh," said Frank. He hesitated, asked finally, "You want me to leave the room or something?"

"That depends," Liz answered. "When do I have to get up?"

"We can't do anything until daylight," Frank replied. "That's still two or three hours away."

"Then if it's all right with you," said Liz, snuggling deeper into the sleeping bag, "I think I'll just stay where I am for a while longer."

"Good idea," Frank said, unable to suppress a shiver. "It's cold out here."

Liz turned her head and looked at Frank, suddenly alert to what she had been missing. He was huddled on the dirt floor, hugging himself with his hands jammed under his armpits. She ran her eyes over his lightweight windbreaker and saw his breath condensing in the air, which made her fully aware of the cold stinging her own cheeks. She glanced at the nearly dead fire, nothing but a heap of feebly glowing ashes. There was a single blackened twig on top of it, venting a plume of hissing steam. She looked back at Frank and asked, "The wood's all gone?"

"All the dry stuff." Frank nodded down at the little pile of green branches at his side. "If I use any more of this, we'll suffocate in the smoke."

Liz's eyes traveled to the doorway.

"They're all right," Frank replied in answer to the unspoken question. "They've got the blankets Alfredo left and the other sleeping bag."

"What about you?"

"I'll survive." Frank attempted a brave smile, but the effect was undone when his teeth began to chatter.

Liz turned on her side and gave Frank a hard, appraising look. She was alarmed by the heavy shadows beneath his eyes and the white, pinched appearance of his mouth. "You didn't get any sleep, did you?"

Frank shook his head. He did not trust himself to speak.

Liz stared at Frank. He tightened his grip on his chest in an effort to control his trembling.

Liz sat upright and began to unzip the sleeping bag.

Frank caught a glimpse of something white and filmy against a long, coppery thigh as Liz leaned to undo the zipper. He continued to tremble, not entirely because of the cold.

Liz lay down on her side. "You'd better come here," she said. There was a tiny catch in her voice when she spoke.

21

PAUL STENMARK gazed at his reflection in the smoky mirror. As usual, he was vaguely discomfited by what he saw. The face peering back at him from among the bottles stacked on the other side of the bar was a shade too callow for his liking. He wished there were a little more steel in those blue eyes, a little less flesh on the rounded cheeks. He set his jaw and gave himself a hard-eyed squint, then stopped abruptly. He glanced furtively around, embarrassed by his boyish posturing. He looked down at the glass cradled in his hand on the bar and was mildly dismayed to find it half empty. It was already his second. Or was it the third? He would have to slow down before he made an ass of himself.

Paul swirled the vodka around the ice as his thoughts drifted back to Alfredo, just as they had been doing ever since he walked out of the ambassador's office earlier in the day. There was simply no way around the man. He had gone over it again and again, searching for the path that would allow him to move ahead with the project in the hills. But every trail he followed eventually, inevitably, wound back to Alfredo.

Paul lifted his glass and drank moodily, forgetting the warning he had just given himself. Alfredo was the key. His influence was paramount. As long as Alfredo felt the way he did, there was no chance of swaying his people. As long as Alfredo's people felt the

way they did, there was no chance of denying sustenance to the
insurgents. As long as the insurgents were free to act with relative
impunity, there was no chance to prevent them from striking at the
project.

Paul took another sip of his drink. No matter which way he
played it, backward or forward, the result was always the same. The
dams could not be built because the insurgents would not allow
it . . . because that was the most effective method of maintaining a
hold on the allegiance of the local population . . . because the local
population believed the dams threatened their very existence . . .
because that was what Alfredo believed.

Paul drank. It was infuriating. The man was purblind. He was
chaining his own people to a life of backwardness and deprivation
because he lacked the vision to see what the future held and reach
an accommodation with it.

Paul drank again. It was also depressing, on a very personal
level. For those chains Alfredo was forging were also binding Paul
to his desk back in Washington. There would be no more rubbing
shoulders with admirals and generals and ambassadors. The admirals and generals and ambassadors he was thinking of would not
even want to talk to him. And when would another opportunity
like this arise? Maybe never.

Paul muttered and raised his glass. It was empty. He signaled the
bartender, who appeared before him with alacrity. "Gimme
another one," Paul said gloomily. As the bartender turned, Paul
said, "Put something in it this time."

"What'll it be?" the bartender asked with a smile. "Tonic?
Soda?"

As Paul was about to answer, he noticed out of the corner of his
eye a figure sliding onto the stool beside him. The bartender's
glance shifted; the smile on his face grew almost sycophantic.

"Evening, Mr. Veloso," said the bartender, oozing servility.

"Evening, Rick," Veloso replied. The voice was deep, rasping.

"Will it be the usual, sir?" the bartender asked.

"That's right." Veloso glanced at Paul. "When you're through with this gentleman."

Paul looked. He found himself being regarded by a heavy, middle-aged Filipino. There was a pleasant smile on the man's face, which did not quite rescue it from conveying an overall impression of brutality. The man had a lantern jaw, a flattened nose, and the high cheekbones and cruel eyes of a Tartar warlord. He was dressed expensively in the local style, in a banana-colored *barong* so fine it was almost transparent. But there were too many flashes of gold at his neck, wrists, and hands. It suggested well-heeled vulgarity.

Faintly repelled, Paul nevertheless managed a polite smile. He turned back to the bartender, who was regarding him.

"You wanted something to go with your vodka, wasn't it?" the bartender asked.

Paul hesitated, deciding.

"Why not try it with kalamansi juice?" intervened Veloso.

Paul turned and gave the man an inquiring look. "Sorry," he asked, "what did you say?"

Veloso smiled apologetically. "I was suggesting kalamansi. It's a local lime. Goes good with vodka." He spoke English fluently in the American manner, with only a trace of an accent.

Paul nodded. "Okay," he responded, a little reluctantly. He was not completely convinced that he welcomed the intrusion.

Veloso turned to the bartender. "A kalamansi and vodka for the gentleman. You know what I want." He paused. "Put 'em both on my tab, Rick."

"Thanks," said Paul, groaning inwardly. He had a feeling that he did not want to be in this man's debt.

"It's nuthin'," Veloso replied with a negligent wave of his wrist, which exposed a heavy gold bracelet. He extended a large hand, aglitter with rings. "My name's Francisco Veloso. My friends call me Chico."

Paul grasped the outstretched hand. The grip was firm, and confident. "Paul Stenmark."

"Been here long, Paul?" Chico inquired amicably.

"Not long," Paul answered. "A couple of weeks."

"You here on business or pleasure?"

Paul smiled noncommittally. Undecided about the attention he was receiving, he was not anxious to encourage it.

The tactic backfired. Paul felt a nudge in his ribs. He looked up in time to catch the end of a knowing wink in one of the Tartar eyes.

"Maybe a little of both, huh?" Chico smirked.

Paul's smile became awkward.

If Chico noticed, he gave no sign. He continued, undeterred. "This is one helluva town for mixing business and pleasure." There was another nudge. "But I guess I don't have to tell ya that."

Paul's smile grew strained.

Chico once again missed the signal. He was no longer regarding Paul. His attention was on the bartender, who was arriving with the drinks. " 'Bout time, Rick. A man could die of thirst around here." He looked at Paul, shoved a glass awash with ice and a pale green liquid in his direction. "Try that."

Paul looked hopelessly from the drink to Chico. He was feeling trapped. He raised the glass and sipped. He smiled grudgingly. The drink was tart, refreshing. It helped to restore his humor. "You're right," he admitted. "Hits the spot."

Chico grunted with satisfaction. "What'd I tell ya?" He raised his own glass, tipped it in Paul's direction. "*Mabuhay*, as we say."

Paul tipped his glass, took another sip. He sat savoring the taste.

After a moment of silence, Chico asked, "Where you from, Paul?" His tone was friendly, conversational.

"Minnesota, originally," Paul replied, beginning to accept his fate.

"Brrr, Minnesota. Too damn cold for the likes of me."

"You know the place?"

"Only by reputation. You still live there?"

"No. Washington's my home now."

"Washington, huh? You must be with the embassy."

"No."

"Government?"

Paul shook his head. "Not exactly."

Chico inspected Paul. "You don't look like military."

Paul chuckled. "I'm not." He was enjoying cloaking himself in some mystery. He was also enjoying the drink and the fact that for the first time in hours, he was not worrying about Alfredo.

Chico fixed Paul with a friendly look. "You gonna keep me guessing all night, right?"

Paul regarded Chico. The eyes were looking a little less intimidating. Perhaps his first impressions about the man had not been entirely accurate. He took another drink and finally relented.

"I've been working on a project up in Luzon."

"Oh?" Chico asked casually. "What project is that?"

PAUL LEANED back, drained the cognac in the large balloon-shaped glass, and let his hand, with the glass in it, drop back onto the table. It struck with a force that startled him. He stared in puzzlement at the glass for a moment. Then he swung his head in the direction of Chico, who was seated on the other side of the small round table. He had some difficulty focusing.

"So the real problem," Paul stated with conviction, "is this Alfredo character."

"Sure sounds that way," Chico agreed. He lifted a bottle of cognac from amid the detritus of what had clearly been a sumptuous meal. He poured a large dollop into Paul's empty glass. He swirled the cognac in his own and raised it to his nose, sniffing appreciatively. He put the glass back down on the table without drinking from it.

Paul and Chico were seated in a restaurant, where they had retreated at Chico's suggestion after many drinks and much conversation at the bar. The restaurant had a cozy, clublike feel to it. The floor was carpeted in thick burgundy, matching the leather cushioning the chairs. The walls were paneled in dark wood and decorated with circular patterns of lacquered cowrie shells. The shells shone quietly in the subdued lighting. It was the kind of place that encouraged whispered confidences.

It had worked its spell on Paul, whose defenses were not what they normally would have been as a result of the alcohol he had consumed. During the course of the dinner, with a little coaxing from Chico, Paul had spilled out the story of the dams in the hills and his involvement there. He had not left out many details, nor had he been reluctant to deliver his own views.

Chico sat contemplating Paul, who was staring morosely into his glass after passing judgment on Alfredo. Chico suggested softly, "It's a pity something can't be done to . . . *neutralize* this man Alfredo's influence."

"How's that?"

Chico toyed with his glass. He raised it, inspecting the cognac. "I guess you'd probably be able to proceed with this project of yours if that guy wasn't around to foul things up all the time."

"There's something to that," Paul agreed.

Chico lifted his glass to his lips and drank deeply. He rolled the cognac around in his mouth. As he did so, there was a distant, speculative gaze in the Tartar eyes.

22

FRANK WALKED through the stand of oak, wondering why he did not feel as blasted as the gnarled and twisted trees around him. He knew that something had ended for him. It had been a long time coming, but he no longer had any doubts that it was over now. There was a time when it had been important, the most important thing in his life. He felt he should be appalled, prostrate with grief, at least empty. He kept telling himself he wanted to feel that way. It was no use, however. No matter how hard he tried, he could summon nothing stronger than a kind of wistful regret, a melancholy longing for what might have been.

Frank moved out of the trees, onto the meadow. He saw Liz and stopped. She stood with her arms folded across her chest, gazing down the hill to the point where the slope dipped and dropped out of sight. As he looked at the slight, dark figure, her hair loose and blowing in the morning breeze, he began to understand why he was feeling the way he was. It was not endings that occupied his thoughts: it was beginnings. He smiled, struck by a sudden awareness that the future, which he had grown accustomed to viewing with a certain despair, no longer appeared to be as bleak as he had imagined.

Liz turned as Frank approached. There was a hint of trepidation in the look she gave him, as if she was a little fearful of what she might find in his face.

Frank was conscious of similar doubts about Liz as he reached her. He said awkwardly, "I was wondering where you were."

"Couldn't sleep," Liz answered tightly. She searched Frank's eyes.

"You should have waked me."

"I thought you needed the rest." As soon as the words escaped Liz, she blushed furiously. She looked away, toward the unseen valley beyond the lip of the slope.

Frank stepped to her side and placed an arm tentatively around her shoulders. He pulled her gently to him. She sank gratefully against his chest, dropped her head onto his shoulder, and took a deep, shuddering breath. He leaned his face against the top of her head and began to stroke her hair. The two of them remained like that for some time, watching the breeze chase the last wisps of morning fog down the hill.

"I've been thinking," Frank said at last.

"No kidding," Liz murmured.

Frank gave Liz's shoulder a shake. "I'm serious," he said. "This is important."

"I'm listening."

"Do you think it's too late to start over?"

"Too late?"

"Well," said Frank, struggling, "what I mean is, I'm kind of set in my ways."

"If you're asking me if I think you're too old, Frank," said Liz without raising her head from Frank's shoulder, "the answer is no."

"It's not so much the years I'm talking about," Frank went on. He swept his eyes around the landscape, which was looking damp and forlorn under an overcast sky. "Do you know how long I've been in these hills? When I first came here I was not much more than a boy. Aside from supply trips down to Manila and the odd visit home, I've spent my entire adult life here."

"I know that."

"I'm not sure I know how to function doing anything else." Frank threw an arm toward the bedraggled hills. "I came here to help these people. For the better part of my twenty years, that's what I thought I've been doing."

"You have," Liz objected. "You've given these people a lot: the mission, the school, the clinic, the action groups."

"That's not what these people need now."

"If it's those dams you're talking about . . ."

"Of course it's the dams. What good is a prayer in the face of that kind of threat? Hell, Ka Larry's accomplished more with his gun than I have with a thousand prayers."

"You've provided more than prayers, and you know that," Liz said heatedly. "You've taught these people how to organize. You've made it possible for them to resist."

Frank glanced at Liz. "Have I made it possible for them to resist Ka Larry?"

Liz did not respond.

"Exactly," Frank went on, nodding his head. "And you want to know something else? Lately I've found *myself* almost believing that Ka Larry and his kind are right after all. And that really alarms me, because despite what they say about me, I've never been one of your liberation theologists. Maybe I'm old-fashioned or something, but I have no illusions about what would happen to people like me, or the things people like me believe in, should Ka Larry and his friends ever manage to pull off their revolution."

"Aren't you exaggerating?"

"I don't think so, but that's not really the point."

"What is the point?"

Frank turned from Liz and stared down the hill. "The point is, that's why I've been thinking that maybe the time has come to start over." He dug his hands deeply into his trouser pockets. "And I was wondering . . ." he began with difficulty. "I was wondering . . ." He took a deep breath and turned back to Liz. He gave her a helpless look. "Hell," he complained. "I guess what I'm trying to say is, 'You want to start over with me?' "

Liz laughed. She was on the point of flying into Frank's arms when he jerked his head back in the direction of the valley.

Liz followed his look. "What is it?"

Frank cocked an ear. "Can't you hear it?"

"Hear what?" Liz asked, peering around.

"I'm not sure," Frank replied. He nodded down the slope. "It's coming from the valley."

In a moment, Liz was hearing it too. It was a muffled, rhythmic thumping, emanating from beyond the lip of the slope, where it dipped out of sight. "Yes," she whispered. "I hear it now."

"It's getting louder."

Liz silently agreed. The noise was swelling, filling her ears with a distant, thrashing sound. "What is it?"

Frank shook his head, straining to listen. "It sounds like . . ."

"Look!" Liz shouted. She pointed down to where a figure was appearing on the lower edge of the slope. They watched a bobbing head gradually emerge into view, then moving shoulders and arms, finally pumping legs. The figure paused for a moment, glanced back in the direction of the mounting noise, then continued up the hill.

"He's in a hurry," said Frank.

"Who is it?" Liz asked.

"I can't make him out yet."

"It's not Alfredo?"

"No."

"The boy?"

"Maybe," Frank answered hesitantly.

At that moment, the figure waved an arm at Frank and Liz.

"It *is* the boy!" Frank cried, returning the wave.

"Thank goodness," Liz breathed in relief.

"But wait," said Frank, a note of budding concern in his voice. The boy laboring up the slope continued to wave, but there was no greeting in the gesture. His movements were frantic, edged with desperation.

Liz caught it too. "Something's wrong."

The boy staggered, fell to one knee. He pulled himself to his feet with effort, stumbled forward.

"He's exhausted," said Liz.

The boy began to wave both of his arms. He motioned Frank and Liz into the trees. When they did not move, he gestured to his rear, to the invisible source of the crescendo. It pummeled the air now with measured, sibilant strokes, like the beat of a thousand giant wings. Neither Frank nor Liz had any more doubts about what was causing it.

"Better get back to the hut," said Frank. "See to the girl and the child."

"Be careful, Frank," said Liz, backing slowly toward the line of gnarled trees.

Frank set out for the boy. He had gone no more than a few steps when the helicopters reared into view. They rose straight up out of the valley, like a pair of startled, angry wasps. They hovered for a moment above the lower edge of the slope, rocking nose to nose in the air.

The boy looked over his shoulder, fell to his hands and knees in the long, coarse grass.

Frank increased his pace.

The helicopters pivoted, thwacked side by side up the slope. They skimmed the meadow, riffling the long grass as they moved. On reaching the spot where the boy was kneeling, they halted in midair above him. One rotated, shot upward. The other banked, began to plane sideways at him.

Frank saw the soldier clearly in the helicopter's open hull door. He wore an olive-green jump suit and a helmet with a black visor that was pulled down over his face. He stood spread-eagled, gripping with both hands the machine gun mounted on the cradle in the hatchway. Frank watched him load and cock the gun and train it on the boy. He began to run toward the kneeling figure.

The boy stared up at the helicopter skidding sideways at him through the air. He raised his arms, in a gesture of surrender.

Frank pounded down the slope. He watched the weapon begin to spit tiny flames, saw it jumping in its cradle. It jolted the gunner's arms and shoulders. He looked toward the boy and saw him picked up and flung aside, as if he were made of rags.

Frank shouted as he continued to tear down the hill. He saw the gunner swivel the weapon in the helicopter door until it was pointed directly at his head. Frank waved his arms and screamed at the man. But the face was a mask, invisible behind the black visor.

23

THERE WAS an elfin gleam, mingling mischief and malice, in the girl's eyes as she stretched an arm behind her back and began to fiddle with the fastening on the short shift she was wearing. When she withdrew her arm, the shift plunged to her ankles. She stepped daintily out of the garment, raised a hand, then the other, and slipped brassiere straps the color of ivory off shoulders the color of burnished bronze. Both hands disappeared behind her back, her shoulders twitched, and the brassiere fluttered down to join the shift at her feet. She hooked two thumbs into the waistband of ivory panties, fringed with ivory lace, and slowly drew them downward. She stooped to slide one foot out of the panties, then rose. She lifted the other foot, holding it out in front of her. The ivory lace dangled from her upraised toe like a flag of surrender. She flicked her foot, flinging the panties upward and forward.

They flew directly into Paul's face. He snatched at them, but the movement was no more than a reflex. His attention was riveted to the girl. He could not take his eyes off her, nor could he decide which part of her merited the closest scrutiny.

The girl giggled. She spread her legs and placed her fists on her hips, challengingly.

Paul swallowed. There was a tightness in his chest and an ominous stirring in his loins.

The girl arched her eyebrows expectantly, as if awaiting a move on Paul's part.

Paul wanted to do something, but he was not entirely sure how to proceed. He was preoccupied, and the situation was a little beyond his experience. He did not really find either of these two conditions surprising under the circumstances. It was becoming distressingly routine every time he crossed paths with Harry Quayle.

THE REUNION occurred in the lobby of Paul's hotel, late in the afternoon of the day following his long and boozy session with Chico Veloso. Paul had been aimlessly wandering the lobby, wondering when the throb in his head was going to subside, when he felt a resounding whack across his shoulders, as if someone had thumped him with a two-by-four. He staggered under the blow. As he did, he heard a booming apology, delivered in a familiar antipodean twang.

"Bloody hell!" shouted the voice. "Sorry about that, mate."

Paul turned and looked into Harry's broad, battered face. There was an expression of regret written upon it. He held aloft, by way of explanation, his thick forearm, which was encased in a plaster cast.

"I keep forgetting I'm armored now."

Paul grinned. "Harry!" he cried. "How are you?"

"Not too bad, my old son."

Paul glanced at Harry's arm, recalling the wound he had received in the highlands. He asked solicitously, "How's the arm?"

"Feels all right," Harry replied nonchalantly. "But I'm going to have to learn to wank with one hand."

Paul chuckled. He was happy to see Harry again, so pleased that he almost forgot about his hangover.

"But what about you?" Harry inquired, peering at Paul. "You look terrible."

Paul raised a hand to his forehead, fingered the few tiny scars. "I just took the bandages off this morning."

"That's not what I was talking about," said Harry, darting a glance at Paul's brow. "It's the rest of your mug. You been through a war or something?"

"Oh, that," Paul replied, reminded once again of the dull pounding inside his skull. "I'm feeling a little under the weather today."

"Nothing serious, I hope?"

"No," Paul replied. He gave Harry a sheepish smile. "I guess I had a bit too much to drink last night."

Harry chortled. "You been celebrating?"

"Not exactly."

Harry cocked an eye at Paul. "You're not abandoning us already, are you?"

"No," said Paul. "Not yet, at least. As a matter of fact I was planning on going back to the valley tomorrow morning to give the project one last look."

"Is that so?" Harry beamed. "Me too. We might as well make the trip together."

Paul found the news delighted him and he was suddenly struck with the realization that he shared something mysterious with Harry, a bond that had been forged that night on the terraces.

Harry interrupted Paul's thoughts. "In the meantime," he said, "what are your plans for this evening?"

"I don't have any."

"Good," declared Harry. "Join me. I'm treating myself to a night on the town. I think I've earned it. I think you have too."

"Great idea," Paul replied. "There are a few things I have to tell you about."

"Such as?"

Paul hesitated. "I don't really know where to begin."

Harry rubbed his hands together in eager anticipation. "A drink is always a good beginning."

*   *   *

"ERMITA!" HARRY announced. "Get a good grip on your pecker and your wallet. Both are in dire peril."

Paul glanced around, resisting an irrational urge to follow Harry's advice. It was well past midnight, the day's monsoon deluge had finally ended, and he was walking by Harry's side down a sodden street. The street was normal, of the kind found in any city. What was happening on it, however, would not have been happening on many normal city streets, particularly at that hour.

The place howled with a desperate energy. An unbroken row of bars lined each side of the street. All were more or less identical but seemed to be striving to compensate for this uniformity by blazing with multicolored lights and bellowing with pulsating music. Young, scantily clad women thronged the doorways, screeching at the crowds, mostly composed of young men, who jostled for space on the sidewalks. Gaudy jeepneys, yellow taxis, and rainbow-streaked pedicabs jammed the central strip of pavement. A blue-and-white police car moved slowly through the turmoil, cruising like a shark through a shoal of tropical fish.

"You are now deep in the evil heart of one of the seamiest red-light districts in Asia," Harry shouted at Paul. He threw his plaster-encased arm out expansively. "What is now afflicting your eyesight is one gigantic bordello. There's more sin per square inch packed into these two city blocks than most anywhere else in the East." He surveyed his surroundings with an expression of feigned disgust. "Depraved, isn't it?"

Paul was not fooled. He shot a skeptical glance at Harry. "And what do we do now?"

Harry grinned at Paul. "Why, we enjoy a little depravity, of course."

PAUL WAS not feeling particularly depraved as he gazed at the girl in front of him. But he was enjoying himself, even though the naked creature was not particularly beautiful. There was something hard and shrewd in her face, as if the racial memory of a thousand generations of peasant toil were reflected there. But Harry had insisted on her, and Paul had learned from experience that when Harry insisted, he was usually right.

"YOU WOULDN'T want to take her home to meet mum, I'll grant you that," Harry had conceded, beckoning the girl to join them. When she did, he patted her rump affectionately. "But our little Jenny here is what you need. She'll make it seem almost real."

The girl named Jenny had glowed, as if she had just been paid a compliment.

Harry, Paul, and Jenny were perched on high round stools at the corner of an L-shaped bar in a small, dim club. There was a threadbare quality to the place, a suggestion that grim struggles were waged there in an effort to retain a precarious hold on a prosperity that was inexorably slipping away. But the bar was relatively quiet, which was a welcome relief from the other stops that had punctuated their noctambulation. A jukebox thrummed in the background, competing with the murmur of a dozen clients sitting at the bar and scattered around a handful of tables. A knot of young girls sat in a corner close to the bar against the backdrop of a huge black spiderweb that had been painted crudely on the wall. A huge black spider patrolled the web above the girls heads. In the gloom, they looked like moths stoically awaiting their gruesome fate.

Harry had recommended the bar when Paul began to indicate that he was growing impatient with mere observation of the living habits of the subterranean continent they were exploring.

"If a knee-trembler is what's on your mind, then we'd best retire to a little place I know," Harry advised. "One can't be too careful in matters of this sort."

Paul had no reason to doubt Harry's judgment. The Australian had demonstrated that he knew every gulch and valley, every hidden fold, of the terrain. He seemed to know most of the population as well, the vast majority of whom were nubile women intent on shedding their clothes for reasons often as flimsy as the few garments they wore.

It was a netherworld that Harry introduced to Paul. In no way was it complete. It dealt only with the senses, and only extravagantly. Paul and Harry had dined in a roisterous restaurant staffed entirely by roisterous dwarves. They had poured beer into a somnolent tiger with a sailor's thirst, smoked potent weed under the baleful glare of a monkey-eating eagle, fended off the advances of an alarmingly amorous orangutan.

Initially, Paul did not quite know what to make of this world. He was unsure whether he was horrified or exhilarated. But as the evening wore on he began to warm to the environment. There was something contagious in the air, and he eventually caught it.

Harry did not. While Paul grew steadily more enthusiastic, the Australian moved in the opposite direction. He became more pensive, withdrawing to some quiet place of his own. It took a while for Paul, preoccupied as he was with the spectacle unfolding around him, to notice. But he did, finally.

"Is something troubling you, Harry?" Paul asked. They were seated at the L-shaped bar under the shadow of the spiderweb. The girl named Jenny sat on a stool between them.

Harry raised his head from the glass of beer he was staring moodily into and blinked. He glanced at Paul, at Jenny, at Paul again, reorienting himself. "No, it's nothing," he said at last, unconvincingly. "Run along upstairs with Jenny."

Paul looked at Jenny, a trace regretfully. What he wanted to do at that moment was exactly what Harry advised. But he also wanted to find out what was wrong with a man he now regarded as a friend. He didn't have many of those.

"There's plenty of time for that," Paul said. "Maybe you'd better tell me what's on your mind first."

Harry contemplated Paul, lips pursed in thought. He replied

after a moment, "You're right. I'm a little concerned."

"About?"

"About what the hell is going on back in the valley."

"Why?"

"Because of all the things you told me this evening."

"You mean Colonel Rosales . . . and his suspicions?"

"Partly. Rocky's a mean son of a bitch. He's also a crazy son of a bitch. That's always a dangerous combination." Harry took a sip of beer. "But it's not just Rocky and his fantasies that bothers me."

"What else?"

"It's the cast of characters, one in particular, who seem to have developed an unhealthy interest in our little project."

"You mean all those important folk who have been chasing me around?"

"I have to admit that I'm impressed with the company you've been keeping lately."

"There seems to be one of them who doesn't impress you very much."

Harry grunted.

"Which one is it?"

Harry glanced at Paul, then looked thoughtfully at Jenny. He dug a handful of coins out of his pocket and shoved them across the bar at the girl. "Why don't you go play us a few tunes, Jenny."

Jenny scooped up the coins and smiled brightly at Harry. She slid off the barstool. As she did, she pressed a warm breast into Paul's arm and blew into his ear. Her breath was hot.

Paul watched Jenny glide toward the jukebox. There was a light, tingling sensation in the middle of his chest.

Harry sighed. "I guess we can talk later."

Paul's gaze swung from Jenny to Harry and back to Jenny, where it lingered. It took some effort to return his eyes to Harry. "No," he said decisively. "First I want to know which of my new friends you don't like, because I have a hunch I can guess his name."

Harry gave Paul an inquiring look. "Who?"

Paul took a swallow of beer and turned to face Harry. "It's my dinner companion of last night . . . Chico Veloso."

"How'd you guess?" Harry asked with surprise.

"I don't really know. There's something about Veloso that bothers me. I had a bad feeling when I met him. When I think about the night I spent with him, it's worse."

"Can't say I blame you."

"Why? What's his story?"

"The usual." Harry shrugged. "Before the current regime came to power he was a small-time businessman. I think he was in chewing gum. Might have been cigarettes. Whatever it was, it was a fringe operation."

"He seems prosperous enough now."

"You can say that again. He's worth millions."

"How'd he manage that?"

Harry snorted. "A simple biological accident."

"Huh?"

"He's related to the ruling family, some kind of distant cousin I think."

"That's all?"

"That's all you need in this place," Harry declared with feeling. "Half the fortunes in the country, maybe more, are based on nothing more than a blood relationship to the people who hold the power. Not much happens around here unless there's a rakeoff in it for one of the relatives. And the bigger the project, the bigger the rakeoff." He took a sip of beer, added bitterly, "It's just one big happy family, gorging themselves stupid at the public trough."

"I knew it was bad, but I didn't think it was that bad."

"It's so bad they even have a name for it. Your friend Veloso is one of the prime beneficiaries of what people here call 'crony capitalism.'"

Paul considered this for a moment, then glanced in alarm at Harry. "You don't think . . ."

Harry watched Paul.

"Oh shit!" Paul exclaimed. "I knew it! I've been suspecting it all day long. That meeting last night was no accident. That sonofabitch got me drunk deliberately."

"I'd say that was a fair guess."

"He was sniffing around, trying to find out what's going on with the project."

"There's an awful lot of money involved," said Harry. "And when one of the cronies smells a buck, it's like a thirsty buffalo who's caught the scent of water."

"But how can he expect to cut himself in?"

"That's what's been worrying me ever since you mentioned his name."

"Why?"

"There seems to be some kind of link between Veloso and someone else we both know."

"Who?"

Harry took a breath. "Rocky."

"Rosales!" Paul cried, so loudly that he startled the moths entrapped in the spiderweb. They stirred, struggled feebly, subsided; as did Paul's voice. "What the hell is the connection between those two?"

"I don't know," Harry replied, "but they have a history."

"A history?"

"Yeah, they have a disturbing habit of popping up together in some very murky places." Harry sipped at his beer. "Some time ago there was trouble down in Negros with the sugar workers, which just happens to be an industry where Veloso is heavily involved. Rocky was sent in, and he resolved the problem. Same thing happened in Mindanao, pineapples I think, and over in Quezon with the coconut trade. There are other examples, enough to set a pattern and start a few tongues wagging."

"It's talked about?"

"Only in whispers."

"Why?"

"Because of Rocky's methods."

"There was bloodshed." Paul hesitated. "People died."

"*Salvaged* is the term."

"How does he get away with that?"

"That's easy," Harry replied. "Rocky does the dirty work, Veloso makes sure that nobody important asks too many questions."

"Christ," Paul murmured. He lifted his beer, sipped reflectively.

Harry turned and contemplated Paul for a moment before he asked, "You didn't tell me that you got drunk with Veloso."

"Yeah." Paul sighed regretfully, staring into his glass.

Harry continued to study Paul. "I guess he asked a lot of questions?"

"Mmm-hmm."

"What did you tell him?"

Paul lifted his eyes and looked uncomfortably at Harry. He was searching for an answer when he felt the pressure of two warm breasts snuggling into his back like a pair of kittens. Two bronze arms snaked around his waist and squeezed.

"Have you finished yet?" Jenny whispered into Paul's ear with her hot breath.

Paul squirmed, managed to reply, "No."

"Good," Jenny crooned. "Neither have I. We can finish together."

Paul glanced at Harry, more than a little relieved by the interruption.

Harry regarded Paul and Jenny. "Take him away, Jenny," he said without a trace of envy. "I'd say the lad's ready."

PAUL WAS more than ready. He was just a shade intimidated by the manner in which the naked Jenny was facing him across the room. He was also having some difficulty concentrating on the problem at hand. He was thinking of an answer to Harry's question.

Jenny resolved his dilemma. She heaved a deep, impatient sigh and dropped her fists from her hips. After contemplating Paul for a long moment, she strode purposefully across the room. On reaching him, she slid her arms around his waist and wrapped her legs around one of his thighs. She rested her chin on his chest and looked up into his eyes. She began to grind herself into him.

"Is that better?" Jenny whispered.

If Paul could have spoken, he would have admitted that it was better. Jenny's face, inches from his own, seemed to have lost its peasant coarseness. Her breath danced lightly across his mouth. There were two soft mounds of warmth pressing into his chest. Farther down, against his thigh, there was another kind of warmth: a jungle heat, dark and moist and mysterious. Paul's body began to talk for him.

Jenny noticed. She dropped a hand from Paul's waist and caressed the rigidity between his legs. "Mmmm," she murmured. "It *is* better."

Paul moaned softly. He thought fleetingly of Harry's question.

Jenny reached up with her free hand and began to undo the buttons on his shirt, slowly at first and then with increasing haste. As his shirt fell open, she ran her mouth and tongue across his chest and belly, lingering around his nipples, delving into his navel.

Paul moaned again. He attempted, briefly, to remember what it was that he had wanted to tell Harry.

Jenny dropped to her knees and unfastened Paul's trousers. She reached in and slowly drew out his erection. Cupping it in both of her hands, she wandered along its length with her tongue. She hesitated for a long time over the tip. Then she took him gently, entirely, into her large, warm mouth.

Paul groaned loudly. He stopped thinking about Harry.

PART THREE

Typhoon

24

HARRY QUAYLE sensed it first. He brought the truck, one of the few working vehicles left in his rapidly diminishing fleet, to a halt at the top of the rise, just past the point where the ocher track curved before it rolled downhill into the settlement. He sat with his hands on the steering wheel, staring down at the station with a thoughtful frown creasing his brow. He switched off the engine and cocked his head slightly, like a dog straining to listen.

"What is it?" Paul asked, glancing uncertainly at Harry.

"Can't you hear it?" Harry replied, scanning the buildings scattered along both sides of the roadway in the distance below.

Paul followed the direction of Harry's gaze. He examined the collection of thatched huts, the school, the clinic, the grain depot. There was no movement. The flag on the pole above Colonel Rosales's headquarters hung lifeless in the stifling heat. The great metal cross on the steeple of Frank Enright's church winked joylessly in the bright, merciless sunshine. It was absolutely quiet.

Paul ran the back of his hand wearily across his forehead. He had started to sweat again the moment the truck stopped. There was no breeze, not a breath of wind other than that created by the truck's movement. It exacerbated the vague irritability that had gradually overtaken him as they had spiraled up into the highlands. He complained, a shade testily, "I can't hear anything."

"Neither can I," Harry answered softly.

Paul darted a puzzled look at Harry before he suddenly understood. The silence was total, unnatural. There was no noise save for the gentle creak of the truck's cooling engine. He surveyed the surrounding jungle. It teemed with life, he knew, but was as still as death. No creature uttered a sound, no leaf stirred. "It *is* awfully quiet," he said, shifting uncomfortably in his seat. His shirt was plastered to his back. He added, "And hot."

Harry glanced up at the sun directly overhead, squinting as he looked into a perfect molten disk, without rays. The sky was clear, cloudless and pale, almost white, as if the blue had been seared out of it. Harry muttered under his breath, restarted the truck.

"What is it?" Paul asked.

Harry eyed Paul as he threw the truck into gear. "You ever seen a typhoon?"

"No," Paul responded grumpily.

"Well, I think you're about to," Harry declared as they began to roll downhill.

"What?" asked Paul, startled out of his grouch.

"There's one out there someplace," said Harry, nodding toward the line of peaks in the east. "And unless I'm very badly mistaken, I'd say it's headed this way."

Paul searched the mountains on the valley's eastern rim, looking for whatever it was that Harry saw there.

"This is the time of year when they rip in from the Pacific," Harry continued as the truck gathered speed. "All the other signs are right too. Look at that clear sky." Harry gave an upward nod. "When there's a typhoon circling in the neighborhood, it tends to suck up all the dirty weather for miles around."

Paul regarded the metallic sky, blistered by the metallic sun. He wiped his brow another time. "It is so bloody hot."

"That's another sure sign," said Harry. "The oppressive heat; that and the unholy calm." He shook his head wonderingly. "It's always the same before a really big blow. Things get tense and quiet." He slanted a look at Paul. "It's apt to make people a mite peevish."

Paul did not catch the look, but he smiled guiltily all the same.

"I don't know why it's so hard on the nerves," Harry went on. "It's almost as if everything in a typhoon's path somehow *knows* what's coming."

Paul looked out of the truck's window. As he surveyed the passing scene, he was struck by the accuracy of Harry's remark. They were entering the settlement, rolling by the thatched huts on their stilts that lined the approaches on either side of the dusty red track. Nothing moved, not even the skinny gray dogs lying in the shade beneath the elevated huts. They silently watched the truck trundle past, eyes round, ears alert, snouts buried in their outstretched paws. There was a wary vigilance in the air, as if the entire village were crouched in wait like the dogs under the huts.

"You know something, Harry?" Paul whispered. "I think you may be right."

Harry did not respond. He was peering intently at the passing huts. There was a worried look on his face.

Harry's silence prompted a glance from Paul. He saw the expression on the Australian's face. "What is it?" he asked, a trace of concern in his voice.

Harry shook his head.

"There's something else, isn't there?" Paul persisted.

Harry frowned. "I don't know," he murmured. "Maybe it's just a little *too* quiet . . ." His voice trailed off.

"But you said it would be like this . . . the storm and all."

"Yeah," Harry replied slowly, musingly. "Still . . ." His voice died again.

"Maybe it's just your imagination, Harry," Paul said, a shade anxiously, not entirely convinced.

Harry shivered violently, as if shaking something off. "You're probably right," he said. "We're coming up to my place. Let's drop off my gear, then wander over to see Frank. He'll give us all the latest gossip."

"Okay," Paul replied, relieved.

Harry shifted down, swung the truck off the track, and pulled up in front of a low single-story bungalow. The house was not particularly attractive, but it looked sturdy, functional, reliable, much like the tenant.

Hauling a battered duffel bag from behind the driver's seat, Harry climbed down from the truck. He paused outside, plaster-encased forearm resting on the open door, and looked back at Paul. "You want to come in for a minute?" he asked. "I've got a pair of talking bookends you might want to meet." Something mischievous slid into the tired brown eyes. "Like Jenny, only double the trouble." Harry turned without waiting for an answer and strode toward the bungalow, whistling ostentatiously.

Paul watched him go, feeling a hot flush rising on his cheeks, reminded of the ache in his overused loins. The pain was not at all unpleasant; nor was the memory. Paul smiled mellowly, climbed gingerly down from the truck, and followed Harry. He reached him just inside the bungalow's doorstep, where the Australian stood holding open a screen door that was mounted on springs. Harry's puzzled frown was back.

Paul's mellow smile vanished. "Something wrong?" he asked uneasily.

"It's Gloria and Lourdes," Harry muttered, surveying the bungalow's interior.

Paul followed Harry's look. He saw a sparsely furnished living room, devoid of personal touches. It was like an arid room in an anonymous hotel, the kind of place anonymous people camp out in for a night or two and then move on, leaving no trace of their passage, except maybe the burned-out end of a cigarette.

"Gloria and Lourdes?" Paul inquired.

"My bookends," Harry replied dully. "They've skipped."

"Oh," said Paul. He studied Harry, attempting to read the expression on his face. It seemed to call for condolences. "Sorry," he added lamely.

"Something really *is* wrong," Harry continued in the same flat tones, as if unaware that Paul had spoken.

Paul felt compelled to offer comfort. "They were only . . ." He hesitated, groping for a euphemism.

"Whores," Harry stated brutally.

Paul winced inwardly but shrugged his agreement. "Whores," he concurred reluctantly.

"Exactly. And a whore is like a shipbound rat. When she starts to swim, you know you're in trouble."

Paul said nothing, but his face betrayed a faint sense of disapproval.

Harry noticed, clucked. "When you've wasted as much time as I have chasing whores, you'll understand." He threw an arm at his arid living room. "I know it isn't much," he conceded, "but it sure beats the hell out of gobbling half the American Navy every night."

Paul glanced into the bungalow's interior. He was inclined to think Harry might be right. But he was not convinced. "Maybe the storm . . ."

"It'd take more than a typhoon to blow those two back to Olongapo," Harry said impatiently. He tossed his duffelbag onto the floor. "C'mon," he said. "We'd better go and see Frank." He moved out of the doorway and released the screen, which slammed shut behind him. In the hush, it cracked loudly, like a sudden slap across the face.

"It sure is quiet," Paul murmured as he and Harry walked away from the bungalow, heading down toward the track and the big frame house behind the church that stood on the other side of the roadway a short distance away.

"Yeah," Harry responded, also in a murmur, as if a little daunted by the silence.

They reached the track, began to move along it toward Frank's house. Neither spoke. There was no movement but their own slow pace down the track. There was no noise save for the muffled thud of their feet in the ocher dust. The dust rose in puffs around their ankles and hung suspended in the still air. The sun, a disk of brass in the white sky, glowered remorselessly, casting no shadows.

"Hulloo, Frank!" Harry cried as they approached the doorway to the priest's house. They could hear the river now, soughing quietly behind the house. But that was all they could hear. The house stood mute, unresponsive, implacable.

Paul glanced uncertainly at Harry.

"You home, Frank?" Harry called again. "It's me, Harry . . . Harry Quayle!"

Silence.

Paul and Harry reached the doorstep. They paused, looked at each other. Harry grunted, entered the house. Paul followed.

"Frank!" Harry shouted. He stood in the center of the priest's spartan living room, directly beneath a large electric fan suspended from the ceiling. The fan hung motionless.

There was no reply to Harry's call.

Paul joined Harry beneath the fan. He offered, not very hopefully, "Maybe he's sleeping."

Harry strode toward Frank's bedroom, swung the door open, peered in. He looked back at Paul, shaking his head negatively. He walked toward the entrance to the room where Paul had been staying, did the same thing. He turned, headed back across the living room, and disappeared into the kitchen.

Paul waited beneath the fan. When Harry did not reappear, he followed him. He found Harry standing beside a circular table covered with a floral-patterned oilcloth. The Australian was staring down at something on the table. Paul could not see what it was from where he was standing. There was a rectangle of glare, luminous with motes of dust, falling across the table. It came from an open doorway behind Harry, which led from the kitchen to an outdoor terrace overlooking the river.

Paul walked to Harry's side. On reaching him, he saw a dark green bottle and clear glass sitting on the table. The bottle was half full, like the glass. The liquid appeared to be whisky.

"It's Laphroaig," Harry murmured.

Paul regarded the bottle and glass.

"Frank has a single case of it shipped to him once every year. He guards the stuff with his life," Harry reached down and lifted the glass, inspecting it. "He *must* be here."

"The drink's not Frank's," said a deep voice, at the same instant that a shadow fell across the table.

Paul and Harry, both startled, glanced toward the open doorway to the terrace. There was somebody standing in it, outlined in black against the bright exterior light. Neither Paul nor Harry could identify the individual's features because of the glare. But they both knew who it was all the same. There was no mistaking the short figure with the too-broad shoulders and the outsize head, upon which was perched an outsize baseball cap.

"Rocky!" Harry whispered.

"Welcome back, Harry," Colonel Rosales said quietly. He remained in the doorway, face hidden in the shadow cast by the blinding light behind him. The large head moved slightly. "You too, Mr. Stenmark."

Paul and Harry stared without speaking.

"I've been waiting for you both," Colonel Rosales continued in the same quiet voice.

Paul and Harry remained silent.

Colonel Rosales moved out of the glare. He walked toward Harry, accompanied by a soft creak of leather. On reaching the Australian, he lifted the glass out of his hand. "That's mine," he said.

Harry did not respond.

Colonel Rosales walked to the table, sat down on the side opposite Harry. He pushed the dark green bottle toward the Australian. "Help yourself."

Harry watched the colonel. "It's Frank's."

"Frank won't be needing it anymore," Colonel Rosales replied. He leaned back in his chair, and a faint smile crossed his lips. "Not where he is now."

25

FOR A moment, there was no sound other than that of the river purling softly in the background. Nothing moved, not even the motes of dust glittering in the sunlight that fell through the kitchen doorway and across the circular table. Harry Quayle and Colonel Ricardo Rosales faced each other within the bar of slanting light as if trapped there.

"What did you say?" Harry whispered at last.

Colonel Rosales lifted the glass in his hand. "I said Frank wouldn't be needing this anymore."

"What's happened to Frank?" Harry asked.

Colonel Rosales raised the glass higher, inspected it in the light. "I'll say this for that priest," he mused, "I like his taste." He sipped from the glass. "Both his whisky . . . and his women."

Harry's lips set, tightened. "Where's Liz?"

Colonel Rosales put the glass back down on the table. "With Frank." He looked up at Harry. "With Alfredo."

"What have you done to them?"

"Nothing," Colonel Rosales replied. He smiled coldly. "Yet."

"Then they're alive?" Harry asked tensely.

"They're breathing, if that's what you mean."

Harry relaxed a shade. "Where are they?"

"I've finally got them where I want them, the whole cabal."

"Where?"

"They won't be meddling in things around here anymore."

"Where are they?"

"I've solved our problems," said Colonel Rosales. He poked a thumb at his chest. "Mine." He pointed a finger at Harry. "Yours." He nodded toward Paul, standing wordlessly at the end of the table. "And his."

"Where *are* they?"

Colonel Rosales looked smug. "In my jail."

Harry took a breath, expelled it noisily. "That explains why this place feels like a pile of tinder waiting for a match."

Colonel Rosales waved a dismissive hand. "Don't worry about those *Igorots*," he said. "I'll handle them."

"Yeah," Harry muttered acidly. "You sure know how to do that."

"What's that supposed to mean?" Colonel Rosales asked tightly.

Harry looked at the colonel, suddenly alert. "Nothing," he said warily.

Colonel Rosales regarded Harry with narrowed eyes. He said, in a voice heavy with menace, "Don't *ever* suggest I don't know how to do my job."

"Right," Harry replied. He moved carefully to the table, pulled out a chair, and sat down opposite the colonel.

Colonel Rosales watched Harry.

"Why have you arrested Frank and Liz and Alfredo?" Harry asked.

Colonel Rosales ran his eyes over Harry's face, as if a little unsatisfied with the man's behavior. "I'm no lawyer," he said finally, "but when the judge advocate general's boys get around to preparing the charges, I guess they'll involve conspiracy." He paused, added, "Several different kinds of conspiracy."

"Conspiracy?" Harry asked. There was a hint of resignation in his voice, as if he suspected what was coming.

Colonel Rosales shrugged. "That's the usual in these cases."

"Conspiracy to do what?"

"Conspiracy to commit rebellion, for a start," Colonel Rosales replied. He took off his hat, wiped the sweat off his brow with the back of his hand. "Then I suppose there'll be conspiracy to commit sabotage, sedition, maybe murder."

Harry raised his eyebrows sardonically. "Murder too?"

"Murder," Colonel Rosales confirmed.

"Who the hell did they conspire to murder?"

Colonel Rosales replaced his hat, looked at Harry. "You." He slid a glance at Paul. "Him." He looked back at Harry. "And of course Ot and the rest of your crew."

"I was afraid you were going to say that." Harry sighed wearily. "You haven't seen the evidence."

"What evidence?"

"Wait until the arraignment."

"I can't," Harry answered sarcastically. "I'll have a long gray beard by then."

The suggestion of a smile crossed the colonel's mouth, but he did not respond.

"Why don't we stop beating around the bush?" Harry continued. "I don't know what it is that you've trumped up against—"

"I haven't *trumped up* anything," Colonel Rosales cut in sharply. "I've caught those three bastards red-handed this time."

"Rocky—" Harry began patiently.

"It's *Colonel*," Rosales snapped.

Harry took a breath. "Look, Colonel," he said, "I can't believe—"

"What is it you can't believe?" Colonel Rosales broke in again. "You can't believe Frank has been working hand in glove with the NPA?" He gave Harry a fierce stare. "That cassock of his fools you, does it? Well, it doesn't fool me. It never has."

Harry, taken aback by the look in the colonel's eye, did not respond.

"And that refined little piece of ass he travels with?" Colonel

Rosales went on, voice rising. "What the hell do you think a woman like that is doing up in these hills? Peddling aspirins?"

Harry stared at the colonel.

"No," said Colonel Rosales, shaking his head. "They're CT, all right." He reached for the dark green bottle on the table. "Just like the other sonofabitch." He raised the bottle, pointed it at Harry. "I suppose you can't believe that Alfredo is one of them too?"

Harry remained silent.

Colonel Rosales jerked the bottle toward Paul. "Well, ask your friend here. *He* knows."

Paul gaped at the colonel.

"What the hell are you looking so surprised for?" Colonel Rosales asked Paul. "*You* fingered him."

Paul frowned, shook his head.

"C'mon, don't play dumb with me. Who'd you tell me was responsible for all our problems?"

"But that's not what I —"

"Right," said Colonel Rosales, pouring a dollop of whisky into his glass. "Just like I've been saying all along."

Paul reached for a chair by the table to steady himself.

Colonel Rosales eyed Paul. "I owe you one, by the way," he said. "I've been hollering about Alfredo for months. I've been telling Manila there was no way to settle things up here without nailing that bastard to the wall. But they wouldn't listen to me."

Paul watched the colonel, heart sinking.

"They listened to *you*, though." Colonel Rosales tipped his glass at Paul. "Thanks."

Paul sat down heavily in the chair he had been holding.

Colonel Rosales took a drink. He smiled with satisfaction. "And now I've nailed the bastard good."

Paul slowly closed his eyes.

Colonel Rosales swept his glance around the table. "You two

should be grateful," he said. "Those dams are going to be built now."

Paul opened his eyes. He asked, his voice subdued, "What happens to Alfredo and Frank and Liz?"

"You don't have to worry about them anymore," Colonel Rosales replied.

"But I am worried."

"Relax," said Colonel Rosales, taking another drink. "Alfredo will be locked away somewhere safe and sound for a long time. Liz too. Frank's case is a little different. He's American."

"What will be done with him?"

"I'm not sure."

"He'll probably be deported," said Harry, breaking into conversation. "If he isn't, the church will move him out of the country. They get a little sensitive about these kinds of things."

"Whatever happens," said Colonel Rosales, "we're rid of all three of them."

"You're sure about that?" Harry asked.

"Of course I'm sure."

"You must have a pretty good case."

"Watertight."

"Mind telling us?"

"Not at all," Colonel Rosales replied. He helped himself to some more of Frank's whisky. "We start with the fact that all three disappeared mysteriously shortly after the attack on your construction site."

"That's all?"

"No. After the attack we found all three of them, more or less together, in very suspicious circumstances."

"Suspicious circumstances?"

"Uh-huh," said Colonel Rosales. "We nabbed them way up in the hills in the heart of bandit country, miles from anywhere."

"So?"

Colonel Rosales glanced at Harry, mildly irked. "So what were

they doing wandering around in the back of beyond after everything that happened?"

"What did they say they were doing?"

Colonel Rosales took a drink. "They had some cock-and-bull
story, something about a difficult childbirth."

"Maybe it was true. Liz *is* a doctor, you know."

Colonel Rosales regarded Harry a moment before he answered.
"We didn't find any mother, or any newborn baby."

Harry searched the colonel's eyes. "I see," he said quietly.

"But that's not all," Colonel Rosales went on after a time.

"Oh?"

"I've also managed to find an eyewitness who saw what they were
really doing."

"And what does this eyewitness say they were doing?"

Colonel Rosales smiled. "He's prepared to testify that all three
were in the company of Ortigez and his band of CTs right after the
attack."

"Ortigez?" asked Harry, surprised.

"Right."

"Paul and I saw Ka Larry after the attack. We didn't see Alfredo
or the others."

"You saw Ortigez much later."

Harry's eyes narrowed. "Who was it who saw Alfredo and the
others with Ka Larry?"

"He's right here in the settlement."

"Where?"

"Over at the grain depot."

"Chan's grain depot?"

Colonel Rosales nodded.

Harry leaned forward. "Your witness wouldn't be Winthrop
Chan himself, would it?"

"What of it?"

Harry leaned back into his chair. He glanced at Paul, looked
back at the colonel.

"You got a problem?" Colonel Rosales asked.

"No," said Harry softly. "But you do."

Colonel Rosales frowned.

"You're going to have a hard time proving Chan saw Alfredo and the others with Ka Larry right after the attack."

"Why's that?" Colonel Rosales asked, glancing suspiciously from Harry to Paul and back.

"Because there are other witnesses who can swear they saw Chan somewhere else at the very same time."

"What other witnesses?"

Harry flicked a glance at Paul. "Him," he said. He smiled at the colonel. "And me."

Colonel Rosales darted a look full of consternation at Paul. "But you didn't tell me . . ."

Colonel Rosales had no chance to finish his question. He was halted in midsentence by the sound of three quick shots, which shattered the quiet and reverberated off the surrounding hills. All three men sitting around the circular table jerked their heads in the direction of the original noise. None could be sure, but it seemed the shots had come from across the road, at the grain depot owned by Winthrop Chan.

26

NONE OF the three had any difficulty identifying Winthrop Chan, even with the mess around what was left of the man's mouth. The bald head, the wedge-shaped face, and the taut yellow skin as translucent as a piece of old amber were all the same. So were the eyes: hooded, reptilian. They wore an expression of the most profound surprise.

Paul Stenmark recognized the look instantly, although he would have preferred not to have done so. It summoned memories he wanted to forget. He had seen the same thing once before, when he had briefly cradled in his arms Ot's smashed head.

Wherever Ot had gone, Chan had now followed. The Chinese lay slumped in a large wooden chair mounted on swivels. His head rested on the back of the chair, chin tilted slightly upward. It was secured there by a copper wire that had been wrapped tightly around his throat. The wire had punctured the skin on his neck, causing thin rivulets of blood to trickle down from it.

But that was not what had killed Chan. They could all see that clearly enough. The Chinese had been shot directly in the mouth, at close range and with something more powerful than a hand-gun. The man's cold smile was gone, replaced by a glistening red hole.

Colonel Rosales stared at Chan's ruined face, speechless with rage. His fists were balled tightly at his sides, his mouth was clenched in a grim line, and all the muscles along his jaw were working convulsingly. He muttered and kicked out at the chair to which the Chinese was lashed. The chair skidded across the floor into a wall, rocked violently a couple of times, and gradually subsided into a gentle swivel. Chan's head swung with the chair. His body slid lower, tightening the wire noose, accelerating the flow of blood from the line around his neck.

There was a sharp intake of a dozen breaths coming from behind where the colonel, Paul, and Harry stood. All three turned, found that the room in the grain depot had filled with native inhabitants of the settlement. They stood among the stacks of piled rice bags, silently studying the scene in front of them. Their gaze strayed repeatedly from Chan's bleeding corpse, rocking slowly in the chair, to the colonel. The look in every pair of dark eyes was one of satisfaction, verging on triumph.

Colonel Rosales glowered at the villagers, trembling with anger. His face was the color of newly fired brick, only a shade less fierce than the blood vessels throbbing on his temples. His olive-green shirt was black with sweat.

"Out!" the colonel snarled. "All of you, get out!"

The crowd did not move.

"I said get out of here!" Colonel Rosales shouted, flinging an arm at the door.

They stood, black eyes fixed on the colonel.

"Out!" Colonel Rosales screamed, spittle hurtling from his mouth.

There was no movement, no sound.

Colonel Rosales stood glaring for a moment, then charged into the crowd. The villagers parted to allow him to leave, but without any particular hurry.

"Christ!" Paul whispered breathlessly once the colonel had gone. He glanced around, looking for Harry. He found him bent over Chan, peering into the man's destroyed mouth.

Paul glanced at Chan, looked quickly away. "I wonder who did it."

"No doubt about that," Harry replied, straightening. "That's why Rocky's so bitter and twisted." He nodded toward the villagers, who were beginning to filter out of the room. "And why all the locals look like the cat who swallowed the canary."

"Who was it?"

Harry turned, contemplated Chan's corpse again. "Revolutionary justice."

Paul followed the look, suppressed a shudder. "The NPA did . . . that?"

"It was an execution," said Harry. "His mouth. That's an NPA trademark."

"They shoot everybody in the mouth?"

"That's a special treatment," Harry replied. "Reserved for those with loose or lying tongues."

Paul's gaze was finally drawn back to Chan. "The eyewitness," he murmured. "He was killed because of what he was willing to say about Alfredo and the others."

"Not the others so much," said Harry. "But certainly Alfredo. Tamper with that man and you are touching something very deep among these people. Rocky may not have been able to figure that out, but the NPA have. They know how to keep these people on their side."

Paul stared at Chan. "Didn't *he* know that?"

"Chan knew all right. He was a nasty piece of work, but he was no fool."

"Then why did he agree to those lies?"

"He probably didn't have much choice."

Paul looked at Harry. "Rosales."

"Rocky's methods are not very subtle, but they are often effective," said Harry. "He somehow got Chan to cooperate, either by enticing him or by pressuring him. Probably a bit of both."

"But Chan must have known that we could deny his story."

"Given our interests, he may have been under the impression that we might be willing to play along with anything that removed Alfredo from the scene." Harry paused. "Rocky certainly seems to have believed that." He watched Paul. "And it appears he had some help in reaching that conclusion."

Paul looked back at Harry with some dismay. "All I told him was that I didn't think there was any way to proceed with the project unless something was done to change Alfredo's mind or . . ." His voice trailed off.

"Or?"

Paul sighed. "Or his influence."

Harry continued to watch Paul. "You told Veloso the same thing?"

Paul nodded bleakly.

"Shit," said Harry quietly.

"I had no intention—"

"People like Rocky and Veloso live in a black-and-white world," Harry interrupted. "There are no colors, not even any shades. You have to understand that." His gaze drifted back to Chan. "The price of a miscalculation can be high."

Paul shot a nervous glance at the dead man. "Let's get out of here."

COLONEL ROSALES slouched in the chair, mirror-bright boots atop the battered desk, and stared fixedly at the red telephone as if it were something alive and venomous.

"There sure are a lot of people out there," said the young woman, who was peering through the venetian blinds on the window that looked upon the courtyard under the flagpole.

"Shut up, Connie," Colonel Rosales snarled without taking his eyes from the telephone.

The woman turned and regarded the colonel with wide, innocent eyes. "What do they want?"

"Will you get away from that window," Colonel Rosales growled.

The woman shrugged and sauntered to the dingy sofa behind the colonel's desk. She sat down, crossed her legs, and picked up a magazine that was lying there. She began to flip idly through the pages. A delicate foot, toenails painted bright red, bounced.

There was a long silence, broken only by the riffle of the magazine pages and the gradually swelling murmur emanating from the courtyard.

Colonel Rosales glanced toward the sound and scowled. He looked back at the telephone. "Where's Martha?" he demanded.

"In the kitchen," the woman replied.

"Go tell her to make me something to eat."

The woman rose, tossed the magazine aside, and strode toward the door.

"Get me a drink while you're at it," Colonel Rosales ordered as the woman approached the door.

The woman reached the door, opened it.

"Connie!" Colonel Rosales barked.

The woman turned and regarded the colonel, who did not look up.

"Bring the bottle."

The woman left the room.

Colonel Rosales heaved a deep breath, as if bracing himself. He reached out and picked up the telephone. "Sergeant Cruz," he said. "Get me Manila . . . the back channel."

"WHAT ARE they doing?" Paul asked as he ran his eyes wonderingly over the crowd.

The courtyard outside Colonel Rosales's headquarters was thronged with hill people, squatting on their heels in the red dust beneath the flagpole. They chatted quietly among themselves and cast occasional expectant glances at the building's entrance, which was being guarded by two nervous young soldiers who looked as if they devoutly wished to be somewhere else.

"They're waiting for Alfredo," Harry replied.

"He's going to be released, just like that?"

"If he isn't, there's going to be trouble."

Paul gave Harry a puzzled frown.

Harry answered with a nod toward the hills behind the settlement.

Paul looked, and his eyes were rounded with surprise.

The terraces were alive with tiny figures. They were all slowly picking their way downward, moving along the terrace walls, heading toward the courtyard.

"There'll be thousands of them here by this evening," said Harry, "as soon as the news spreads about what's happened."

Paul chuckled with amazement.

"If Rocky doesn't let him go, they'll simply take him."

"They'd do that?"

"You can count on it," said Harry. "There's no holding them now." He shook his head slightly. "When the NPA put that bullet into Chan's mouth, they did more than destroy one not very likable Chinaman."

Paul looked at Harry. "You mean the dams?"

"What do you think?" said Harry with a nod at the crowd. "When Alfredo walks out of that door, he's going to be even more of a hero than he was when he was dragged in."

Paul turned, surveyed the people, felt the buoyant tension in the air. He asked, "And then?"

Harry smiled. "And then there's going to be one hell of a party."

"Yes," said Paul ruefully after a moment, "I guess everybody's going to be in the mood to celebrate."

Harry's smile faded as his eyes traveled across the assembled heads to the window with the venetian blinds that looked on the courtyard. He murmured, "Not everybody."

＊   ＊   ＊

COLONEL ROSALES smashed the telephone into its red cradle and
glared at it. He rose abruptly, yanked open a drawer in his desk, and
pulled out a chrome-plated automatic with pearl grips. Gun in
hand, he strode across the room to the window. He studied the dark
faces beneath the flagpole for a time until his gaze strayed to the
surrounding hills, which were bathed in the fire of a setting sun.
An enormous red orb grazed the peaks on the western horizon. It
shimmered behind a rippling veil of heat. The heat lay upon the
valley like an affliction.

27

PAUL STENMARK examined the bowl in his hands and realized, with mild surprise, that it had been fashioned out of a coconut shell. Some time ago, he thought, judging from the feel of the thing. Wondering idly how many thousands of fingertips had been required to produce the satiny burnish, he raised the shell and sniffed gingerly. It was, as he had feared, full of the rust-colored liquid the locals elevated to the status of wine. He stared into the bowl, recalling his seared throat, which, in turn, prompted thoughts of Alfredo. He lifted his eyes and peered through the flames at the *pangat*.

Alfredo sat with his wife, one arm thrown casually around her shoulder. The firelight flickered across his bony face, accentuating the hollows on his cheeks and temples, throwing the area around his eyes into deep shadow. His head was nodding gently, in time with the beat of the bronze gongs, as he watched his people dance.

Paul's gaze wandered in the same direction. The dance was not what he had expected. It was a delicate thing, a kind of rustic minuet, that was being performed under the stars on the grassy meadow beside Frank Enright's church. Alfredo's people were circling the fire, atop which sat the spitted, sizzling carcass of a water buffalo. They moved around the blaze and the roasting *carabao* with a stately rhythm, measured by a handful of male

210

elders wielding the gongs and a pair of crones fingering wooden flutes. In time with the gongs, the villagers shuffled forward. In tune with the flutes, they dipped and wheeled while fluttering hands and arms up and down, like gulls riding a breeze.

"HOW ABOUT a break, Liz?" Frank puffed. "These old bones of mine aren't used to this sort of thing."

Liz looked up into Frank's face and laughed. "Already?" she cried with mock scorn. She tossed her head, flinging aside her long black hair.

Frank stared at Liz's hair, marveling at the play of the firelight across it. He suppressed an urge to reach out and touch it. Peering around, he spotted Harry sprawled on his back on the grass just beyond the circle of dancers. "I'm not the only one," he said, pointing a finger.

Liz regarded Harry's prostrate form and clucked. She began to move in his direction. As she did, she took Frank's hand for a moment. "C'mon," she whispered, a little huskily.

Frank stood, watching Liz go. He did not notice the dancers surging around him. He did not hear the gongs, nor the flutes. He was oblivious to everything save Liz's receding figure and his own heart, which was lurching.

Liz reached Harry, dug a toe into his side. "Get up, Harry," she ordered. "You're ruining your image."

Harry opened his eyes, saw Liz standing above him, closed his eyes, and groaned, "Only if you promise you're not going to ask me to dance."

"Who'd want to dance with an ugly brute like you?"

Harry chuckled. He opened one eye and cocked it up at Liz, preparing to return the insult.

"Feeling a little tired, are we?" Liz asked, sitting down. She hugged her knees against her chest.

"Tired," Harry confirmed, rising to an elbow, "but not yet

emotional"—he paused, yawned—"although I'd like to be. Where's the beer?"

"Sorry, Harry," Frank interjected as he joined the two of them. "This is a night for rice wine." He sat down beside Harry and folded his legs beneath him. He looked across the Australian to Liz.

Harry caught the look and wondered, as he had been wondering throughout the evening. He glanced at the villagers circling the fire. "Yeah," he said after a moment, "I guess you're right, Frank. It's their night."

Frank and Liz followed Harry's look. All three sat silently contemplating the dance. The villagers, silhouetted against the fire, cast wavering shadows into the night.

Harry pulled up a blade of grass and began to chew on it ruminatively. He glanced furtively at Liz. In jeans and white T-shirt, with her hair loose, she seemed younger than usual. He looked at Frank, who had abandoned his cassock and was dressed much like Liz. He thought that Frank, too, was looking a little vulnerable. He began to think that the suspicion that had been growing on him might well be true.

Harry let his gaze wander skyward as he contemplated the implications of what he was thinking. The night was hot and close. There was no moon, but the sky blazed with stars. They were gigantic and staring, as if the heavens had moved closer to the earth.

"There's a typhoon on the way," said Harry.

Frank looked up. "Yes," he agreed. "Tomorrow probably, maybe sooner." His eyes returned to the villagers. "They're very happy."

"Yes," said Harry.

"It's been a while since I've seen them like this."

"It must make you feel pretty good."

"I feel good for *them*," said Frank, "but I'd feel better if things had happened . . . well . . . differently."

"Chan," said Harry.

Frank shook his head regretfully.

"Ka Larry knew what he was doing there."

Frank hesitated before saying, "He's won again."

"I suppose he has."

Frank drew a frustrated breath.

"And that poor boy," Liz broke in.

"They murdered him," Frank said dully. "Right in front of our eyes."

Liz looked at Harry. "You think they did the same with the girl and the baby?"

"I told you what Rocky said," Harry answered quietly.

Liz clenched her jaw and swung her eyes in the direction of the low building on the other side of the road from the church. She murmured, "What kind of man could do that?"

Frank and Harry followed Liz's look. The building was in darkness except for a solitary light. It gleamed in the window of the office occupied by Colonel Rosales.

PAUL SCANNED the faces whirling by, wishing he could share in some of the joy he saw reflected there. But he could not. He believed they were wrong, perhaps fatally so. In the future he was contemplating, he saw little that gave him cause for cheer. He was not entirely sure, however, whose future it was that concerned him most—that of the people dancing past, or his own.

Paul looked across the fire at Alfredo, who continued to sit with his arm around his wife's shoulders. He was assailed by conflicting emotions as he watched the man. He wished him no harm, but he could not rid himself of the conviction that things might have been different if Alfredo had been different, or at least somewhere else. It gave him no comfort to realize that the only other individual who seemed to share his opinion was Colonel Rosales.

Paul ran a finger around his shirt collar, wiping away the sweat. The heat was oppressive, and there was no wind, not the faintest whisper. He glanced up at the sky, ran his eyes over the multitude of stars. They were huge and still.

Paul felt suddenly confined, in need of a walk. He rose and wandered aimlessly into the darkness beyond the circle of dancing light thrown by the fire. Once in the shadows, he heard the river gurgling at the foot of the meadow. Drawn by the sound, he strolled down the meadow's slope to the riverbank. On reaching it, he sat down and gazed at the stars sliding liquidly around the water's undulating surface. He could hear the subdued buzz of conversation coming from the fireside behind him, but the fire itself, and the people by it, were screened from his view by the rise of the meadow. He was soon lost in thought.

Paul was startled out of his reverie by the noise of footsteps crunching in the scree by the river's edge. He did not know how long he had been sitting, motionless. It could have been a few seconds, a few minutes, even longer. He looked up and saw a woman profiled in the dark a dozen yards away. She was peering into the gloom on the river's far shore.

Paul thought there was something vaguely familiar about the woman. He was sure he had seen her somewhere before, but he could not remember where. He was about to speak when a thin pencil of light shot from her hand, stabbing the darkness across the river. It flashed once briefly, then again.

Paul froze. He recalled the last time he had seen such a light, when Ot died, and it chilled his blood. He jerked a look at the opposite shore. He sucked in his breath when he saw an answering beam.

Paul glanced frantically around, looking for a place to hide. There was none. He stared up the slope, debating how long it would take to dash to the fire. Then he heard a splash, looked back at the river, and realized it was too late.

There were three of them, crossing what must have been a ford. They moved quickly through the water, which was no more than knee-deep. They were hunched low, cradling weapons. For one brief, paralyzing instant, Paul thought of the sparrow team. He surveyed the three figures, searching for a bushy head and a red bandanna. He did not find it. But what he did find gave him no cause for relief. He recognized the first of the three men to emerge from the river. It was Ka Larry.

28

ALFREDO DANTOG'S gaze lingered with interest on the young woman who stood with the three young men in the doorway of the hut. He nodded, reminding himself that he should not have been surprised. His eyes traveled back to Ka Larry, whom he studied for a moment before saying, "You are a man of many resources."

Ka Larry smiled thinly. "The *revolution* has many resources, *Apo Pangat*."

The two men exchanged a wordless stare, as if they were measuring each other the way the gongs and the flutes in the background were measuring the dance proceeding there.

"You sent for me," Ka Larry said finally, breaking the silence.

"Yes," Alfredo replied. "We have a lot to discuss."

Ka Larry glanced at his two male companions, who began to position themselves on the floor of the hut on each side of the doorway.

"Your friends will be hungry," said Alfredo. He gestured with his head to the entrance to the room behind him. "My wife has prepared a meal."

"They will stand guard," Ka Larry answered, a little brusquely.

"Against whom?" Alfredo asked quietly.

Ka Larry darted a quick look at Alfredo, alerted by his tone.

"You have something to fear out there?" Alfredo continued,

motioning toward the sound of the beating gongs and whistling flutes.

Ka Larry did not respond.

"Or perhaps you feel your enemy is somewhat closer?"

"The troops—" Ka Larry began.

"The troops will do nothing as long as my people are there," Alfredo interrupted. "You know that as well as I do."

Ka Larry shifted uncomfortably.

"Your friends will join my wife," Alfredo stated firmly. He glanced at the woman. "All *three* of your friends will join my wife."

The woman and the two men looked from Alfredo to Ka Larry.

Ka Larry contemplated Alfredo for a time. He nodded finally at his companions, who left the room.

"Come," said Alfredo, lowering himself to the floor beside a glowing lantern. "Sit down."

Ka Larry walked across the hut, sat.

"You want something to eat?" Alfredo inquired. "To drink?"

Ka Larry shook his head. He regarded Alfredo warily, said, "You're angry with me, *Apo Pangat*."

"Yes," Alfredo bluntly replied.

"You have no reason to be."

"Oh?"

"I have won a victory for you."

"For me?"

"I have inflicted a serious defeat on those who would build the dams."

"The price was very high."

"A few soldiers," said Ka Larry dismissively. "A thief with a lying mouth."

"And unarmed workers."

"They carried no weapons, but they were enemies of the people."

"Were the boy and the girl and the child 'enemies of the people'?"

Ka Larry gave Alfredo a puzzled look. "What boy?"

"The boy I was trying to help when Rosales found me."

"He was killed?"

"Yes," Alfredo replied. "And his woman and his child." He paused, murmured sadly, "His firstborn."

"I'm sorry, *Apo Pangat*, but that was not my doing."

"It was not your hand that dealt the blow but you were responsible all the same."

"But—"

"Just as you were responsible for almost killing the American."

"I rescued the American!" Ka Larry exclaimed.

Alfredo shot a dark look at Ka Larry. "You rescued him from whom?"

Ka Larry avoided Alfredo's eyes.

"They were your own people, were they not?"

"They have been punished," Ka Larry muttered.

"Nobody would have needed to be punished if you had not done what I forbade you to do."

Ka Larry bristled. "Is your precious American dead?" He threw an arm toward the source of the muffled sound of music and conversation that was reaching their ears. "Isn't he sitting out there right now?"

"That's not the point."

"What *is* the point?"

"I warned you not to do this thing."

"I see," said Ka Larry acidly. "I have defied the mighty *pangat* and am now to be reprimanded."

"If you want to put it that way."

"Reprimanded for what?" Ka Larry demanded. "For putting a stop to those dams?"

"No."

"Is that not what I have accomplished?"

"For the time being."

"For the time being?"

"Yes," said Alfredo, "and *that's* the point."

Ka Larry frowned.

"You did not end this struggle when you embarked upon your little escapade," Alfredo continued. "You merely managed to raise the level of violence up another notch."

Ka Larry stared at Alfredo.

"You think Rosales is going to slink away now with his tail between his legs?"

"No."

"He's going to hit right back, isn't he?"

"Yes."

"Which will provoke another response from you?"

"Yes."

"And when Rosales spills his brains, what happens?"

Ka Larry shrugged.

"They send more people like Rosales up here, with more troops like Rosales has," Alfredo said.

"I'm prepared for that."

"Of course you are!" Alfredo snapped. "It's what you want!"

Ka Larry did not respond.

"You want this whole valley turned into a battleground."

"Armed struggle is—"

"Spare me your ideology," Alfredo cut in impatiently.

Ka Larry took a breath. "I will simply say then that it is necessary."

"Necessary for whom?"

"To build a new society."

"And will your new society be any more sympathetic to the aims of my people than the current one?"

Ka Larry remained silent.

"I think not," said Alfredo. "Your prophets make no allowances for the kind of things I want to preserve, do they?"

Ka Larry continued to stare wordlessly at Alfredo.

"Well, you are not going to build your new society on the bones of my people," Alfredo declared. "I'm not fighting to save the terraces to see them transformed into a graveyard."

"There is no other way to save them."

Alfredo's gaze drifted away from Ka Larry. He was silent for a time, then murmured softly, "Yes, there is."

Ka Larry studied Alfredo. He asked, "What are you going to do?"

Alfredo looked back at Ka Larry. "Do you recall that I once told you that our paths would someday diverge?"

Ka Larry did not answer.

"That day has arrived." Alfredo rose, lifting the lantern with him. He looked down at Ka Larry sitting cross-legged on the floor. "It's time for you to take your revolution elsewhere."

Ka Larry slanted a look up at Alfredo through the veil of dark hair falling across his eyes. "Do you really think you can stop me now?"

"I'm going to try," Alfredo replied as he was joined by his wife. He threw an arm around her shoulders, and they began to walk toward the hut's door.

"You're too late," Ka Larry called to the retreating figures.

Neither Alfredo nor his wife turned. They walked out of the hut without a backward glance.

"You might as well try to stop the rain," Ka Larry told the empty doorway.

29

IT WAS no more than a caress, a breath of air that lightly touched Frank Enright's cheek, as if the breeze had blown him a kiss. But it was enough to cause him to halt in midsentence. He understood the meaning. He saw instantly that Alfredo had felt it too, as had Harry. They were both craning their necks, peering up toward the valley's eastern rim.

Frank looked in the same direction. The mountain peaks formed a dark, crenellated line against the moonless, star-bright sky. Thin, ragged strips of cloud were racing across the stars, tearing gashes in the firmament as they moved.

"She's coming now," said Frank, gazing upward.

"Yes," agreed Alfredo. "I guess it's time." He dropped his glance from the sky and looked toward the fire.

The fire was dying. It had subsided into a glowing heap of embers, from which an occasional flame flickered up, licking at the remnants of the buffalo carcass. The villagers were scattered in repose around the fire. Some scanned the eastern horizon, as Alfredo had done previously.

Alfredo rose. He reached out, assisted his wife to her feet. "We'd better be going."

"When will it come?" asked Frank, rising.

Alfredo looked back at the notched line of dark hills. As he stood, the wind riffled the long meadow grass, loosening for a moment the heat's tight clasp. "Tonight. Before daybreak, probably."

"Then we'd all better get moving," Harry declared. He joined the others in standing, stretched a hand, and pulled Liz to her feet. "You too, my little lady. There's work to be done."

"As usual, the *little lady* has done all her work," Liz retorted. "My bungalow's shuttered, and so's the clinic." She raised an eyebrow at Harry. "How about your place, big fella?"

Harry grinned sheepishly.

"Neither is the church," Frank interjected. He looked at Liz. "You want to give me a hand?"

"Sure," Liz answered, pausing as her glance fell upon Alfredo and his wife. "That is, unless Alfredo wants a ride up to the bridge?"

Alfredo shook his head, threw an arm around his wife's shoulders. "I think we'll walk."

Frank nodded, regarded Harry. "You want to sit it out at my place?" You can keep me and Liz and Paul company." He glanced around, suddenly aware of the American's absence. "Where *is* Paul, by the way?"

"I saw him earlier down by the fire," said Alfredo. "I was going to talk to him until I realized that conversation was not what he required."

Frank, Harry, and Liz gave Alfredo an inquiring look.

Alfredo shrugged. "He looked to me like someone who wanted to be alone."

"Well, I guess he'll show up sooner or later," said Frank. He looked at Harry. "You going to join us?"

"Why not?" Harry replied. "Let me secure my place and I'll be right back." He turned to Alfredo, gave him an affectionate thump on the shoulder. "And we'll be seeing you, China, after the blow." He wheeled, lumbered off.

Alfredo watched him go for a moment, then turned to the

others. He regarded Liz closely before he inclined his head at her. He smiled at Frank and seemed to be on the point of saying something. But he chose not to. He walked toward the road. The villagers were moving along it, heading in the direction of the rise that curved up and out of the settlement.

Liz joined Frank, stood by his side. The heat was dissipating rapidly, and there was less caprice in the breeze. It rustled through the long grass, stirred the tops of the trees at the edge of the meadow. The leaves on the treetops began to whisper urgently among themselves.

Frank swung an arm around Liz's shoulders. She surrendered to the gentle pressure and leaned into him. They stood together like that, watching Alfredo lead his people up the hill and into the night.

Liz glanced up at Frank, found him gazing into the sky. She did the same. The strings of ragged cloud had spawned. Swarms of them whirled across the face of the stars. Her eyes wandered after a time until they settled upon the solitary light burning on the other side of the road in Colonel Rosales's office. The light glared.

COLONEL ROSALES lifted the bottle and poured what was left of its contents into the glass he held in his other hand. He raised the glass to his lips and drank, emptying it in a single swallow. He set the glass heavily back down upon the desk.

There was a knock on his office door.

Colonel Rosales's eyes did not stray from the red telephone. He barked, "Enter!"

The large head of Sergeant Cruz poked around the corner. "I still can't get any response from Manila, Colonel."

Colonel Rosales's eyes sparked and his grip on the bottle and the glass tightened.

After a pause, the sergeant asked, "You want me to keep trying?"

Colonel Rosales shook his head.

The sergeant hesitated. "Any further orders?"

"Yes," said Colonel Rosales. "Find Ramirez. Bring him here. When you've done that, assemble a squad. Full combat rig."

"Yes sir," the sergeant replied, withdrawing his head and gently closing the door.

Colonel Rosales rose unsteadily to his feet and hurled the bottle in his hand against the wall, where it smashed into a thousand fragments.

FRANK AND Liz walked, hand in hand, across the meadow toward the church. The great metal cross on the steeple glimmered palely in the starlight. They entered the church beneath the cross and swung the big double doors shut behind them, which prevented either from noticing the lights winking on across the road in all of the windows at Colonel Rosales's headquarters.

Frank and Liz moved down the church, securing the storm shutters. The shutters were heavy wooden affairs built to withstand the brute force of a tropical cyclone's hundred-mile-per-hour-plus rotating wind. It took some effort, therefore, to slam the shutters into place. It also made a lot of noise. Neither Frank nor Liz, as a result, heard the engine on the military truck across the road cough into life; nor did they see it pull up and stop and die again in front of the entrance to Colonel Rosales's headquarters.

It was dark inside the church with the doors shut and the windows sealed. The only light came from the belfry at the peak of the steeple. Starshine slipped through the belfry's embrasures, suffusing the interior of the church with a silvery luminescence.

Frank and Liz stood within this light, staring at each other. They were at the front of the church near the altar, which was a simple wooden table bearing a wooden cross. High on the wall above their heads, half hidden in the shadows, was a huge crucifix, also made of wood. It was crudely done, in the local fashion, but whoever had carved Christ's face had known something about agony.

Frank stepped in Liz's direction and was reaching out a hand to touch her when his arm froze, struck immobile by the quiet creak of a door opening. They looked into each other's widened eyes for an instant, then glanced in the direction of the noise. It came from the opposite corner of the church, on the far side of the altar, where there was a small side entrance. The altar blocked their view of the door itself, but they could see a shaft of faint starlight reflected on the church's interior walls. They watched as the beam widened. Then they heard a voice.

"Father Enright?" the voice called quietly. It was a woman, and her tone was a little tremulous, as if uncertain, or afraid.

"Yes," Frank answered.

"It's Martha," said the voice, a clear note of relief in it. "Martha Innog."

Frank glanced at Liz, who looked back with downturned lips and upturned eyebrows. Frank shouted, "Over here, Martha, by the altar."

The door closed, snuffing out the starlight on the wall, and Martha shuffled into sight at the opposite end of the altar rail. She was bent with age, beyond being merely old. No one in the hills knew exactly how old she was; she did not even know herself. But everybody knew there was nobody older than the woman who worked in Colonel Rosales's kitchen.

"Over here, Martha," Frank called again as he saw the old woman hesitating at the far end of the altar rail.

Martha peered into the feeble light. She said, the tremble in her voice renewed, "But you're not alone, Father."

"Don't worry, Martha," said Liz, moving toward the woman. "It's only me, Dr. Elizabeth."

Martha grasped the altar rail, steadying herself as Liz walked toward her. She did not speak until Liz reached her. She scrutinized the doctor's face, as if reassuring herself that she was not being deceived. She whispered at last, "Thank heaven I've found you both."

"What's the problem, Martha?" Frank inquired as he joined the two women.

Martha glanced nervously around the church. "There's nobody else here?"

"Nobody," Frank assured her.

Martha continued to stare uneasily into the church's darkened interior.

Frank reached out and grasped the woman's elbow. "Why don't we sit down," he said, attempting to steer her to a pew.

"There's no time," Martha replied, shaking off Frank's grip.

"No time?" Frank asked.

"You must hurry," Martha answered, "or it will be too late."

"Too late for what?"

"To save Alfredo."

Frank shot a quick glance at Liz, looked back at Martha. "To save Alfredo?"

"They're going to kill him."

30

FRANK ENRIGHT saw the boulder, reflected in the Land Rover's single working headlight, a moment too late. It lay at the side of the track, a chunk of jagged rock the size of a refrigerator. He jerked the steering wheel in an effort to avoid it. But his front wheel struck the rock and bounced violently off it, which slewed the rear of his vehicle sideways and sent it plunging toward the cliff edge on the opposite side of the road. He jammed on the brakes and turned into the skid. For a breathtaking fraction of a second he thought he had lost it. But the sturdy old Land Rover crunched to a halt amid a cloud of dust on the lip of the precipice. The dust rose and drifted lazily through the lone beam of light that pierced the darkness.

Frank could not see into that darkness, but he knew there was nothing there but a half-mile drop to the floor of the valley. He shut his eyes and gripped the steering wheel tightly, giving his racing heart a moment to recover. He reopened his eyes, slipped the Land Rover into reverse, and backed gingerly away from the cliffside. Once safely back on the track, he told himself he had been going too fast. He threw the vehicle into forward and slammed the accelerator to the floor anyway. He knew he had no alternative, not if he was going to reach Alfredo in time.

It was not that he trusted entirely in Martha's judgment, but there was a disquieting ring of truth in her story. It was just like

227

Rosales to drink himself into a volcanic rage. And there was no denying that something was afoot. He had seen the preparations himself: the lights, the waiting truck, the telltale signs of bustle. Martha said the colonel had summoned a squad. She claimed she had overheard the colonel tell that young lieutenant that they were going to "teach Alfredo a lesson." He frowned. What kind of lesson?

Frank geared up, pushing the Land Rover ahead, punishing it. He had to reach Alfredo, explain things. He would get Alfredo out of the way, at least for tonight. It was the safest course. He peered into the darkness ahead. Where *was* Alfredo? He could not be that much farther ahead. The shaft of light from the Land Rover's lone eye bounced erratically.

Frank thought of the others. Liz would find Harry and Paul. The three of them might be able to talk some sense into the colonel. Frank ran a hand through his hair, wondering how they were going to do that.

WHICH WAS exactly what Harry was wondering as he stood outside the entrance to Colonel Rosales's headquarters, staring up at the two young soldiers guarding the doorway. Liz was haranguing the pair in Tagalog, the lowland dialect they all shared. Harry possessed only an imperfect knowledge of the language, but it was sufficient to persuade him that their chances of getting to see the colonel personally were slim. The two nervous recruits had been given their orders. The orders were clear. What's more, they came from the colonel himself. The soldiers had not been around the battalion long, but they had been around long enough to know what *that* meant.

Harry glanced around, irritated anew by Paul's continuing absence. What a time for him to disappear. His presence might have helped to tip the scales. He was an American, and even a pair of raw youngsters knew that you had to be careful with Americans.

Americans often had friends, and sometimes those friends out-ranked notoriously vindictive colonels.

Harry looked back at the soldiers. They were clearly uncomfort-able with Liz's hectoring. But it was just as clear that what they *were* suffering was preferable to what they *would* suffer if they yielded.

Harry had a thought. He stretched out a hand and placed it on Liz's shoulder, silencing her. He stepped in the direction of the troopers.

The soldiers stiffened, raised their weapons.

Harry stood before them, towering over the pair. He reached into his pocket, pulled out a pack of cigarettes, offered it.

Both troopers shook their heads warily but, at the same time, relaxed a shade.

"Look," said Harry confidentially, shaking a cigarette from the pack. "We've all got a problem here." He pointed the cigarette over his shoulder at Liz. "Me and the lady need to see the colonel." He leveled the cigarette at the two soldiers. "You can't let us do that." He placed the cigarette in his mouth. "All *four* of us are going to be in deep trouble if we don't see the colonel." He lit the cigarette. "There must be some way around this problem." He took a deep draw, exhaled the smoke slowly.

The soldiers stared.

Harry regarded each in turn. "You got any ideas?"

The soldiers remained silent.

"Why don't you let me make a suggestion?"

A receptiveness crept into both pairs of black eyes.

Harry slid a furtive look around, leaned closer to the two. "Go fetch Lieutenant Ramirez," he said. "Tell him we want to have a word with him." He paused. "In private."

The soldiers glanced at each other doubtfully.

"You do like I say," Harry went on, "and both *your* asses are covered." He smiled, sharing a secret. "Anything goes wrong, you got an officer to blame."

The soldiers exchanged another quick look, but they did not move.

Harry shrugged. "Have it your way," he said, turning. "It's your funeral."

"Wait," said one of the soldiers.

Harry looked back.

The soldier studied Harry for a moment, then said to his companion, "Go get the lieutenant."

FRANK CAREENED around a bend and saw them, frozen in the Land Rover's solitary beam of bouncing light. They were gathered by the edge of the track in front of the old shack where the bus used to stop in earlier, more pacific times. They were preparing to descend what Frank knew was the long flight of stone steps that led down the cliff face to the footbridge that crossed the river. Their faces were turned inquiringly into the light.

Frank heaved a sigh of relief. He was too far away to identify individuals, but he knew Alfredo would be among the crowd somewhere. He flashed the Land Rover's light and pounded urgently on the horn.

THERE WAS a strained expression on Lieutenant Ramirez's narrow face as he regarded Harry and Liz. He darted a glance at the two soldiers on the doorway, who immediately averted their eyes and stared studiously into the night. The lieutenant nodded toward the truck, which stood near the entrance. He led Harry and Liz to the far side of the vehicle. Once they were out of the sight of the guards, he asked with irritation, "Do you think I like this any better than either of you?"

"Then why the hell won't you help?" snapped Liz.

Lieutenant Ramirez regarded Liz coldly. "Don't you think I've tried?"

"Then let us try," said Liz impatiently. "Let us talk to the colonel."

"He won't see you."

"Take us to him."

"I can't do that."

"Why not?"

"Because you will make things worse."

"He's bad, huh?" Harry asked.

Lieutenant Ramirez fixed Harry with a look. "I've never seen him this angry before."

"So you're just going to sit, doing nothing, while Rocky goes up the *barrio* and murders Alfredo," said Liz accusingly.

"Nobody's going to sit doing nothing and nobody's going to be murdered," Lieutenant Ramirez retorted.

Liz threw an arm at the truck. "Then what the hell is this all about?"

Lieutenant Ramirez looked uncomfortable. "It's a police action."

Liz muttered in disgust.

Lieutenant Ramirez was on the point of an angry response when Harry intervened.

"What *are* you going to do?"

Lieutenant Ramirez looked at Harry. "I'm going to make certain that things don't get out of control." He glanced back at Liz. "I can promise you that much."

"You sure you can manage it?" Harry asked.

"I'm sure." There was a confidence in the lieutenant's voice. It was not matched by the expression in his eyes.

FRANK STARED into Alfredo's eyes, where two tiny replicas of the candle's wavering flame were mirrored. He had seen that look in those eyes before. He knew what it meant, but he could not prevent himself from trying one more time.

"There's going to be trouble," Frank said. "Why don't you come back to the mission with me? Stay there, just for the night."

Alfredo smiled. The light from the candle that sat on the table between them flickered across his bony face, glimmering on the coral beads wrapped around the corded muscles of his neck. "If there's going to be trouble for my people, Frank," he asked, "do you really think that my place is with you and not them?"

"You're the one that's in trouble, Alfredo, not your people. Old Martha says Rosales is coming to kill you."

"You told me that."

"She may be right."

"I suspect she is."

"Then why don't you do something?" Frank demanded, exasperated.

Alfredo contemplated Frank for a moment before he allowed his gaze to wander around the dilapidated shed where they sat. His eyes settled finally upon the shack's solitary window, where a steadily rising wind was whistling hollowly through broken panes of glass.

"At least get out of the way," Frank urged when he received no response.

Alfredo continued to gaze at the window. "The violence has begun," he said.

"I know."

"There is more on the way," Alfredo went on. "I can feel it coming. It's going to wash over my valley and destroy everything I value, unless I do something to stop it."

"You won't be able to stop anything if you get in the way of a bullet from Rocky."

Alfredo swung his eyes back to Frank. "You're wrong."

Frank's brow creased in puzzlement.

Alfredo gave Frank another of his quiet smiles. "What would you say if I told you that I wanted Rosales to kill me?"

"What?" Frank exclaimed.

"It's the best solution."

"What are you talking about?" Frank cried.

"Think about it," said Alfredo. "Imagine the consequences if I am murdered by government troops."

"I'm not going to think about any such thing," Frank retorted angrily.

"Try to keep your emotions out of it."

"Alfredo . . ." Frank began.

"Be objective, just for a moment."

Frank shook his head.

"There would be an uproar, would there not?"

"Well . . . yes," Frank admitted grudgingly.

"There would be such an uproar that it would be impossible for them to find *anyone* willing to supply the money for those dams."

Frank stared at Alfredo.

Alfredo added, a conclusive note in his voice, "And those dams are the root of all of our trouble."

Frank was silent for a long time. He said at last, "You can't be serious."

"But I am."

"You'd sacrifice yourself?"

"I've already sacrificed much more than my life," Alfredo replied softly.

The wind gusted, rattling the broken panes of glass in the window. Frank glanced toward the sound, listened to the hollow whistling for a moment. He asked, his voice subdued, "Do you want to die?"

"No," Alfredo replied.

Frank did not take his eyes from the window. "Are you afraid?"

There was a pause. "Yes."

"So am I."

"I know." Alfredo paused again. "Thank you for that."

Frank looked back at Alfredo. They regarded each other silently until there was another gust of wind. It carried some rain this time, which splattered heavily on the shed's tin roof. Both men glanced up.

"You'd better go now, Frank," said Alfredo, "while there's time."

"Yes," Frank murmured.

31

FRANK ENRIGHT did not even have to ask. Everything he wanted to know was staring at him, written in Harry's glum expression and in the tense set of Liz's mouth. He sagged a little, allowing his grip on the doorknob to loosen. The wind immediately ripped the door from his hand, slammed it against the exterior wall of the house, and swung it back again. It thumped heavily into Frank's shoulder. He barely noticed. He glanced at the door quizzically, as if wondering what he had done to provoke the blow. He caught the door on the point of another trajectory and closed it.

"No luck with Rocky?" Frank asked, stepping into the room. His voice was dispirited. He already knew the answer.

"No," Liz replied tightly.

"And Alfredo?" Harry inquired.

Frank shook his head. He ran a hand wearily down his face, wiping away the rain. The water dripped from him, puddling at his feet.

"You're soaked," said Liz. She rose from the sofa and walked across the room to Frank. On reaching him, she grasped his hand and began to lead him to his bedroom. "You'd better get out of those wet clothes."

Frank looked down at himself, as if a little surprised by his state. "Yeah," he murmured distractedly.

"I'll make you a drink," said Harry as Frank and Liz disappeared into the bedroom. He walked to Frank's makeshift bar. He stood, staring down at the lonely green bottle on the little rattan table. He muttered to himself, "We all need a drink."

As if in reply, the house groaned. Harry looked up and cocked his head. The rain drummed on the roof's wooden shingles. The wind prowled, scratching at the walls, rattling the storm shutters, snuffling under the doorways. The big ceiling fan overhead quaked on its brackets.

Liz reemerged from the bedroom and caught the direction of Harry's look.

"It won't be long now," Harry said. He lifted the dark green bottle. "You want a drink?"

"Yes," said Liz. She walked across the room, fell heavily into a sofa.

"Water?" Harry asked. "Ice?"

"Neat," Liz replied. She slid lower down into the sofa, rested her head on its back, and closed her eyes.

Harry walked to Liz, handed her a glass with two fingers of whisky in it. He sipped his own whisky, studying her for a moment. He asked, "How is he?"

"He'll survive," said Frank.

Both Harry and Liz looked.

Frank stood in the doorway to the bedroom, dressed in dry clothes, toweling his hair. "The question is," he asked from under the towel, "will Alfredo survive?"

Liz dropped her head back onto the sofa, closed her eyes. Harry stared down into his drink. Frank let the hand with the towel in it fall to his side as he leaned into the doorpost. Nobody spoke.

The front door suddenly swung open with a loud bang. The wind sprang. It whistled into the room, carrying a spray of rain. Frank, Harry, and Liz looked at the door in surprise.

Paul was standing in the doorway, drenched. His blond hair was plastered to his skull, and his clothes clung to his lean frame. He

stared at the three of them, wide-eyed. He seemed to be bursting
with news. But when he opened his mouth to speak, the door
slammed into his back. He staggered forward and his glasses, his
one spare pair, fell from his face, clattering to the floor.

"Jesus!" Paul gasped.

Frank and Harry rushed across the room. Frank wrestled the
door shut while Harry retrieved Paul's glasses and pulled the American upright.

"You all right?" Harry asked, handing Paul his glasses.

Paul took the glasses and rubbed his back, wincing.

Frank gave Paul the damp towel he was carrying. "You'd better
go get changed."

"Yeah," Paul replied, accepting the towel. "But first there's—"

"Later," Frank interrupted. He began to steer Paul to his bedroom.

"But you've got to know—"

"First get dried off," Frank cut in again. "Otherwise you're going
to catch a bad cold." He glanced at Liz. "Isn't that right, Doctor?"

"Pneumonia probably," Liz replied. She said it as if it would not
have made an awful lot of difference to her if Paul did catch
pneumonia.

Frank pushed Paul toward his room. "Don't worry," he said.
"We'll all be right here."

"But . . ." Paul objected.

Frank gave Paul another shove in the direction of his room.

"Listen . . ." said Paul with a backward glance.

Frank pointed a finger, commanded, "Go!"

Paul reluctantly obeyed.

When he had gone, Frank turned to the others. "Where were
we?"

"Alfredo," said Harry.

"Right," Frank replied with a sigh.

"You couldn't convince him?" Liz asked.

"You know Alfredo."

"What did he say?"

"He said he wasn't going to hide out in the mission if there was going to be trouble in the *barrio.*"

"That's all?"

Frank regarded Harry and Liz for a moment. "No," he replied quietly, "that's not all." He walked to the rattan table and poured himself a drink from the dark green bottle.

"Did you tell him what's happening here?" Liz asked, directing her question at Frank's back.

"Yes," Frank answered as he lifted the glass to his lips.

"Doesn't he know what Rocky may be planning?"

"He knows."

"And he doesn't care?"

Frank turned to Harry and Liz. "He *wants* Rocky to murder him."

PAUL FROZE when Frank's words reached him inside the bedroom. He remained absolutely still as he waited for more, hoping that he had misunderstood. For a time, he heard nothing but the stunned silence that had greeted Frank's announcement. There was no sound but the wind pawing at the house and the rain ringing on the shingles.

And then Frank began to recount for the others his conversation with Alfredo.

As Paul listened, he sank slowly onto the edge of the bed, beside which he had been standing. As he began to comprehend, the towel he held fluttered to the floor. He stared sightlessly at it, numb with horror. He recognized the hand that had helped to create the current situation. It was his own.

"I DON'T care what Alfredo thinks," said Liz when Frank had finished. "We cannot let this happen."

"I agree," said Frank. "But what can we do?"

"We have to make contact with someone important enough to stop Rocky," said Harry.

"How?" Liz asked.

Frank began to pace. He halted after a moment, looked at Harry and Liz. "Rocky's telephone?" he asked. "Can we get to it?"

Harry and Liz exchanged a glance, looked back at Frank with negative expressions.

There was a distant growl of thunder. Everyone in the room looked in the direction of the noise.

"And the road will soon be impassable," said Harry, voicing the common thought.

Frank resumed pacing. "What about Ramirez?" he asked. "Maybe he *is* capable of doing what he says he can do."

Neither Harry nor Liz responded.

Frank glanced at them both. "What do you think?"

Harry, who had been gazing disconsolately into his glass, raised his head until his eyes found Frank's. "What do *you* think?"

Frank sagged. He balled his fists in frustration. "There must be *something* we can do."

"What?" Liz cried.

Paul appeared in the doorway to the bedroom. If he had been more careful, less blinded by his own concerns, perhaps all of this could have been avoided. Well, he would go no further. He would attempt to undo what he had done. He stepped out of the bedroom door and announced, loudly and with determination: "I know a way."

32

"WHAT DID you say?" Harry asked, his voice hardly more than a whisper.

Paul stood in the doorway, arms folded across his chest. "I said, I know a way."

Harry, Frank, and Liz stared at Paul.

"It might work," Paul continued, "but there are some risks."

"Risks?" asked Harry.

"Yes," Paul replied. "Somebody could get hurt." He hesitated, then added, "Maybe worse." He took a breath. "Somebody might get killed."

"What are you talking about?" Liz demanded.

"I'm talking about saving Alfredo's life," Paul answered calmly.

"And who the hell is going to get killed?"

Paul's look grew level. "*Not* Alfredo."

"But—"

"Let him finish, Liz," Harry interrupted. He regarded Paul with interest. "Go on. Tell us how you think you can save Alfredo's life."

"I can't save Alfredo, but I think I know someone who can." Paul glanced at his little audience. "I think we all know someone who can."

"Who?"

"Ka Larry."

"Jesus, Mary, and Joseph!" Frank whispered. "Do you know what you're saying? You want to set Rocky up for an NPA ambush!"

"I said somebody could get hurt."

"Killed, you mean."

"But it won't be Alfredo," Liz intervened quietly, contemplating Paul with a look that was different from the one she normally reserved for the American. While it fell short of outright admiration, it did suggest a kind of budding respect.

"Aren't we getting a bit ahead of ourselves here?" said Harry. They looked at him.

"It seems to me this discussion is a little on the academic side," Harry went on. "No matter what we may think of Paul's idea, there's a key element missing. It won't work unless we can locate Ka Larry, and . . ." He nodded toward the building storm outside. "How are we going to find him with that going on out there?"

"Finding Ka Larry won't be a problem," said Paul. "He's right here."

"What?" gasped Harry, Frank, and Liz almost in unison.

"He's in the settlement," said Paul. "He has three companions. One of them is a woman. There's a native hut behind Chan's warehouse. It looks abandoned, but it isn't. Ka Larry's in there with the others." He paused, glanced around. "He met Alfredo there."

The others exchanged quick looks. Harry asked, "How do you know all that?"

Paul regarded Harry. "I followed him there. I saw Alfredo come out a little later, with his wife. I was sitting down by the river when you were all having that party. I saw Ka Larry and two others wading across the water from the far shore. There was a woman waiting for them on this side. She gave them a flashlight signal before they crossed."

"Nobody saw you?"

"That's right," Paul answered. "I guess I wasn't moving much." He smiled sheepishly. "Actually, I was petrified."

"Go on."

"After Ka Larry and the others met the woman, they all headed up the hill toward the settlement. They kept to the shadows. I followed them until they reached the hut I was telling you about. They entered, and I sat outside for a while, watching. That's when I saw Alfredo leave with his wife. I hung around some more until it started to rain. Then I decided I'd better let someone know what was going on." Paul shrugged. "You know the rest."

"Are you sure it was Ka Larry?" Harry asked.

"That's one face I'll never forget."

Harry nodded. "Did you recognize the other two?"

"No."

"Were they armed?"

"Yes, except for the woman."

"Did you recognize her?" asked Liz.

"No, I never got close enough." Paul paused, looked at Liz. "But you know, I had a funny feeling that I'd seen her before."

"And what about Alfredo?" Frank inquired.

"He must have been inside waiting for them, because I didn't see him enter." Paul hesitated, smiled faintly. "But I'll tell you I could have been knocked over with a feather when I saw him come out later with his wife."

"Was he in there long?"

Paul shook his head. "Not long."

"How did he look when he came out?"

Paul gave Frank a puzzled look.

"I mean, did he appear angry or anything?"

Paul raised his eyebrows as he considered the question. "No," he said finally. "He just looked the way Alfredo always looks."

"When did all of this take place?"

"It must have been during the dance," Paul replied. "I could hear the gongs and the flutes."

There was a long silence, broken only by the sound of the wind and the rain and the rumble of approaching thunder. Frank, Harry, and Liz watched Paul, as if each was seeing something there they had not noticed before.

"You know, you could have gotten yourself in a lot of trouble, doing what you did," Harry said finally. "Why did you do it?"

Paul regarded Harry for a moment before he answered. "I'm not sure," he said. "Amends, maybe."

Liz rose from the sofa. "We have to go to him."

Nobody moved.

"We have to go to him *now*," Liz insisted. "While there's still time."

Frank and Harry exchanged a long look. Frank turned to Paul. "You can find this hut again?"

"Yes."

"You're prepared to go there?"

"Yes."

Frank looked back at Harry.

"It has to be you, Frank," Harry said quietly.

Frank pressed his lips together.

"He won't believe *me*," Harry went on in the same voice. "He'll smell a trap."

Liz walked to Frank's side. "I'll go."

"No," said Frank with a small shake of his head. "He won't believe you either."

"Then let Paul go alone," Liz urged.

"There's a chance it will work, Frank," said Harry, "but not without you. You're the only one who can convince Ka Larry that it's not a lie. He *knows* you, the way you *know* him." He paused. "He'll believe you because he'll know what it cost you to go to him."

Frank heaved a defeated breath.

Liz reached out and touched Frank's arm. "You're not doing it for Ka Larry," she said. "You're doing it for Alfredo."

"Then you have no doubts?"

Liz tightened her grip on Frank's arm.

"He'll be a hero." Frank paused. "He'll win again." He looked at Liz. "Can you tell me why it always has to be that way?"

Liz did not have an answer.

33

THE RAIN, plunking slowly down onto the plank floor from the leaky thatch, measured the lull in the conversation like a metronome. All three men gazed silently at the candle, which was anchored to the floor in a pool of melted wax. It cast a tentative light, barely enough to illumine the corner of the hut where they sat in a circle facing each other. Beyond the circle the dwelling was in darkness, as immune to the candle's feeble efforts as the wind and the rain outside to a plea for mercy.

Ka Larry lifted his head finally and regarded Frank Enright and Paul Stenmark, his eyes straying from one to the other. He asked, "Is there anything else you want to tell me?"

Frank looked up, exchanged a glance with Paul, and shook his head. "There's nothing," he replied. "You know everything that we know."

Ka Larry nodded wordlessly, but he continued to watch Frank and Paul carefully.

There was a crack of lightning, a roll of thunder. A flash of light the color of bleached bones flooded the interior of the hut. In that instant, Frank caught a glimpse of two of Ka Larry's companions. They squatted on either side of the entrance, weapons cradled across their laps, just as they had been doing when he and Paul had entered. There was still no sign of Ka Larry's third companion, the woman Paul said he had seen.

Frank's glance was drawn to the rectangle of deeper shadow over Ka Larry's shoulder, which marked the doorway to the hut's other room. He was speculating privately on what might lie within that shadow when his thoughts were interrupted.

"May I ask you both a question?" Ka Larry inquired.

Frank looked at Ka Larry. As he did, he realized there was an austere quality to the man that summoned a distant echo in the back of his mind. He nodded.

"I'm curious to know why you chose to bring me this information," said Ka Larry.

"That's obvious, isn't it?"

"To you, maybe; not to me."

"We want to save Alfredo's life."

Ka Larry leaned forward, resting his forearms on his legs folded in front of him. With each hand, he grasped the toes on his bare feet. He looked at Frank. "But why come to *me*?"

Frank did not answer. He glanced down, taking note of the thick calluses that covered the soles of Ka Larry's feet. They were worn and cracked, like old boot leather.

"It's not because you have finally realized we are both on the same side?" Ka Larry asked.

Frank looked up. He replied sharply, "We're not on the same side."

"We have the same goals."

Frank was about to deny the assertion when Paul cut in. "But our methods differ."

Ka Larry turned to Paul and shrugged. "Does that matter?"

"It matters very much," Paul declared.

"Not always, apparently," Ka Larry answered, smiling faintly.

"There was no choice," said Paul, bristling.

"No choice?"

"There was no other way, no one else."

"So in this case at least you are willing to tolerate my methods."

Paul looked uncomfortable. He fell silent, stared at Ka Larry.

Ka Larry stared back, his smile a little less faint.

Frank studied the pair confronting each other across the candle's guttering flame, struck by their similarity. One was dark and one was fair, but they were like the positive and negative photo prints of the same image. Both were young and lean and committed and so awfully sure of themselves.

Ka Larry finally released Paul's eyes, straightened, and asked lightly, "Do either of you smoke?"

Frank and Paul exchanged a puzzled look before shaking their heads.

"Then neither of you has cigarettes?" Ka Larry asked with a hint of resignation.

"No," said Frank.

Ka Larry sighed wistfully. He reached into a pocket of the sleeveless tunic he wore, pulled out a soiled cloth pouch. He shook the contents onto the floor beside the candle. There were a few scraps of yellowed newspaper and some shreds of rough black tobacco. "It's a weakness, I know," he said dolefully as he surveyed the meager mound of tobacco and the curling slips of newsprint, "but how often I wish I had something better than this to smoke."

Ka Larry leaned forward, and a lank of black hair fell across his face, glistening in the candlelight. With his immense thumbnail he sliced a scrap of paper, then scattered tobacco on it, moistened an edge with his tongue, and sealed it. The procedure was performed in a few seconds with a spare economy of movement.

Frank, watching, glimpsed the rigors of the man's life, which set echoes ringing in his mind once more.

Ka Larry slanted an apologetic look up through the screen of shining hair. "It's the only luxury I permit myself," he said before bending to the candle to light the cigarette.

Frank stared at the long dirty thumbnail and listened to the echoes.

Ka Larry rose from the candle, puffing the cigarette into life, and caught the direction of Frank's look. He smiled and flourished the thumbnail. "It has many other uses," he said. "It's particularly good for digging the lice out of your hair."

"What?" Frank asked distractedly.

"I was talking about my thumbnail," Ka Larry replied with some amusement. "You seem to be interested in it."

Frank stared as the echoes grew louder.

"My thumbnail," Ka Larry repeated, a little puzzled now. "I was telling you it's good for getting at my lice."

Frank suddenly understood. It was the reference to lice. The man he was looking at was not merely austere, he was ascetic. He was an anchorite in a lice-infested hair shirt. His life was one of abstinence, self-denial, self-discipline. Frank's eyes widened as the awareness dawned. It was a priest's life.

"Are you all right?" Paul asked.

Frank glanced at Paul and saw another youthful version of himself.

"Is there something wrong?" Paul continued.

"It's nothing," Frank muttered, regathering his control. He glanced around, experiencing an urgent desire to be somewhere else, far away from these two ardent young men. He thought of Liz and realized where it was he wanted to be. He had a lot of lost time to make up. He rose.

"There's no rush," said Ka Larry.

"Don't you have . . . uh . . . things to do?" Frank asked.

"There's time," Ka Larry replied easily. He drew deeply on the cigarette, blew the smoke out rapidly. It billowed around his head.

"The colonel . . ."

"The colonel is in his lair. He won't be moving for a while yet."

"All the same, we'd better be on our way." Frank cast a look at Paul.

Paul glanced at Frank, then at Ka Larry. He rose to his feet reluctantly, as if disappointed that the conversation was ending.

"As you like," said Ka Larry, who remained seated.

Paul looked down. "May I ask you a question before we go?"

Ka Larry flashed an accommodating smile. The smoke from the end of his cigarette curled lazily upward in a thin blue plume.

"What are you going to do . . . about what we've told you?"

Ka Larry's smile faded. "I will do what has to be done."

"Then you will stop this thing?" Frank asked.

Ka Larry looked up at Frank. "Alfredo is necessary."

"You will save him?"

"He will survive," Ka Larry declared. "I will make certain of that."

FRANK STOOD in the entrance of the house that had been his home for most of his adult life. He stared across the room at Liz, as oblivious to the wind's attempts to wrench the buffeting door from his hands as he was to the rain sheeting around him.

Liz, gazing inquiringly at Frank, rose from the sofa.

Frank released the door and strode toward Liz. He did not take his eyes from her face, as if the room he moved through and all that had been accumulated there no longer interested him.

Liz looked up into Frank's eyes when he reached her. "It's done," she said. It was a statement, not a question.

Frank nodded and reached out for Liz.

Liz placed her hands in Frank's and smiled.

Frank drew Liz toward him, wrapped his arms around her. He pressed a cheek to the top of her head and closed his eyes, content at last.

Paul appeared in the entrance, dodged the swinging door, and finally managed to wrestle it shut. He looked across the room to where Frank and Liz were embracing. He lifted his eyebrows in surprise. He glanced around, found Harry standing by the kitchen door.

Harry silently beckoned Paul and disappeared into the kitchen.

Paul followed. "Jesus!" he whispered as he gently closed the door behind him. He gestured toward the living room. "What's that all about?"

"What do you think it's all about?" Harry muttered, pulling Paul away from the door.

Paul cast a backward glance. "But I never thought . . ."

"It's a little detail that must have escaped your attention," Harry said. He gave Paul an irritated look. "Not the only one, I'm afraid."

Paul, alerted by the edge in Harry's voice, turned and looked. He pressed his lips together. "Look," he said, "I know—"

"Ah, forget it," Harry cut in again. "How'd it go with Ka Larry?"

"All right, I guess." Paul shrugged.

"What's he going to do?"

"He didn't spell out any details."

"But he *is* going to do something?"

"Of course he is," Paul replied. He gave Harry a puzzled look. "Why wouldn't he?"

THE YOUNG woman emerged from the rectangle of shadow and slid to the floor beside Ka Larry. She joined him in staring pensively at the entrance to the hut, through which Frank and Paul had disappeared into the wind and the rain.

"My, my, my," the woman whispered with amusement.

"You're surprised, Ka Connie?" Ka Larry asked, without taking his eyes from the rain slashing across the open doorway.

"Very much," Ka Connie answered. "They're the last two people I would have expected to betray the oaf."

"Why?"

"A priest," Connie replied. "An American." The way she spoke she made it sound as if the words produced a bad taste in her mouth.

"You find priests and Americans so contemptible?"

"I do."

"Why is that?"

"They are our greatest exploiters, our principal oppressors."

Ka Larry did not respond.

Ka Connie glanced at him, wondering at his silence. She asked, "Are they not?"

"I suppose they are," Ka Larry answered in a weary voice. He was quiet for a moment, then asked, "When will Rosales move?"

Ka Connie glanced at the watch on her wrist, which was, in itself, a source of secret satisfaction. It had been given to her by the colonel. "They depart in just under two hours."

"You're certain."

"I was there when he issued the orders."

"Then I must go now."

"You have decided?"

"Yes."

"May I know what you are going to do?"

"Merely observe."

Ka Connie regarded Ka Larry with heightened interest. "That's all?"

"That's all."

"Why?"

"The central committee will need a full report, all of the details," Ka Larry paused. "For the propaganda."

Ka Connie began to smile.

"They will have to know exactly what happens when Rosales kills Alfredo."

Ka Connie's smile spread across her beautiful face. "So you lied to them."

"No, I didn't lie."

"But you told them Alfredo was necessary."

"He is."

"You said you would make sure he survives."

"And I will," Ka Larry replied. "I'm going to make sure Alfredo outlives us all." He swung his gaze slowly from the doorway to Ka Connie. His eyes looked enormous in the candlelight, and they glistened blackly, as if unshed tears were trapped there. He said:

"The revolution is about to acquire a martyr."

ALFREDO DANTOG was buried in keeping with the customs of his people. The day was bright, washed clean by the passing typhoon, and the ceremonies were minimal. The *pangat* wore no shroud, only the clothes he had been dressed in when he died. Across the chest of his blue denim shirt, there were ragged holes encrusted with dried blood the color of rust. He was lowered into a circular pit on a patch of level, stony ground in front of his hut. When his body had been arranged in a sitting position, a wooden spear was placed upright in one hand and secured there. The metal tip of the spear trembled, glinting in the sunlight, as clods of earth were shoveled into the grave.

"They won't lay him out properly until his death has been avenged," said Harry.

Paul, who stood beside Harry on the crest of the knoll that overlooked Alfredo's hut, did not comment. He watched in silence, feeling as dirtied and as bruised as the corpse that was being slowly entombed before his eyes.

"We'd better go now," said Harry after a time. "The jeepney's waiting."

Paul shook his head wordlessly. He had chosen to remain until this was over and he intended to see it through. He felt he owed it to Alfredo, as well as to himself. He stared intently at the scene unfolding at the foot of the knoll, as if he might find something there that would help him understand, or at least convince him that he had been wrong. He watched them finish the grave, seal it with a pyramid of small rocks. He saw Frank and Liz, supporting Alfredo's wife between them, lead the shattered woman away. He searched the dark faces of the departing mourners—until his eyes fell upon Ka Larry.

Paul straightened. "I didn't expect to see *him* here," he said.

"Who?" Harry inquired.

Paul gestured toward the lean, barefoot figure in the midst of a crowd of young men who were in the process of separating from the main body of mourners.

Harry grunted with distaste.

The young men, Ka Larry among them, formed a circle and squatted on the ground. As they passed the bowls of rice wine, a village elder entered the circle. There was a red, flapping chicken in his hand, held upside down by the feet.

"What are they doing?" Paul asked.

"Selecting an avenger," Harry replied. "The old man is going to set that chicken down in the center of the circle and slit its throat. The bird will stagger around for a while as it dies. Whoever it's pointing at when it falls will be responsible for executing the vengeance."

Paul nodded, murmured, "So it does not end."

"It's only beginning."

Paul and Harry watched the old man cut the chicken's throat, followed the bird's desperate reaction, until their attention was diverted by the sound of distant, rhythmic thumping. They glanced in the direction of the noise, which was coming from the far side of the valley. A pair of military helicopters beat slowly upriver, silhouetted against the terraces that climbed the valley's wall. The terraces, brimming with water dumped by the typhoon, sparkled in the sun.

"Rocky?" Paul asked.

"Or his replacement."

Paul looked back at the circle. The chicken's grotesque dance was drawing to a close. It fluttered feebly, tottering around the blood-stained dust in a drift of golden down and russet feathers. Paul scanned the ring, looking for Ka Larry. He found him staring upward, tracking the progress of the helicopters with a watchful, almost eager eye. The dying creature at his feet was of no interest.

"C'mon," said Harry a little impatiently. "That jeepney won't wait forever and our bags are on it."

Paul made a half-turn and hesitated, glancing back over his shoulder. He stared down the slope of the knoll for a moment, chasing the thought, before he gave up. With one small, puzzled shake of his head, he turned and walked quickly away.

About the Author

BARRY CAME, who began his writing career as a journalist in Canada, has been a foreign correspondent in Asia, Africa, and Latin America. From 1977 to 1982 he served in the Far East, first as a correspondent for *Newsweek*, later as that magazine's Hong Kong bureau chief and regional editor for Asia. During this period much of his time was spent covering affairs in the Philippines. He has also served in Beirut, Cairo, and Rio de Janeiro. He lives in Rome with his wife and two children.